Ashley:

My best &
cutest fan:

Jerry Everett

Jesus

of

Cottondale

By: Jerry Leverett

Copyright © 2006 by Jerry Dennis Leverett

ISBN 0-7414-3332-X

Published by:

INFIN∞ITY
PUBLISHING.COM

1094 New DeHaven Street, Suite 100
West Conshohocken, PA 19428-2713
Info@buybooksontheweb.com
www.buybooksontheweb.com
Toll-free (877) BUY BOOK
Local Phone (610) 941-9999
Fax (610) 941-9959

Printed in the United States of America
Printed on Recycled Paper
Published June 2006

Words have the power to hurl us onto the brightest
or darkest of paths.

My thanks to Hester whose words started the
journey of this book.

The words of my daughter who always encouraged me.

And the words from all the friends I met along the way,
especially Shelbie, Jenny, and Sue the BBG's.

All the words from my son Chad growing up,
and lastly, my son Jon we didn't talk enough.

Circumstance may either subvert or fortify the soul.

Author's note:

I held a conference with the characters in this novel before the first draft. I explained that under no circumstances would I tolerate any sex, violence, or cussing. No one listened...

PROLOGUE

The supervising nurse hung up the phone. Whoever said that the nightshift was uneventful, bloody-hell didn't work at Cottondale General. The words spoken by her lead maternity nurse replayed in her mind. "Get down here. If this woman pulls this off, we'll either be sued or become the laughing stock of the community."

Details followed; details beyond her comprehension and thirty-odd years' work experience.

She headed toward maternity. In route she considered that she would retire in six months, and neither situation nor circumstance would cock it up.

Arriving at her destination she took a second to compose herself, then taking a deep breath she stepped inside.

A beautiful blonde sat up in the designated bed. The nurse breathed a sigh of relief, she recognized her from multiple admissions to the psych unit. And sitting by the side of the bed, making a study of his trembling hands sat her husband, Ralph.

She spoke to the patient. "Hello, Martha, I understand there's confusion regarding the paternity of your child. Who's the father?" The words caused Ralph to jerk, bend almost into a ball, and cover his ears.

With a delicate finger Martha pointed upward.

The nurse grabbed Martha's chart and calmly wrote Ralph's name in the provided place on the birth certificate. As she wrote she thought, *Not today Mrs. Martha-- and not on my bleedin' shift.*

Feeling back in control, the nurse smiled warmly at Martha, and said. "Okay, last question. What will you name your baby boy?

In a strong resonate voice, she answered. "Jesus."

1

SEVENTEEN-YEARS LATER

Jesus walked outside and sat on the porch. Icy tendrils of dread gripped his heart. Blue eyes, red rimmed from lost sleep and worry.

Construction sounds pounded and blasted at his nerves. Across the street stood beginnings of the new Cottondale aircraft assembly plant; the old one exploded into flames one night, burning to a black crisp. Around-the-clock rebuilding was an invasion of sound and light.

He swiped shoulder-length hair away from his eyes. Sweat beads formed on his pale expressive face. He pulled his knees up to his chest and rocked back and forth. Jesus lived in a two-story brownstone. Next door its clone, only red in color. Separating the front yards was a dilapidated picket fence–gapped like a punch-drunk boxer's smile. Back yards had eight-foot wood planking bisecting the properties.

He spotted John Henry walking in the distance. Instantly, his boyish face transformed. White even teeth flashed from a dimpled, mouth-stretching smile, he stood to greet his friend.

John Henry was big. Muscle-ripped body cut from countless long days of hard work. Obsidian black skin and a bright grin turned lopsided by a lightning-bolt shaped scar. The scar started on the right side of his scalp and ended at a point on his chin, contrasting vivid white, it gave him a decidedly different look. His short nappy hair was streaked gray by the passing of time.

Jesus leapt from the porch and landed in the big man's rib-bending embrace. John Henry messed up his hair with a gorilla-sized hand.

"Happy birthday, sonny boy," said John Henry.

"Thanks."

"So how blankin' old already?"

"Seventeen."

He rubbed his scar. "Don't think I can remember back that far."

"Been playing chess?"

John Henry pointed upward and said, "Once in a while with You-Know-Who."

Jesus loved his outrageous stories about hanging out with God and their chess games. John Henry could make him smile, no matter how bad he felt.

"When you teaching me to play?"

"When you learn to cheat." John Henry ruffled his hair and added, "Where's that dark haired beauty with the lovely smile?"

He blushed and stared at his unmatched sock-covered feet.

"She's out for your scalp. And from where this old cowboy's standing, that's a good thing."

Jesus nervously changed the subject. "W-What else you been d-doing?"

"Just blanking around, sonny boy."

"Why do say *blank* all the time?"

"Momma told me swearing was for losers. A body needs to listen to their momma. But tensions well up in a man and he needs letting them go–blank is my way of doing that. So shut the blank up."

He laughed.

John Henry swatted him on the back, and said, "I've got to hit the trail." Glancing upward, he added. "He's got me on a blankin' time clock."

Jesus opened his mouth and couldn't find words. His eyes took on a pained expression.

John Henry squeezed his shoulders. Seeking, then holding eye contact with an eyebrow arching, reassuring look, he said, "Don't worry, sonny boy, I just dropped by to check on you. Take things slow and get some rest. Everything will be fine."

Deep lines dug furrows of concern around Jesus' eyes. He doubted it, something felt wrecked inside him. And there was something else...

John Henry said, "Hey now, if you're going to pout, I'll be forced to beat the blank out of you."

"Sorry, just thinking."

"Well take it easy with that. Might set your hair on fire."

***

He waved as John Henry left. In his entire life, no adult had treated him as good as he did. Jesus loved and trusted him without thought or reservation. Slowly, he turned and went back into the house. The sheet he had wrapped around himself started coming loose. He cinched the belt tighter. It dawned on him that, even in this strange apparel, John Henry never questioned him.

A broken washing machine meant he'd have to wash some stuff in the tub. He went about finding dirty clothes and reflected that his entire lifetime had been spent here on Garden Street.

Jesus' thoughts turned to what bothered him most. Mom was having another nervous breakdown. She'd been gone four days now. Usually, when she came home, her eyes would be unfocused and she'd walk trance-like into her room. The last time Mom left the house, she only wore a wrinkled blouse and pants. Frequently, she came back nude.

He didn't think he could handle this much longer. Not with a murderer on the loose. The newspaper referred to him as a serial killer and labeled him, "The Sole Taker." Rumor had it that he tortured and mutilated victims by cutting the bottoms off their feet. There were eleven murders in the past year, all attributed to this killer. If only Mom would come home. Maybe then she'd forgive him.

He glanced upstairs; Dad hadn't been out of his room since Mom left. The telephone rang and he moved to answer it. "Hello... " He blushed crimson and added, "Dunno... well... maybe. Bye, Maddie."

He hung up the phone and burst into a smile; his sixteen-year-old neighbor, Madeline Mae Bridger called. She'd asked if her handsome man would enjoy a big fat kiss! She had an olive complexion, almond shaped eyes and full red lips. No one on earth was prettier–not even close. She was a sweet little Crackerjack chucked clear full of surprises.

Jesus harbored a secret crush for Maddie Mae. However, this thought was something that he didn't share. The fragmented thing inside left him crippled. Anxiety plagued him. It wasn't just from physical threats. Any amplified stress would short circuit his brain and drop him into some black abyss, effectively snatching his awareness and leaving him no more than an infant lost in the dark. An inky black, life-sucking dark.

Maddie deserved better. Still, he liked her–tremendously. He couldn't find the words to express how very much he cared about this girl. Jesus carried an old frayed hand-me-down wallet that his father had given him. It contained his fondest possession; a picture of Maddie. Every dream or fantasy resided in Maddie Mae and he would care about her until time became only a place where machines could travel to–and backwards at that.

She had a bright bubbly spirit and a voice that could make angels cry. Sometimes she would sing to him. Her notes reached into the workings of his soul; they came as melodic words with the power to enlighten and heal. He felt as though his spirit absorbed the soothing vibrations of her song.

Jesus hoped that one day he could play the piano for Maddie. He possessed a gift similar to hers.

Someone had left an old piano in the basement, and somewhere around seven-years-old, it called to him. He made his way down to the basement and scrabbled up and onto the bench, and began expressing all the misery and hope in his heart. Music flowed in soul-wrenching rhapsodies.

He looked up and saw his mother standing with her eyes shut, swaying with the melody. The look on her face stopped him, part rapture, mixed with incredible pain–he never played again after seeing the depths of her misery.

His thoughts were interrupted with the door opening. "How's my handsome birthday boy?" Maddie ran over and grabbed him in a hug. Her nimble fingers expertly sneaking down his back.

He pulled back, "Maddie, we can't do these things."

She pulled him closer, grabbed his butt with both hands and kissed him hard on the mouth. The kiss ended and she said, "Say my name, lover boy." Her hands were reaching under his sheet and going toward his sex. It felt as though she knew all the sensitive spots. And Maddie's hands were quicker than the person with three walnut shells and a pea at the fair grounds.

He blushed. His groin pounded with the rapid beating of his heart. His thing started inflating with a thump, thump, thump. He waved her off with his hand. "Stop, Maddie, I... we can't... ."

She pulled back and gave him a lower lip pout, dropped her hand down between her legs, and started rubbing while her hips made slow suggestive circles. Her big eyes dropped to the tenting under his sheet. "Come to momma, circus boy.

He wanted her badly–but... .

She went back into his arms. In a probing kiss she teased him with her tongue. Involuntary, he responded in kind. Maddie sucked his tongue deep into her throat, ever-slowly letting it escape, and then repeated the process. He pulled back.

"Blankety, blanking blank," said Jesus.

"What?"

"Just something guys need to say sometimes." Now the sheet resembled a faith healer's tent at the fairgrounds.

Her eyes slowly traveled over his body. "Come to momma and get your present." She started advancing on him with a lusty look on her face.

He ran around the couch, determined to keep her at bay. Her breasts were heaving and she started moaning. In a husky voice she said, "I-I need to use the bathroom." As soon as the door shut, her moaning gained in volume until she shrieked. Jesus became concerned that she might be hurt, but some heretofore latent intuition assured him otherwise. He found his own breath getting ragged listening.

He could hear the water running full blast in the sink and Maddie mumbling words he couldn't make out. Long minutes passed until she came out and said, "Soon now, momma's going to take you out, circus boy. Now help me gather the rest of your dirty clothes, I can't have you running around looking like a ghost on Halloween." They finished bagging his laundry as an exaggerated two-syllable yell came resonating from the direction of her house, "Ma-a-a-a-a-a-a-a De-e-e-e-e-e-e-e-e!"

She grabbed up the bag and said, "Bye-bye, honey pie, next time your sweet butt is mine." She leaned over and puckered her lips offering him another kiss. Knowing that she had to leave, he kissed her a good one. Her mouth felt incredibly soft. Licking her lips she said, "Now you kiss me! You're toast, circus boy."

She smiled, turned, tossed her long hair and went out the front door. He watched her walk away with the bag over her shoulder. She stuck her free hand behind her back and wiggled her fingers in a goodbye gesture.

Maddie vibrated as she moved. Bouncing, playful, energy in motion transitioned into skipping down the sidewalk.

2

On her way home, Maddie yelled, "Co-m-m-m-m-m-m i-n-n-n-n-n-n-n-g!" A laugh escaped her lips and she whispered, "At least four times." She shouted, *"Double gooey woolly-booger!"* It was one of her favorite sayings. As a child she used to play with small colorful hairy caterpillars. They felt so soft that she called them "woolly-boogers." One day another kid flew down the sidewalk on his tricycle and ran over one. The result looked like yellow-green goop. Thus, the saying was born. It ranked right up there with, holy-moly, and green goober snot-suckers.

She neared home and heat returned to her loins. This conjured up early childhood memories. She remembered being around eight-years-old, sitting on her doll's hard plastic head and grinding her sex into its face. Rock-a-bye Maddie! The act comforted her and the doll didn't seem to mind. Things were fine until Mom happened upon a session and banished her synthetic playmate to the burn pile, switched her silly, and then took her to see the family Doctor.

She recalled the words spoken by the bespectacled physician, "She seems overtly sensitive to clitoral stimulation, in all probability, this is simply a phase and she'll outgrow it, just don't traumatize her."

Maddie smiled. She didn't know about the big words, but the heat in her crotch wasn't outgrown. Double bubble nope! She relieved herself frequently. She could stand still, think of Jesus, squeeze her legs tight and orgasm. Absolutely nothing came close to her pelvic explosions and words weren't made that could describe the brain-blasting, panty-soaking experience. But in the past few years other things came afterwards–bad things.

Shaking her head, she turned her attention back to Jesus. She loved his hair. Shoulder length, it shined like spun gold in the sun. And his beautiful hands, they were the long finely-shaped hands of an artist. When he touched her, his gentle heart expressed itself through his fingers. He could only be described as gee golly gorgeous. He most certainly was her soul mate, and she felt green goober snot-sucking sure about that.

Maddie still hadn't experienced intercourse, it being a mortal sin and all, God would chicken deep fry her on the spot, but she LOVED how thinking about IT made her feel. Only one word came close to adequately expressing the sensation—*m-m-m-m-o-o-o-o-r-r-r-e-e-e-e-ee!*

She stashed Jesus' clothes under the porch and opened the front door. "I'm home, Mom."

"I'd better not find out that you've been with him. Do you understand?" Her mom didn't wait for an answer; in a deep voice she said *"A mindful daughter is a blessing unto the heavens."* Then continuing in her usual voice she added, "Maddie Mae, that entire family's crazy. Stay in our yard."

She cringed. Her mom was starting on another rant.

"It takes a mad woman to run off without a speck of clothes, stay gone for days, and then claim Immaculate Conception."

"Mack what? Mother."

"Never mind, miss prissy. I'll tell the world this though: Ralph's not his daddy; it's one of them no account, trash-mouthed construction workers."

The construction workers across the street would always give her mom wolf-whistles while setting out to go door-to-door spreading the word. Mom was an excommunicated Jehovah's Witness turned Pentecostal who never lost the passion to preach. Whenever she heard their lewd whistle's she would stiffen up, clutch her Bible in a white-knuckled grip, and mutter prayers until out of earshot. She watched her mom's eyes narrow at the mention of the men. "It's driving poor Ralph nuttier than pecan pie—his wife's a scarlet woman."

"Holy moly, Mom, that's not very nice." Maddie's head seemed stuffed with her mother's unsolicited sanctimonious sermons. And, in her opinion, Mommy was missing more than a few pieces from the old puzzle box.

"It's the good Lord's truth. And she burned his legs bad when he was only a baby. Jehovah-God only knows what else happened that night. He's brain damaged. I can see it. Don't let me catch you around him, girl. Remember what I told you about men. And don't be cursing–I'll switch you silly and stuff a few soap bars down your dirty little throat.

Maddie winced. She could still remember her mom almost knocking her teeth out, trying to cram one in her mouth for saying 'Darn.' The stuff gagged her just thinking about it. Ivory soap tasted far worse than it looked. Who would have thought that a sweet looking white bar could make a maggot barf?

According to her mom, all men were nasty, filthy beasts. Maddie briefly wondered about her father. He left when she was five. She only knew three things about him: Mom had him committed, he died in the hospital, and asking about him brought on a fearsome whipping, followed by a sermon on sin.

Her mom started back on Jesus again; she said, "Why do you think his feet are scarred pink, and he wouldn't talk for all those years? I'll tell you why. Because he's needed to fend for himself, even with his stinky diapers falling down around his knees."

Maddie felt tears welling up and spilling down her cheeks. She couldn't argue the last part, his bundle of washing attested to that. She helped Jesus out whenever she could. And she wouldn't stop, regardless of what her mom said or did to her.

The mention of his name made her wet again. Maddie wouldn't dare tell anyone, but touching herself gave her comfort. So how could it be wrong? Heck-a-peck, both the preacher and Mom said the penalty for thinking about sex was eternal Hellfire. She loved Jesus and it felt natural, but if her mom and the good reverend were right, she was never-ending toast. Dark black crispy toast. These admonitions were in constant war with her combustive sexuality. She went up the stairs toward her room.

Her mom's voice followed her, "Don't be messing about up there."

"Yes, Mom," she answered. Maddie lie back on her bed and pulled a pink one-inch square piece of Bazooka bubblegum from her pocket. Maybe a good chew would take her mind off her fiery dilemma. Besides, she had a contest going with her best boy to see who could blow the biggest bubble. Jesus could blow them as big as his head.

Before chucking the gum in her mouth, she read the Bazooka-Joe comic strip; a four-step cartoon depicting a basic judo move. She would have to try it on Jesus and see if she could make him squeal like a girl. The thought made her smile. Anytime she got him down, he'd do that.

Thinking about him gave her reason to discard the gum and reach for the ever-hot spot between her legs. Relief found her in minutes as she daydreamed. In the fantasy, she walked hand-in-hand with the absolute handsomest boy in the world–Jesus.

About twenty minutes later, the telephone rang. Maddie could hear her mother talking up a blue streak; it must be her conversation comrade. Mom loved few things more than good old juicy gossip, and her phone cohort absolutely required it for survival.

She believed that if gossiping compared with sexual urges, her mom would be the one slated for the fiery pit. When the conversation got to cooking, Mom would get to rocking, raising her voice until she was shaking in excitement, with rapid booby-heaving breaths.

Her mom's voice became loud and shrill as she said. "No. But I can tell you what the psychiatric social worker said when she came over... .Yes, she's a witness too... Martha's paranoid schizophrenic and Ralph's manic-depressive. Blessed Jehovah knows that's a strange family. Can you imagine someone crazy enough to name their poor baby 'Jesus?' She's the laughing stock of the entire congregation. Oh yes, besides having fits, the boy's supposed to be mildly autistic with a reported savant talent." Her mom laughed. "I don't know, Clair, maybe he can walk on water. But here's my official diagnosis: They're all nuts!"

Maddie placed her fingers in her ears. She hated what she was hearing, and it just wasn't fair. Good golly Molly, her mom and everyone else were wrong. Someday this town would change its mind about Jesus. She knew it. Most of his troubles were from either being teased about his mother, or about his name, but not once had he complained. He radiated an inner grace and quiet composure that belied his situation in life... Unless he was nervous, then the light behind his eyes winked off and he all but disappeared.

She felt happy that summer vacation had finally started; school would be goober-snot right now. Jesus hated school. Simple things like reading in class would send him running out the door in tears; he would start speaking, and freeze. Specialists examined him often, about as often as the beatings he received from other kids.

They held him back two grades. He possessed an advanced intelligence, but the doctors deemed him developmentally challenged. Her mom made a similar claim about her, when she said, "You're not a little girl anymore, Maddie Mae, time to grow up." She even took her to see a battery of doctors and, ever since then, she dropped the subject.

Following the examinations, her mom started asking the preacher to lay hands on her. She hated being dragged up to the pulpit. He would manipulate her head with his oversized fingers like a basketball player with a ball fetish, pulling her clear off the floor in his religious zeal, damning unseen demons and twisting neck muscles, while her flailing legs searched in vain for purchase. It reminded her of watching Mom pull the heads off chickens. Silent, flapping, headless bodies ran blindly around in circles– Maddie felt certain that she was headed for a similar fate every time he snatched her up.

A frown jerked at one corner, then settled on her lips. She didn't know how to cope with a recent event. A few nights ago, the sounds of loud voices coming from her mom's room woke her. She crept up to the door and inched it open. Inside, her mom gestured wildly. Long hair flying around her pale nude body Maddie had seen neither before then. Any memories of Mom included dresses covering her feet with braided-hair coiled tightly and pinned to the back of her head. Tears fell in streams down her mom's cheeks as spit sprayed from her mouth and the screwy parts. The noodle-baking, screwy-Louie parts were that her lips weren't moving and the words coming out of her mouth sounded nothing like her.

Willfully, she pushed the memories away and searched for a pleasant thought.

A smile came to her lips. She remembered kissing Jesus, and her hand found its way back inside her panties.

Shame, shaking a long bony finger, stalked Maddie into troublesome sleep.

3

Jesus woke up with a warm feeling on his face; rays from the morning sun flooded through his window.

Jumping out of bed, he hurried up the stairs to his mom's room. Her door stood open confirming the emptiness within. A troubled look settled into open misery. He hoped she'd return soon. If he could apologize, he'd feel better. He wanted her safe–badly. He whispered a prayer. Trying not to wake his dad, he slid silently down the banister.

In the basement, he walked toward the small bathroom and opened the shower door. After adjusting the water, he peeled off his clothes and jumped in.

Bending down, he located the special bar of soap he kept in the corner. After rubbing it on his feet and calves, he replaced it. His scars repulsed him. Both legs were damaged below the knees.

A voice once whispered in his head that it happened in a fire. Without thought or will, he banished that voice. That information must never reach the light of consciousness. The inner-child in Jesus sat with his back guarding that dark door in his mind, with fingers jammed knuckle-deep in his ears and chanting at the top of his lungs as if his life depended on it.

Using a scrub brush, he started cleaning. He didn't want to touch either foot, especially the right big toe, misshapen and chewed looking. Without a toenail, it resembled a spit-out, distorted, hunk of pink bubblegum. It reminded him of the loathsome, malformed mass of fear, ever-ready to erupt from his gut, and he hated both.

He stood and tossed the brush onto the floor in disgust.

Jesus' thoughts returned to yesterday. Maddie always made him feel good no matter what was going on in his life.

Whenever she came around, he'd end up smiling. She'd been doing that all his life. He could never quite figure out how or why, but that was her way. A slow smile started at the corners of his mouth, and stretched into a full-blown grin.

Grabbing a bottle of shampoo, he squirted it all over his body. In short order, he became a human soap bubble. He moved back under the hot water and stood with his head down, relaxing in the steamy bliss.

Suddenly a very nude Maddie jumped in with him. "What the... ?" She reached out for him. Ignoring her intentions, he took her hands in his and said, "How come they look all cut and red?"

She pulled loose, bunched her small hands and struck a boxer's pose, then replied, "From punching out pretty boys with stupid questions." Her passion-filled eyes signaled the end to his questions as she gazed openly at his nudity.

Looking slowly up and down his body, she added. "I told you I'd be coming, sugar pie. Don't scream like a girl, you'll only wake your dad, and force me to put my new judo hold on you." She swatted him on the butt. "Nice ass, what else you got for me?"

He opened his mouth to admonish her, even as his eyes found her breasts, and, almost of their own accord, dropped and fixated on her sex. Every thought in his brain slowly drained downward. Wow! His breath sucked in as the unseen pump started inflating his thing again, thumpty, thump, thump... . With his last shred of will power he said, "We can't... ."

She blinked her eyelashes and looked at him. "I know we can't, retardo. It wouldn't be right. And my mom would know just by looking. She'd switch me stupid, tell the preacher, he'd tell *You-Know-Who,* and I'd be a bubbling brimstone, baby. Let's rub bodies instead."

She took his hand, placed it on her sex, then found and caressed his. Her light touch felt like a slow erotic electrocution. His hand trembled on her small hot furnace. She pulled and squeezed him against her. His breath became erratic again.

With her hands, she moved his hips back and forth; grinding her crotch into his groin each time their bodies met.

The sounds in the shower were dominated by the wet slapping of flesh. His breath came faster.

She smacked him on his butt hard with her hand, and said, "Who's your honey?" Jesus felt pressure welling up inside his loins. She slapped him harder, "Say my name." In an orgasmic explosion he said, "M-a-a-a-a-a-a-a-a-a-d-d-d e-e-e-e-e-e-e-e-e-e-e-e-e-e." As if on cue, her body shuddered and she answered, "Ye-e-e-e-e-e-s-s-s-s-s... "

They slid down the shower wall in spent bliss.

Jesus said, "Blank me."

She put her arm around him and stuck a breast in his face. "Kiss it," she said.

He turned red with the realization of what just happened, and stood up to leave the shower. She jumped up, squeezed his butt, and then planted a wet kiss on his neck. "Good gravy, Maddie," he said, and stumbled from the shower.

"You loved every minute of it," She retorted.

Freshly done laundry greeted him. "Thanks, Maddie."

"That was your second present. Want your third?"

He didn't respond, but she was the bee's knees all right. He said, "I have to clean house." He jumped into some short pants with a pair of his dad's old socks pulled clear up to his knees, added a T-shirt, and went into the kitchen. He opened the door to the fridge and found a not-too-ancient apple. Munching away, Jesus could hear her moaning in the shower again. He found the broom and started sweeping.

Maddie showed up proclaiming, "Woman's work," and took his broom. He started cleaning the sink. She said, "Look at this glass. Did you break all the dishes?"

He didn't respond at first. Then Jesus remembered why his mom left. He said, "Mom was having trouble sleeping because the construction noise bothered her. She came downstairs, asked me to be quiet, and went back to bed. I wanted to surprise her and clean the kitchen. I started washing dishes. When I finished, I tried putting a stack into the cupboards and they fell."

His eyes took on a sad look. "She ran back down. 'Told me that I did it on purpose, slapped me, and left. I haven't seen her since." Tears streamed down his face. He grabbed his stomach and crumpled onto the floor in a ball. His last words were, "Now the killer probably has her and it's my fault."

Maddie went to him, picked his head up, and placed it on her lap. She ran her fingers through his hair. He felt her sweet kiss. She explained to him that he'd only been trying to help, and mistakes happened to everyone. She started singing. Repeatedly, her song came to him; it replicated her words in pictures, floating inside his mind, reaching him on a cellular level. The song sounded heavenly. He loved her singing more than anything. It warmed the very core of his being.

He subsided and she said, "Your mom isn't well. Sometimes, when people are sick inside, their pain makes them do mean things. She loves you, Jesus. And I'm sure she regrets what happened. Never forget that. Just like I'll always be here for you." She reached down and squeezed his sex. "That's if you're a good boy and mind your Maddie."

They spent the day cleaning house, sharing a sandwich that she had brought, and a late nap. When he woke up, she had scooted her butt up against him. He could feel the ever-present fire, even through her clothes. While she slept, he caressed her hair and imagined they were together in a special world where all their dreams came true; a place where people loved them and they were safe. Jesus sighed.

She left. They'd made plans to meet in her playhouse at midnight. Maddie had a small one-room shack, built on the back of her mom's property under an ancient apple tree.

He went into the kitchen, found a boiled egg in the fridge, peeled it, dropped his prize into the peanut butter jar, shook and spun it expertly. Rolling the brown egg into his mouth, he transferred it to his cheek, sucked off the peanut butter then slowly ate the egg, first the white and then the yoke. Gourmet dinner complete, he fooled with the broken washing machine until bedtime. When he started, it made humming sounds. When he finished, it stood white-faced and mute with its door agape in shock.

Jesus went to his room. Before getting in bed, he set the alarm. He tried for sleep without much luck. The expectation of seeing Maddie kept exciting him. It seemed like every time he closed his eyes, memories of the shower would replay in his mind. He never knew what she'd do next; this thought brought a smile to his face. After what seemed an eternity, he fell asleep.

It felt like only minutes had passed when the alarm sounded. Jesus sat up in bed. Glancing at the clock, it read 11:30P.M. Yes! He got up and tiptoed up the stairs. Mom still wasn't home and, still, no sound from his father's room.

Using the ever-trusty banister, he ghosted downstairs and went into the kitchen. Finding one slice of dried bread, he made a peanut butter sandwich. Crunching away, he headed to the basement for a quick shower, brushed his teeth, and found some good-smelling stuff to put on. Slipping back into the same clothes that he wore earlier, Jesus walked toward the backyard.

Reaching the fence, he gave the secret whistle Maddie had taught him. She whistled back. He found the loose board, and moved it aside and started stepping through. She yanked him the rest of the way and planted a kiss on him. Her hot lips left him dizzy.

They walked holding hands toward the playhouse. The moon shone bright and a comet lit up the night sky. It streaked across the heavens and Maddie said, "Double-bubble dibs on the wish."

A small entrance necessitated crawling into the single room, and a four-foot ceiling left sitting the best option. With barely enough space to lie down, their feet stuck out the door. Maddie spread out a blanket and said, "Take off your clothes." She began to unceremoniously strip off her own and added, "Hurry up, tiger, momma needs some loving."

Jesus tossed things out the door as fast as he could take them off, fumbling with buttons and zippers. He looked over at Maddie. She lay naked with her hands stretched over her head in the moonlight, her beauty made him all shaky. She arched her body. Soft skin shined silver-blue. Golly! Her nipples even looked glossy.

She sat up and placed a small ring on his pinkie finger, the adjustable kind. He felt her squeeze it tight. "Now you're branded, Jesus." He looked closely admiring the ring until her roaming hands snatched his attention elsewhere.

He reached over and caressed her breast. The familiar erotic shock treatment started happening between his legs as she found him again. He placed his hand on her sex to return the favor and explored her velvet softness. He must have pushed too hard because she said, "No. Not inside. We need to be mar– it w–would be sinful, j–just rub softly." Her voice sounded deep and husky.

She started kissing his neck, shuddered and moaned, then pushed his hand away. Urgently, she pulled him atop her. He felt as though all the heat in her body centered at the burning apex between her legs. She tilted her hips. Without prompting, he moved in a slow natural rhythm. She placed his hand on her breast and said, "Kiss it." His mouth found her breast and soon she reached another body-rocking explosion, shortly followed by his own.

She shuddered, turned away, and rolled up into a ball, he could tell something was wrong and lightly touched her shoulder. She pulled away. Making whimpering sounds while she held her knees and rocked.

Jesus listened to her for more than an hour, and then slowly his thoughts turned to his immediate apprehensions. The more he considered it, the more he became frightened. Their sexuality was getting out of hand. They were getting too close, and something bad might happen.

He enjoyed being with her more than anything, but the imagined realities of caring for her set his mind ablaze with fear, incinerating hopes, wishes, expectations, and childhood dreams. Smothering the wonder he felt with her left only cold, ashen despair.

This had to stop. Hate pounded in his veins–for himself; a rotten no-account coward. He already believed that he'd wrecked his mom's life, and now the same thing was happening to Maddie. His stomach knotted, then cramped.

She sat up and looked at him. Her eyes were wet and soft, almost imploring. She said. "Tell me you love me, Jesus."

He looked down, avoiding her gaze. Words tumbled from his mouth in an irreversible harsh stream. "I don't–I never did."

She seemed to recoil from an invisible blow. He heard a sharp intake of air. Maddie said, "I-I hate you, Jesus... you... bastard!"

She pulled on her clothes and crawled from the room. Maddie ran around her house and onto the sidewalk. In all the years he'd known her, this was the first curse word that he'd ever heard her say. He felt numb and shocked. He lay there dazed, half wanting her to return, the rest wanting to die.

Why did he say that? It wasn't what he meant. How could fear turn his mouth into a traitor, betraying both his heart and the one good thing in his life. And how could he live without Maddie?

His vision clouded as his body jerked, danced, and quaked in an electrified boogey.

4

She wandered the streets. Jesus' heart-breaking remark had propelled her farther from home than ever before.

Downtown Cottondale looked scary to her; everywhere she looked, people stared with gleaming predator eyes. She knew she possessed a vivid imagination, but the men's drooling faces were very real. Had she found the wicked side; the part her momma always preached about? *"Mark my words Maddie. Fornicators and perverts abide on the evil side of town."*

Night scared the snot out of her. The slightest noise would send her running, heart-pounding, and ready to scream. Every darkened alley seemed full of horrible things ready to leap out at her. Finally, sleep would not be denied and she found an open car and jumped in. Maddie awakened to a banging on the door that sent her bolting away in terror. A man yelled after her, "Hey, are you all right?" She wondered how he could ask that after scaring her half to death.

She kept on the move in the predawn light. It wasn't physically cold but another kind of chill cloaked her. Something about this place and how she stood out from everyone else, Maddie could see it in the eyes of people she passed. She didn't belong here, and they knew it.

Sunrise erupted into pinks and blues as the new day began. She headed for a wooded area. It turned out to be a small park.

The smell of freshly-mowed grass and warm sun brought thoughts of Jesus, conjuring intimate feelings expressed in warm tears sliding down her cheeks. She wondered about his ability to compose songs. Maddie could explain what feeling she wanted articulated, and he'd write deeply haunting lyrics. She found that so paradoxical, because when she questioned his obvious feelings for her, he remained mute. However, his expressive eyes always communicated the truth hidden seemingly just behind his frozen tongue... until last night.

Several times, she fell asleep merely to have some noise send her bolting for the bushes.

Maddie watched a young couple with their new baby. After carefully placing her infant on the grass, the woman pulled a large blanket from a wicker basket and playfully tossed one end to the man. They spread a blue-blanket world, peopled exclusively by their small family. Picnicking and whispering bright-eyed secrets, laughing, touching, and kissing often into late afternoon. Watching them made Maddie's heart hurt; their love overtly apparent as they played with their newborn. She missed her best boy.

A mental picture of Jesus as she cussed him still clung fresh to her mind. He looked incredibly shocked. Life without him didn't seem possible.

She went to the restroom, washed her face, and tried using her fingers to comb tangles from her hair.

Walking into one of the stalls she had a good cry. Color this double goober-snot green. Sitting on the cold toilet seat, Maddie looked at her environment. A litter-strewn cement floor and graffiti marked walls blended nicely with the backed-up sewer smell coming from somewhere to her right.

Something caught her attention up by the ceiling. Between the walls and roof was a large gap for ventilation, covered with heavy wire. Spider webs were in abundance for trapping insects drawn to this place. What caught her eye turned out to be a wet-looking butterfly emerging from a white cocoon. Maddie found it ironic that something so delicate could still be living among these predators.

It crawled onto the wire and slowly opened its wings to the air. She noticed that hers weren't the only eyes attracted to this display; a rather large spider moved slowly toward the newborn insect. She picked up a twig and tossed it. The spider scurried back to wherever it came from. The butterfly started beating its wings and, after minutes of this, flew. It circled a few times in the setting sunlight, refracting golden colors from its gilded body before disappearing from sight.

She wondered if the butterfly viewed the twig as some cosmic intervention. With that thought came the realization that if she landed in a similar predicament, none would be forthcoming for her.

Maddie went back outside and sat on a bench. She needed to figure out what to do. She wondered if life would ever change. Jesus suffered from panic attacks and seizures, and she felt that maturity was totally out of her grasp. Besides her singing voice, she had nothing to offer the world that she inhabited. How could she ever have a baby, being little more than a child herself? Life demanded more than being in love. Even the young couple needed to accomplish the basics: getting jobs, a house, and providing for their needs. Cripes!

Before running away, these ideas never crossed her mind. She simply focused on the object of her love. Now that she'd inspected her world, society didn't seem a safe or welcome place. Did this mean her dreams would forever be unrealized? Would Jesus be as lost in public as he was in school? How did people turn the corner into adulthood? She had so many questions. Before, they were tucked safely in the back of her mind, now this hostile environment brought them cascading forth like some monstrous tidal-wave, washing over her soul and threatening to drown her very dreams. Her heart ached.

Jesus would not open up and let her in. And, for Maddie, this hurt the most. She could see the lost boy inside, but he couldn't or wouldn't talk about it. She felt that if he'd communicate, then, possibly, they had a chance. Maybe together they could work through things. But not in silence. She could merely guess at the contents of his heart and, in this crazy world, that wasn't enough.

She regained her composure and went back toward town. Her refuge now transformed with the oncoming night. Shadow-monsters and perverts lurking behind bushes and trees in ever-darkening gloom were now the projected inhabitants of the once friendly park.

Maddie felt clothed in lamb's wool in an asphalt jungle filled with wolves. With the darkening skies, it seemed as though every person she passed gave her the evil eye. The omnipresent recording with her mom's voice played an excerpt in her mind. *"Sin lurks in shadows ever coveting the wayward child."*

She rubbed her head. She could really do without Mom's voice creeping her out. Things were scary enough.

Rounding a corner, she saw a girl not much older than herself. The girl wore a short skirt and heavy makeup. She spoke to Maddie. "Lost?"

Maddie stopped and looked at her. Finally, she decided talking wouldn't be a bad thing, she said, "Nope. Just don't want to go home right now."

The girl offered her a cigarette. Maddie shook her head no.

The girl lit up and blew smoke into the night air, appraising Maddie with old-looking eyes, she said. "Hey, kiddo, how about some food?"

Maddie started to give another negative reply when her stomach growled.

The girl's bright lipstick-smeared mouth stretched into a knowing smile showcasing red-tinged teeth. She dropped her cigarette onto the sidewalk, smashed it with a scuffed high-heel shoe, took Maddie's arm and said, "Come on, kiddo, let's eat."

Maddie followed her new friend and slowly began to relax. Unexpectedly, the girl raised her hand and waved.

Two mean looking men ran from across the street. Bad intentions clearly marked on their scowling faces, as the girl's grip tightened. Maddie doubled up her fist and smacked the snot-faced liar good–right in the kisser–then took off with legs super-charged by fear. The maternal tape played another excerpt; *"Beware false gifts wrapped in a stranger's guile."*

She had always figured her mother to be morally crazed, but now she began to wonder. Either this entire city was filled with devils and freaks, or Mommy had a good point, and she'd landed in it. Maddie realized home was her destination and, like a bat from the hot place, she ran.

The closer she got, the stronger the guilt surged in her chest. The urge felt overpowering. She needed the bathroom, to find her scrub brush and wash her nasty hands, repeatedly, until this feeling went away. Bad girls needed punishing and, because she'd sinned with Jesus, she must say the words and cleanse her dirty soul.

This ritual started long ago in childhood. With Maddie's early sexual awakening came repeated forced trips to the bathroom, countless beatings by her mother and having her mouth washed frequently with soap. So often that diarrhea became the norm.

What scared her most was the assurance that she'd burn for eternity in fire and brimstone, and it would surpass any pain imaginable. In dreams, she was often cast into Hellfire with her small hands inside her panties, trying in vain to extinguish another blaze.

In Sunday school, she scrunched down in her seat and avoided the preacher's stare. His all-seeing eyes seemed to bore straight into her soul, and he could read her every thought—she just knew it. Burn, Maddie, burn.

She tried talking with God directly and begging him to relieve her torture. Solution came in the form of uncontrolled compulsion. With her sexual maturity, she began to question these morals. Her mother was the product of another era, where belief came strict and tightly-wrapped as the ever-present bun glued to the back of her head.

Her scrubbing waned over the past year, especially concerning Jesus after it became clear to her that she loved him. She believed this blindly with the entirety of her being, and enough to risk Hell itself. Maddie aspired to one purpose in her life, and that was loving this boy. She felt that something this natural could not be wrong.

Ever-slowly, Maddie gained voice over ritual, but, for now, it spoke merely in whispers... fading now with her question answered in the dollhouse. Fresh tears filled her eyes as Jesus' last words replayed in her mind.

Passing a familiar street, she lengthened her stride.

5

Jesus sat in the playhouse. Two days had passed since Maddie left. Her intimate smell still surrounded him.

Several times he started to go and talk with Mrs. Bridger. Each time he began hyperventilating. She hated him and forbid Maddie to see him. Whenever they were caught together, Maddie wound up with her body cut bloody from a hickory switch; a crisscrossed memorial to their friendship that she bore without mention or complaint.

He tried keeping a vigil for Maddie's return, fell asleep sitting up, and woke up drooling on the wall with a stiff neck. His bones popped like Rice Krispies in fresh milk as he crawled outside.

Making sure Mrs. Bridger was nowhere in sight, he crossed the fence. Turning on the faucet, he went to the end of the green hose. Waiting until the water cooled, he took deep long drinks. His stomach grumbled, but the hunger was eclipsed by the tremendous pain in his soul.

Jesus' eyes focused on the ring Maddie gave him. It had twin gold colored hearts. Shining brightly in the morning sunlight, they merged into a golden blur as tears flooded his vision.

He turned off the faucet and went looking for his dad. Maybe he'd feel up to talking and help him ease this incredible pain. If Maddie came back, he would apologize and try explaining the unexplainable.

6

Ralph got up from bed and went into the adjoining bathroom.

At the sink, he splashed water on his face, switched on the light and winced in the sudden brightness. Looking back from the mirror were old, blood-shot, sunken eyes. They seemed haunted, peering out from a prematurely aged face.

He bared yellowed teeth at the image. There were more gaps in his mouth than a ten-year-old with a tooth-fairy fixation.

Ralph remembered when he was eighteen, less than twenty years ago. He felt completely normal then, except for being euphoric at times. He still hadn't discovered the depths one could plummet from walking on air.

As a kid, he used to shoot arrows into the sky thinking they stayed there—now he knew better.

Fifteen-year-old Martha was the most attractive girl he'd ever seen. Movie stars weren't as lovely. Willow-slim, blonde, leggy, with huge blue eyes, and like the sun popping through a storm. Where Martha went, faces brightened. At first, she didn't look or act any different from anyone else. The one hardly-noticeable thing separating her from others was her inability to talk about herself.

Some unseen thing that beckoned lovers since the beginning of time drew Ralph to her. When they talked, he expressed his dreams and goals while she listened. She seemed to absorb and resonate with his ideals. She loved hearing him speak about life. If he'd stop, she'd ask questions or tug on his arms and pull him to her in a passionate kiss. Not until late in the relationship did he realized that she remained a mystery, a haunting creature lacking personality. Still, he loved her.

One day, Ralph found her with a tear-streaked face, rocking back and forth, conversing with some unseen thing, mumbling incomprehensible sounds; a singsong chanting in unknown dialect, her unfocused eyes staring into oblivion. Even then, he only wanted to protect and please her.

Ralph had always been talented with his hands and working with wood. With the help of an uncle, he secured a position as an apprentice to a master carpenter. He loved the work but something dark started taking control of his life; instead of showing up on the job, he would wake up on a drinking binge. It seemed as if he'd just forget and become someone else; someone falling with no bottom in sight.

Once, he regained awareness sitting at a black-jack table in Las Vegas. He remembered winning big and then waking up in jail. When he finally returned home, the heartbreak in his wife's eyes all but killed him.

Martha desperately needed a grounded husband. Instead, he kept falling off the earth, often regaining consciousness in the stench of excrement–his own. Ralph felt that their life had reached maximum heartache. He was wrong.

One night she came home with discolored marks on her arms, and semen oozing down her legs. She stood in front of him with arms stretched out; reaching for that unseen thing she communicated with.

Her eyes were unfocused and glassy. She called out for someone named Angel with an awe-filled voice. He felt incredibly hurt. No. Something broke with heart snapping pain–something unfixable. Nine months later, their son came into the world.

Her condition seemed to improve after giving birth to Jesus. For almost eighteen months, all appeared to be going well. Ralph even returned to work and, despite occasional lapses, began slowly mastering his craft and regaining confidence. Then Martha left without reason or goodbye. He assumed that she took the baby.

With her departure, he fell into another depression. He called in sick and stayed shut up in his darkened room. Around the tenth day, he awakened to chimes from the downstairs clock; they seemed unending. Getting out of bed, he heard a scratching sound. Fighting waves of fatigue, he made his way into the kitchen.

The putrid smell of rotting meat filled the room. He turned on the lights. Movement caught his eye by Martha's electric deep-fat-fryer. Large rats squeaked, spit and glared through bulging eyes, apparently in no hurry to leave.

Ralph threw a dishcloth and they scattered. On the countertop lay a decaying chicken and a shitty baby-diaper, side-by-side. Gagging with the urge to puke, he bagged the items in plastic and tossed them outside in the garbage can.

Turning his attention back to the mess, black ashes bore mute witness to the scant remains of a burned baby sock. A stovetop burner remained lit. He noticed a blackened wall socket from the fryer shorting out. Luckily, the house didn't burn down. Apparently, she started supper and then forgot; more and more the norm for Martha. He spent twenty-minutes cleaning the mess up. A faint scratching sound seemed to be coming from somewhere. There! He heard it again.

Walking over to the closet door, he opened it. What he saw seared into his brain like a hot brand through liver.

Jesus lay on the closet floor wrapped in a stinking blanket. His toes covered with yellow-green puss, the mate to the burned sock had holes in it from chewing rats. His bare right foot bore the brunt of the attack. Large chunks of his big toe were missing. Making the noise that drew Ralph's attention in the first place were more rats. Bloody-faced from eating the baby's feet, they stared at him with red reflective eyes. Two stood on hind legs spitting and challenging his right to their food source.

He picked his son up. Blood and puss started oozing from Jesus' bite wounds along with the rancid smell of decay. He stomped a couple of slow-moving rats and hurried to the telephone.

Ralph rocked the child back and forth while waiting for the ambulance. Tears streamed down his face.

It occurred to him that Jesus wasn't making any sound. He looked closer under the blanket. Small round eyes looked back. He would never forget the innocent love reflected in that gaze.

The doctors believed that death was close. Some questioned how an infant could endure this. One told him that newborns could survive weeks feeding off their own body fat, but he knew a miracle when he saw one.

Martha was committed to the State Mental Hospital. He went into a treatment program; declared emotionally disabled and placed on medication. They didn't get their son back until a year later and, when they did, he was mute. Not even crying broke the stillness.

It stayed that way for over five years and then another miracle. In the middle of the night, heaven's own music wafted from the basement. It seemed to Ralph that his depression lifted with the notes. He hurried down the steps and found Jesus' small form sitting behind the piano, tiny hands flying over the keys like fluttering white moths.

Martha stood transfixed in front of the piano, weaving back and forth with the music, the floor around her wet from tears flowing down her cheeks. Before that night, she had never cried.

The memories brought fresh pain to his heart.

And now his worst fear realized; Martha was gone yet again, lost in her disease. Only this time, she wasn't coming back; he felt it in his bones. Ralph turned off the light, wiped his eyes, and went back to bed.

7

Jesus tiptoed up the stairs, placed his head softly against his father's door and listened. He could hear ragged snoring. He didn't have the heart to wake him and quietly went back downstairs.

He changed clothes, went outside and headed toward town.

Heat waves shimmered in a slow-motion dance, ghosting a few feet above the asphalt. The sun started its downswing in the afternoon sky. On his way past Maddie's house, Mrs. Bridger opened her door and stood glaring at him.

He found his voice and said, "Is M-Maddie home, ma'am?"

She gave a stern look and wagged her finger. Using her spooky voice, she said, *"Any child born not from wedlock shall be considered in league with the serpent."* Returning to her everyday scary voice she added, "Maddie's left. She snuck out and never came back. It's your fault. Stay away or I'll call the police." Turning, she slammed the door.

He muttered a perfunctory, raised-to-be-a-good-boy, yet fearful, "Yes, ma'am," and moved on. Mrs. Bridger gave him the creeps.

First his mother and now, this. Hopefully, Maddie had stayed at her girlfriend's house. Losing either woman would be more than he could face. They meant so much to him. The next thought crossing his mind brought a twinge of guilt, *especially Maddie.*

Jesus continued walking up Garden Street.

He stared at the concrete, hands thrust deeply into his pockets. Suddenly, a gang of boys around his age surrounded him. "Look-ee here, fellas, it's the fag, *Jesus*, or is that, *Hey Sues'?"* Lately the kids started bastardizing the Spanish pronunciation of his name. Now, they mostly called him Sue. The biggest boy said, "Give us some money, Sue, and we won't beat your dog-ugly face."

He remained quiet.

Someone hit him from behind in the kidneys. The blow crippled his legs and snatched the air from his lungs. He fell to the ground. A shoe connected with his nose. The burning sensation told him that it bled. Even as he thought of fighting back, burning fear paralyzed him, sucking him down into a vortex, where time seemed to slow and distort...

When his head cleared, he heard screaming from the group followed by the booming voice of John Henry. "What's the matter, you little blanks? Surely you're not all wearing dresses now? If I see you motherblankers again, I'll pull them panties down and spank those blankies." The boy's ran off. John Henry wiped off his cowboy boot, and said, "'Put the spurs to them little blankers." He pulled Jesus up and added, "It's good to see you, sonny boy."

Jesus wiped off his pants and placed the handkerchief offered by the big man over his bleeding nose. "Thanks, John Henry, sure happy you came along. I'm really worried about Mom and Maddie. Now they're both gone."

John Henry put a hand on his shoulder. "I guess that makes it Watermelon time then."

Jesus raised his eyebrows in question.

"My boy, certain things a-body's got to be showed–leave me the showing part." John Henry turned, motioned for him to follow, and Jesus hurried to catch up.

Something about the big man comforted him. He remembered when his life first became unbearable, and John Henry got him to talk. He recalled the day sitting on his front porch. He was ten-years-old and spoke little, with the exception of monosyllable responses to Maddie's teasing, *No! Stop! Bad! More...*

Jesus realized early in life that his mother fought unseen demons and it broke his heart. With his dad lost in depression and his mom gone for days, he badly needed someone to talk with.

He was on the cement steps rocking back and forth and staring into space. All the pressures in the world seemed focused inside him; add much more and he would break. He felt lost.

The big man came right up, sat down next to him, placed a hand on his back, and said, "Tell John Henry what's wrong, son."

Jesus opened his mouth and words came in a rush; every fear and problem in rapid succession. Even now, the ease that he shared with a total stranger amazed him–it was something special about John Henry–a feeling of complete safety. Not once had he felt different.

His hands returned to the bottom of his pockets as his thoughts revisited his fears.

John Henry reached over and tugged on his ear. "Stop with the blankin' thinking. When a person looks inside their own minds, it's the same as using a magnifying glass to look at ants; small nuisances become gigantic monsters. And, if you hold the focus too long, you just might set something afire. So cut it the blank out and follow me."

Jesus skipped to keep up.

They stopped at a store with a flashing red neon sign that read, 'Liquor.' John Henry grabbed two soap bars, plastic glasses, several bottles of Thunderbird wine, a red liqueur, and added a full jar of beef-jerky. Paying the counter man, they walked out the door.

John Henry made long, easy strides toward the country.

Two hours later found them in the foothills under a large Oak tree on the banks of the mighty Fern River. Jesus looked around. There were torn army cots and a fire pit. He saw an old camper shell that didn't make it back with its pickup. The camp felt peaceful.

Colors smeared the sky as the sun lobbed a last-minute bank shot from the backside of the world.

John Henry squatted by the fire pit and motioned for him to sit down. "This here's my favorite spot," he said. Pulling the bottles from the bag, he mixed the two together, and poured a cup for Jesus.

He took the drink and sat on a cot; it looked reddish in color and smelled awful.

"Is this Watermelon, John Henry?"

"Yes, my boy. There's two different ways to make this drink. The easy way is mixing the two. The other way is to buy a large watermelon and cut a hole in the top. Poke a stick inside to make room. Pour in a jug of Thunderbird. Recover the hole. Let the whole thing set for three days in the sun and drink it. I never cared for the waiting part. The closest I ever got was drinking the wine while eating the melon in the first few hours."

Jesus took a sip. The stuff tasted icky-sweet but it made his stomach feel nice. He drained his cup and handed it back to John Henry. "More, please."

"Take it slow, sonny boy. This stuff will sneak up on you." The big man mixed another drink for Jesus, one for himself and held his glass up in a toast. "Here's to bulls that buck and girls who blank."

Four drinks later, Jesus started feeling good. He kept looking at John Henry's fancy black cowboy boots with silver toe and heel-guards. He said, "When I grow up, I'm going to get me some boots just like yours."

"I sure enjoyed kicking those boys' blanks."

Jesus laughed at the memory. Then the drink started taking hold and the problems in his heart needed airing, he said, "John Henry, I think I caused my mom and Maddie to run off. And now maybe the killer has them." The next part was harder for him to say. "I told Maddie I didn't l-lov-care for her. I didn't mean it. I was afraid she'd find out what a coward I am. Something bad is messed up inside me, but I care about her more than anything. She even gave me this pretty ring."

He held up his hand so John Henry could see the ring.

John Henry rubbed his chin in thought and replied. "Your mom's been having problems. Even if you had never dropped the plates, I believe she would still be gone. And just because there's a killer loose doesn't mean he has them. As for Maddie, I think you've hurt her feelings and once she's had time to think, she'll be back. Maddie has loved you all her life and she's no quitter. I'm not quite sure about this fear thing. Sometimes when a person is injured early in life, it takes time to overcome. You're a good soul, Jesus. I can't see down the road of life. But I can see the journey. You've hurt people you love and now you're trying to fix it. Everyone makes mistakes. It takes a good person to correct them. I think you clearly know what needs doing, and this conversation was part of that process... Besides, anyone who can drink that many Watermelons and still make blankin' sense is okay in my thinking."

John Henry pulled off his cowboy boots and tossed them to Jesus. "Here try these blank-kickers on. I'm thinking I'll buy me some new ones."

Jesus kicked off his sneakers and pulled on the boots. He looked down at his feet and did a little dance. "They fit perfect, John Henry."

"Good. Now throw me those tennis-shoes. I can wear them until I get into town."

He tossed John Henry his old sneakers.

Grinning and blushing at the same time, Jesus said, "Gee thanks, John Henry, they're really swell." He danced and spun, mesmerized by the boots.

"Just a suggestion, son. But you might want to pay more attention to where you're going before you fall on your blank."

The words had barely left John Henry's mouth as Jesus tripped and fell over the cot-leg. He held his stomach in laughter. This was sure turning out to be a good time. He pointed to the ring, and said, "Maddie and I are going to be the same as these hearts, John Henry. When she comes back were going to be together always."

"Sounds good, sonny-boy. Just take things slow. A lot of bad things have happened lately and they've happened fast."

John Henry tossed a soap bar and said, "My mother said that washing cleansed a body's spirit." Together they went to the riverbank, cleaned their hands, returned and ate jerky washed down with wine.

Jesus lost track of how many drinks he'd consumed; the stuff now tasted similar to the punch his mom made, and he felt down right thirsty.

John Henry started a fire that bathed them in a warm glow, filled with dancing sparks and the comforting smell of burning wood.

Jesus sat on the cot inspecting his new boots.

While they talked, twilight gave way to crickets singing in the warm moonlit night as good-natured, fire-flung shadows scampered and cavorted among the branches of the friendly Oak.

He felt really good from the drink. Super-duper, actually. The impossible seemed a reality. He would get Maddie back–somehow. The idea made his heart warm, then memories came flooding back from the shower, and other body parts were getting heated. His face grew hot. Bringing his thoughts back to his feet, he grinned, this turned out to be a swell day. John Henry was the best.

Jesus lay down on the cot. He started to ask for another drink when the bed started moving in a circle. Everything seemed okay until he closed his eyes and the spinning started. He looked over at John Henry. The big man seemed unaware of the problem with his bed. Determined not to be a baby, he grabbed the frame and hung on with a white-knuckled grip. Then the movement became so fast that he jumped off the cot. Now the whole earth started spinning! He fell down on the ground and searched frantically with his hands for something to keep him from falling into space. "Help! John Henry, I'm falling off the world."

John Henry laughed and slapped his knee. "No. You're just riding the Watermelon-Bull and he's likely going to throw you, sonny boy."

Jesus felt like everything he'd eaten in the past year came pouring out. He kept puking long after his stomach emptied. "T-This is horrible John Henry, I think I might die."

"No, sonny boy. It won't kill you. People have been gored by that old beast since the beginning of time. Take a good grip and hang blanking on."

The last thing he remembered was John Henry picking him up like a child and laying him back on the cot.

8

George Washington Jones spotted a group of school children waiting for the bus. They appeared to be fourth, maybe fifth graders. He moved toward them.

Pulling the pistol from his shoulder holster, he said, "Okay, kiddies, give up the lunch money, or eat Mr. Bullet."

The largest boy said, "I'm telling my dad, mister, and he's a cop."

George twisted his face into a scowl. "How'd you enjoy attending a funeral, little snitch?" He tapped the gun barrel on the kid's forehead for emphases. "Guess who's in the box?" The boy started crying. George walked away smiling. He wound up with around twelve dollars and it took minutes, there was money waiting to be made in every situation.

He reasoned that the children learned more waiting for the bus than in a week at school. G.W. Jones, instructor in the fine art of social reality. Without looking back, he headed toward town; he had business to complete.

George had developed his own way to walk, and was deep into his patented moves. A little walk step-slide, with his right foot doing a half drag maneuver, simultaneously letting his left arm swing around and lightly touch his ass with his thumb, and his right hand suggestively stroking the blacksnake on the alternate swing. All this blended seamlessly with an extension of his neck, and twisting of his head. His moves described sex in motion. When he slid by women got wet and men turned gay. They knew it, and so did he.

George was a striking black man. Around six-foot-two, large build with hair processed into a huge, shiny, slicked-back pompadour. When he smiled, his teeth resembled pearls, and the front incisors were inset with two-carat diamonds. He possessed a flawless coffee complexion and natural green eyes with long black lashes.

Women loved him. He spent countless hours posing in the mirror; he had the slow provocative wink down to an art. George developed other moves. He'd purse his lips, or gradually use his tongue in a sexually suggestive manor. If faces could talk, his spoke in the sensual language of fuck-speak, with each move designed to bring smoke to a bitch's crotch. He used his face like a street whore working panty-flash.

He loved playing squares and that meant anyone George met. His greatest asset was his innate ability to read people. He relished baiting the hook and sinking it–hard. Usually up some bitch's ass. In his estimation, the world was a fucking stage, and he the master of curtain-calls. He was surely the alpha Mac-daddy in his own mind and a reoccurring nightmare in uncountable others.

Mr. Jones had associates in every bad news deal in town. And, oh yes, for the past year, he supplied victims for a superrich, sick-in-his-white-little-head, genuine, dyed-in-the-fucking-wool, just gots-to-kill-a-motherfucker, homicidal-maniac. The paydays were well into the thousands. It seemed somewhat twisted, even for George, but money could really straighten shit out. He developed the theory that his home delivery system made him the world's first genuine serial-pimp.

He saw his mark up ahead. A seventeen-year-old run-away spending her third day on the streets. He had worked his act a few days prior and left her with a baited morsel of hope, he could tell that she was ready, by the look on her little hook-sucker. She called herself, "Candy." He'd be the judge of that and soon, too.

He gave a slight nod to a black man barely out of sight shadowing her, and supposedly making her street experience a frightening event; the ever-stupid Bobby Bones, a compulsive gambler and dice-man.

Bobby looked graveyard skinny. And what stood him apart from others–besides his huge Afro–were bugged out eyes giving him a perpetually startled look. Bobby claimed his doctor diagnosed him with hyperthyroidism. George deduced that it was more a case of hyperchickenshitism.

When George met the dice-man, he got him drunk and conned him into playing with loaded dice. It took him less than a week and now the gambler owed more than he could ever repay and he'd keep it that way. The man now resided in George's bottomless pocket.

Before moving on Candy, George pulled his most cherished possession from his pocket, what looked like a gold watch engraved with the initials G.W.J. was actually a high quality mirror, and its value resided in the beauty it often shared, reflecting the perfect face--his. Getting his breath sucked away by sneaking a peek in the mirror, he replaced it, and went for the mark.

He slid up on Candy. "Hey, pretty girl. How's life?"

"Hi, George. Not very good. Last night someone ran up and slapped me. And tried to drag me in the alley." Her voice broke. "I g-got so scared." Tears were dripping down her cheeks. George decided that Bobby might actually be doing his job for a change. Time to wiggle the lure.

"Hey, now, sugar sweet. It doesn't have to be that way. Let me take care of you." He watched her eyes as he talked to her. She looked up with appreciation reflected in her wrap-around smile. Bam! Hook line and sinker. Next, he'd show her the pole. He lightly touched her shoulder. "Come on, Candy. I got a special place with your name on it. Shit, girl, people gets hurt on these streets."

Taking his offered hand, she accompanied him down the street and into a restaurant.

Inside, he picked a booth in back and ordered for her. Everywhere he looked people looked away, finding the look in his eyes more than they cared to digest with their meals. If someone forgot and stared too long, he didn't mind going over and refocusing their gaze—not at all.

Choosing the biggest spoon, she ate her food in gulps. He talked and watched. For desert, she gobbled down apple-pie and ice-cream. He smiled; she'd need the sugar rush for the upcoming party.

He paid the bill and with the waitress looking slowly and purposely scooped up tips as they left. Bowing at the door George grabbed and shook his crotch at the patrons in the restaurant before he turned and led Candy down several streets to a sleazy hotel.

George knew the owner and no questions would be asked. Denizens of this establishment minded their own business. They passed several people once inside the building and not one looked at them. Casual eye contact here opened the doorway to adverse social interaction.

She followed him into a room set up for this very purpose. He showed her the restroom and said, "Take a bath. I have some clothes my sister left that might fit you." She kissed his cheek and disappeared into the bathroom. Soon the sounds of running water and happy humming could be heard.

He pulled out the red dress, nylons, and matching heels that he'd purchased yesterday with her in mind.

Laying out the garments, he made a telephone call. "What's up, Fat Tony? I got you a nice one... No. Not Cherry Auction pussy, but five-hundred-clams easy." He listened for a moment and said, "You got a deal." Grinning as he replaced the phone, he rubbed his exquisitely manicured hands together in anticipation.

Fat Tony was the local gangster-pimp. Twice before, he had procured young girls for the auction. Candy's age wasn't a problem, but her face showed hard miles. It took a fine bitch to bring the fifteen-hundred-dollar payday.

The sounds from the bathroom indicated she'd be coming out. George smirked. Time to pass along another free lesson. When he finished, this whore would duck every time someone winked at her. Talk was penny-candy cheap, but his lessons, diamonds that they were, endured forever.

She came out of the restroom with a towel wrapped around her. A huge smile lit her face as she held the new dress up and twirled. All big-eyed and blushing she said, "Wow! It's gorgeous. You're the nicest man I've ever met."

He patted the bed with his hand. "Come here and sit down." Holding the dress in front of her body, she came over and sat an arms length away. Was the lame bitch growing brains? He doubted it. Faster than a snake, his arm shot out and grabbed her chin. Expertly lifting her head up, he applied a chokehold; mustn't bruise the merchandise. Her head fell limply forward and he released the hold.

Working fast, he opened a drawer by the bed and yanked the towel off her. He took out a preloaded syringe of Secobarbital Sodium and shot her in the butt. The drug wouldn't take effect until later, but Fat Tony welcomed getting the addiction process started. Soon she'd be yearning for reds like a fat-boy craving the fresh apple pie that his mom left cooling in the window...

Flipping her back over; he inspected the merchandise. Ah yes. He decided that, some days, things came together better than others–this being one of those days. He slammed his cock into her lifeless body and ten hard thrusts later he was done.

Her eyes opened wide with fear, pain, and question. He said, "Someday, when you're an old pro taking down johns, you'll thank me. Get that fucking look off your face, I did you a favor. A little pain now opens the door for a lot more pleasure later, thanks to daddy George. Now get dressed, we're expecting company."

She gave him the old 'you ran over my dog' look again. Her bottom lip stood out and quivered as she said, "I-I never did anything to you w-why?"

He glared at her. "How's about I kick the shit out of you?" He shook his fist at her. She shook her head and started crying.

Maybe she could use another life lesson. George growled at her, "Get your sniveling ass in the dress or get hurt." She started getting dressed without any more coaxing.

Watching her dress, he changed tactics. "Look, Candy. I probably shouldn't be telling you this, but gangsters had their eyes on you. You may not believe me, but I saved you from a perverted raping at their hands. Now, you'll be trained and learn a profession. One day you can start your own business and buy what ever you want." He watched her eyes, just the slightest widening. George smiled. He could sell a snow-blower in the fucking desert.

A knock sounded at the door. George said, "Who's there?"

"Who the fuck did you call, stickman?"

George opened the door, bent at the waist, and made an elaborate sweeping gesture with his hand. He enjoyed the stickman moniker earned for a certain proclivity for the knife.

Two gangster types walked in with a beautiful, well-dressed black woman bringing up the rear. The tall suit threw him an envelope with money. "Here's your bread, stickman."

George pushed the girl forward.

The black woman placed an arm around her. "Don't worry, girl. It always looks bad at first. Delilah will make it all better." Delilah winked at George, and left with Candy and the suits.

George reasoned that it could have been worse for Candy. If Devil Dan had requested fresh meat she would have went there. He was dead fucking sure about that. He thought back to how it all started...

The way he met Daniel Saurian was unusual; his father had disappeared and was presumed dead. George recalled seeing his arrogant aristocratic face in the local paper launching a huge sailing boat. He'd just busted some perfectly good champagne against the ship and was smiling about it. White people were fucking idiots. His son went from being a ward of the State during the investigation of his father's death to the richest teenager in California.

Daniel Saurian placed an ad for a general caretaker. The job paid well and George's little brother, Sammy, finally found employment.

Sammy received little education. In school, his friends called him Sammy-Sicko. He was little in stature and home ill most of the academic year. It fell to George to pull his slack. If it weren't for Mom–may she rest in peace–he would have showed his brother the fucking door. But he promised on her deathbed that he'd take care of him.

Sammy's finding work freed George up from his despicable big brother duties.

All seemed well for several years and then Sammy started getting suspicious with his employer's habits, came to George, and said, "I've worked a long time for this man. I never see him. And he only talks to me over the intercom or telephone."

George sensed opportunity. "What's wrong with that? I thought he paid well."

"Nothing at first and he does. There's even bonus money. But, he's starting to ask for strange stuff. For the past year he keeps asking for dogs. I deliver them and they disappear." Sammy's eyes got big. "He has me take them into a secret passage behind the mansion. I never see or hear the animals again. Not once has he asked for petfood."

George couldn't believe his ears. "Why the hell do you care? Maybe he eats the fuckers. Ever heard of mutton?"

Sammy shook his head in disgust and continued his story. "Yesterday, he promised to pay me twenty-grand if I would bring a person and leave them chained. Can you believe that, George? I think he's a killer and maybe I should call the police."

George knew the magic word when he heard it, big-fat twenty, followed by all those lovely zeros.

He said, "Look, Sam, this clearly isn't for you. Forget the deal and let me have a go at it. You owe me for all the shit that you've put me through. Didn't I always take care of you? Whatever this is, I'll handle it and you won't be involved. Come on, Sammy, for old times. And because were family. A-And because I-I truly care."

George placed his hand where he figured his heart might be and did his best to look tearful; if Sammy didn't go for this he might just cry for real. Hell, for this kind of coin, he'd suck his grubby little dick.

He softened his voice and continued, "Give the freak my telephone number and I'll take care of this. I doubt he really wants to hurt people. He's probably only testing you. I bet he wants narcotics. And I'm his man, Sam. You know me, Brother. The Thug with the drugs."

Sammy wrinkled his nose. George knew that he hated anything illegal. He batted his eyes, placed his hand on Sammy's shoulder, and gently squeezed, "What do you say, Sambo? Do this thing for me?" Sammy patted his hand, and nodded his head. The same night his boss called.

"Is this, Sammy's... brother?"

"Yes. What can I do for you, Mr. Saurian?"

"Can you bring bad people?"

"Sure can."

"Here's what I want. I call you. You bring offerings. Sammy show you where. I leave money same place after. Never try contact, or see me. Twenty-thousand-dollars each time. Will you obey?"

George closed his mouth to keep the spit in. "I'm your man, sir." He smiled, nothing compared with working for a rich articulate maniac.

Sudden anger stirred in George's gut. Wait a minute. Make that a rich, white, kindergarten-flunking maniac. And what was that 'obey' shit?

George calmed himself and didn't speak. This wasn't time to cop attitude. This was way-too-fucking-much-money time. This was G.W. Jones done-found-the-gold-mine time.

Saurian said, "Bring soon."

"No problem, boss man."

George hung up the phone and waited until dark. He would need to know the layout and Sammy agreed to show him the drop off spot. With his brother's direction, George drove to the property. At the South end of the mansion, they opened a gate and continued up a dirt road, leading to the family cemetery.

Under some tall sinister-looking trees stood a large crypt. On its roof, a statue of a huge white kneeling angel with her airplane sized wings spread. Massive alabaster hands were together in prayer and the marble face seemed to weep. Talk about a frightening bitch!

He left the lights on and cut the engine, and followed Sammy toward the statue and the freak-a-negro-out gravesite.

Inside the granite crypt, a stairway led downward. He could barely make out dim light from below as he trailed behind his brother into the darkness. George's flashlight kept cutting out, and he almost fell twice.

Considerable cussing and banging the cheap-ass flashlight against the wall heralded his passage down the stairs.

At the bottom, a metal chair was bolted into the concrete floor, and a long, dim-lit tunnel disappeared toward some-fucking-where that wasn't on his list of places to visit. The cave, or whatever, looked old, dark, and way fucking spooky. It reminded George of vampire haunts in horror flicks.

Sammy sat down in the chair and said, "Isn't this the weirdest thing? See that long bar? It opens and shut this sliding door, like the concealed one that I showed you on the outside." Sam jumped up and pushed the lever. The door slid on unseen rollers and shut with a soft thud. Reversing the direction, it opened once more. "Didn't I tell you this place was freaky?" Sammy hopped back into the chair and giggled; he was excited as a kid sucking sugar cubes.

George felt so happy that he kissed his brother on the forehead, knocked him unconscious with the fucked-up flashlight, and chained him to the chair. For this kind of crime and money; Sam became a liability that he couldn't afford. Promise to Mom kept, Sammy taken care of at last, and money in the bank. Talk about a sweet deal. Without the slightest feeling of remorse, he went home and waited for the call.

Devil Dan called the next day and assured him that he did the right thing, thus their relationship began over a year ago.

He did break one of the pervert's rules, however. He waited around after one of the early deliveries and got a peek at the killer. George had seen some freaky shit in his time, but whatever birthed this hideous, hairless bastard wasn't fucking human.

He shook his head. He had better shit to do than think about the white-fright. Besides, his bank account would soon improve greatly from delivering the latest victim to the killer.

He pulled out his mirror and copped another peek. A happy tear formed in his eye. Talk about a fine mother-fucker...

9

In a scenic corner office, on the third floor of the criminal justice building sat Chief John Poppelli, not so fondly known as, "The Pope." The room was large and expansive, with an oversized stuffed captain's chair. A huge polished desk set low on luxurious imported carpet, giving the chief a taller stature. Actually, he'd sawed the damn legs half off when no one was looking.

Impatiently pressing the intercom button yet again, he yelled, "Where the fuck are you?"

Bursting in the room, completely out of breath, his summer-break intern from Cottondale High School said, "Y-Yes, sir, Mr. P-Chief."

"For cock-sucking sake, call me Chief, or Poppelli. What took you so long?"

Color came to the young girls cheeks. "I-I started my period, Chief."

He gave her a purposeful look up and down, letting her squirm before speaking. "Rule one is I push the button, and rule two is you appear before the buzzer stops. I suggest plugging the dyke before coming to work to avoid this issue in the future. This is the real world and if you want to be treated like an adult, then act like one. Now get the fuck moving and get me Detective Harlan Prophet."

She scurried out.

The fat man sat back in his chair, rubbing his massive baldhead. At five-foot-seven and 240 pounds, Poppelli looked unusual. Someone compared him to a jack-o-lantern, but he didn't hear it. The doctor, in charge of Forensic Profiling let it slip to his secretary that the chief had a classic God complex. This information also missed his ears.

On the chief's fingers were four thick and heavy rings. They could slice up a face, or, at least he believed they could. He didn't care for fighting. Instead, he depended on bluff and his physical size. Intimidation was his game and he loved it. If all else failed, he'd use authority. Rage lurked just under the surface of his skin, along with a hate for lesser people and, in his estimation, that included everyone on the fucking planet.

Back when he was a beat-cop, he carried a pump-shotgun in a black leather pouch. He had little use for handguns. His infamous motto being, "shoot them all before you make that call." He often practiced looking mean in the mirror, while chomping his teeth down on a fat cigar. His pockets were always bristling with thick Havana's.

A knock came at the door. Poppelli said, "Open the motherfucker."

Into the room walked a six and a half foot tall white man. Scuffed brown cowboy boots created soft tremors throughout the office. Despite his size, the man moved with animal-like grace. He outweighed Poppelli but appeared slim, except his chest and shoulders; they were massive.

Detective Harlan Prophet said, "You called?"

"What's this about the maniac-creep getting another citizen?"

"Yeah."

"Did the idiot cut the bottom off the foot?"

"Yeah. Pre-mortem."

Poppelli rubbed a meaty hand over his brow, and smacked the desktop with a closed fist. "I'm going to get this sick fucker. Who's the victim?"

"Read this." Prophet tossed a manila folder onto his desk.

Poppelli read the report aloud. "A severed human sole. Blah, blah, blah. Right foot as usual. Blah, fucking blah. Long hair strands included, probable female, blah. Paragraphs of technical blahshit. Possible connection with missing persons filed on Martha of Garden street by husband Ralph. Oh shit, Harlan, it's Crazy Martha again! Blah, blah, so what's fucking new? Recommendation: Blah… "

He tossed the report in the general direction of Prophet. "Well, fuck a monkey with a gorilla dick. Looks like the silly bitch ran off one time too many." said Poppelli, stabbing the desktop with a fat finger for emphasis.

"Jumping to conclusions?"

Poppelli gave Harlan a dirty look and said, "When you've been a cop as long as I have, you develop certain instincts." He rubbed to his ample gut and continued. "Besides. If I'm wrong, I'll hire a whore to buff your bone and appoint you acting chief."

Harlan returned his look with an intense stare.

Poppelli thought back to the many calls his office received regarding Crazy Martha. Usually she'd be found in a state of partial dress roaming the streets of Cottondale. She gained a certain infamy when she claimed her son was the seed of the almighty. He'd never seen the boy, but could imagine the adverse impact. Poor little fucker.

Everyone in the department knew her pathetic husband from his many pleas for someone to find his wife. Now it appeared she'd found the town's bizarre killer, or maybe him or her, or fucking it, found her. In his estimation, this proved once and for all that the killer's taste in victims matched his artistic skills.

He recalled the first few bloody soles mailed into his office. Always from the right foot. With the third came a note on the kind of paper found in elementary school art class, on it was a crude crayon drawing of a stick figure in green hanging by its arms, with red scribbling all over the right foot. Small crosses were plastered all across the childish sketch and one in heavy black scrawl where the little stick person's genitals would normally be.

The killer identified himself as, 'The Sole Taker.' It took the highly paid genius of the not-worth-a-fuck Forensic Doctor to diagnose the guy as a dyslexic serial killer with religious fixations, and possible unresolved sexual issues. The doctor's back up–in case I got this shit wrong–diagnosis was: A serial-killer with a latent foot fetish. Who gave a fuck? Could anyone say murderer? Fuck sakes. Poppelli didn't care if it was Mickey-fucking-Mouse with cheese issues. Kill in his town and snort cyanide. Simple 'rithmetic.

He let word get out that the good doctor was a fucking nut with tendencies to suck big fat dicks.

"Okay, Harlan, the office is short-staffed. Let's roll and talk with the husband."

"I'll saddle up."

"Fucking retards and cowboys," muttered Poppelli. Making the remark well after Prophet left.

The big detective had transferred one year ago from Oklahoma. Harlan had a slow, southern drawl expressed with scarce unhurried words. He reminded the chief of someone who stuttered; it took all his patience not to complete the sentence. That's if three-word responses could be called sentences. Lame mother fucker.

Rumors were flying about Harlan. Poppelli figured anyone that fucking big would be automatic gossip material. One popular story went along the lines that Prophet made a stop at a certain brothel, and savagely beat the owners. He rounded up several underage girls and escorted them to his police car. Before leaving, Harlan set the bar on fire. Giving the girl's money and dropping them off at the Greyhound bus station, he gave this advice: *"Don't come back."*

Poppelli chomped on his cigar and muttered, "Yeah. He's a fucking saint alright."

Walking downstairs sent sharp pains shooting through his chest. His cardiologist called him a type-A personality. He hated doctors. A bunch of fucking quacks with the social skills of ten-year-olds. Controlling his anger with an office full of idiots was fucking impossible. Reaching into his pocket, he found his heart pills and took one.

He wheezed his way down to the parking garage. Harlan stood at the rear of his cruiser. The big detective had the trunk open, rummaging inside. His shirt lay on the rear fender; he wore a white sleeveless undershirt that looked painted to his enormous body.

Thick muscle-corded arms seemed ready to explode from under his skin as he pulled on a custom-made twin shoulder holster rig for his Colt Pythons. Poppelli figured there was enough fucking leather to harness a plow horse wrapped around the hulking detective.

Harlan had black hair and dark eyes that rarely blinked. Poppelli reasoned that if Frankenstein had a not-so-scared twin, it'd be Harlan. The big fucker probably gave children panic-attacks on Halloween. Passing by the trunk, the chief noticed two large cases. "What the fucks in there?"

"Chainsaw," Harlan said.

"What fucking for?"

"Little girls… In burning cars."

Poppelli remembered the Forensic Doctor's report on that one. A seven-year-old girl had been kidnapped and molested. The assailant reportedly tried to fondle the scratching little girl in the front seat as the van left the freeway, hit a tree, and exploded.

By the time the ambulance arrived, the child had been pulled from the flaming wreckage and wrapped in Harlan's jacket. The driver was listed DOA. Cause listed as probable heart attack, but suspicion remained. The assailant seemed healthy. During autopsy, the only damage found was a slight bruising to the neck.

Harlan finished with his weapons, slipped back into his shirt, and slammed down the trunk, slowly walked around the cruiser, and got behind the wheel. Poppelli stood by the trunk wiping his brow. It was hot, and he'd be stuck with this fucking Okie Amazon for the next hour. He moved to the passenger side, messed with the lever to get the seat all the way back, and squeezed into the car.

He hated beat work. The chief of mother fucking police didn't belong on the cock-sucking streets. Having three detectives out with the flu put his ass in the seat. He vowed that if they didn't recover quickly, they might as well die. Their careers would be dead.

He lit a cigar and sucked in a lung full. Instead of starting the car, Harlan stared at him. Poppelli said, "What, for fuck sake?" Harlan slowly dropped his eyes to the offending cigar and resumed his stare. Poppelli felt his heart spasm as he found the crank on the door window, rolled it down, flung the cigar and added, "Are you fucking satisfied now? Shit!" Without comment, Harlan started the car and slowly left the garage. They were heading for Garden Street.

While they drove, Poppelli observed the streets. Cottondale was an unusual city. It originally gushed to life on the back of a runaway oil boom. With the fall in the production of black gold, the only industry left was crime and it flourished like fleas on a mange-ridden dog. Glancing over at Prophet, he wondered if the big cocksucker could possibly drive any slower.

Arriving at the address, sweat formed and trickled slowly down his back. Poppelli's shirt felt glued to his body and he was relatively certain that his silk boxers were about an inch up his butt. In his present frame of mind, if his men weren't back on the job tomorrow, he'd kill the lot.

He said, "Deal with this, Harlan. I need to sit this one out." He felt the muscles in his jaws bunch up, and his butt cheeks involuntary flex in an attempt to dislodge his undies. He tried covertly scooting his ass against the seat, as the detective nodded and pulled over to the curb.

***

Exiting the car, Harlan walked up to the house.

He knocked on the door. A few minutes passed before a man appeared. He wore wire-framed glasses and his face looked pale, unshaven, and puffy around the eyes. Harlan said, "Martha's missing?"

The face crumbled. "Yes. Have you found her?"

Harlan shook his head and requested a hair sample. A trembling, hyperventilating Ralph retrieved a hairbrush, hair strands were abundantly evident. Handing the brush to Harlan, he held the door in a white knuckled grip.

Harlan asked a few more questions, and tried comforting Ralph. He hoped the words didn't sound as hollow as his heart felt. For a year now, he both dreaded and detested this part of his job.

He turned to leave. Ralph touched his arm and said, "This is about the killer, isn't it?"

Harlan looked into the man's haunted eyes and nodded.

Returning to the cruiser, he could see the fat man tugging at something out of sight between his legs.

10

When the detective left, Ralph felt all hope leave his body. He felt dead. Heading back upstairs, he fell onto the bed, thrashed around in grief and, in the process, heard a crunch. Rolling over, he found his glasses, broken, bent, and distorted. He knocked them onto the floor. They no longer mattered.

Any reserved energy left in his being, clung hopelessly to the empty words spoken by the detective.

Jesus would be faced with caring for an empty shell of humanity, and he wouldn't have that. Martha was his one single reason for hanging on. In spite of her sickness, loving her brought hope. Now the honorable thing was to let go.

Maybe Jesus could somehow make it without his illness dragging him down. If he stayed, he would only succeed in killing them both. Ralph managed a weak smile. He found it ironic that his death may offer the best chance for Jesus.

His poor son, so badly damaged that he still couldn't sleep in the dark. During a power outage, Ralph found him shaking in the throes of some fit. It took months before he would sleep alone again. Martha nursed his sprit and helped him get better. After that, the fits came with regularity.

Despite her illness, Martha gave them purpose; she had always been the glue holding this broken family together, and Ralph would miss her eternally. Without her, his life was a dream and a bad one at that.

Getting up, he went to his closet, dug under some soiled clothes and found a scarred wooden chest.

Removing the lid, he pulled out a bag of rare silver dollars. He located an old photograph taken in the beginning, and a recent school picture of Jesus. The first one of him and Martha was taken at the county fair. They were holding hands in a small booth; she looked beautiful. He placed them in his pocket. They would forever be next to his heart.

He walked from the closet, put the bag on the bed, found paper, and pen in the desk. Squinting without his glasses, he wrote Jesus a note.

Dear Son; sometimes life gets empty. Without your mom, I can't go on. I fear she's dead. I beg your forgiveness for making life hard on you by never being there, a son should never be required to parent his father. I believe that a broken person can only create a broken life. I tried Son. Even when it didn't look like it, I gave it my best. Sadly, my best fell far short of your simple needs. It's time for me to move on. Any words of wisdom from me now, would only ring empty in your ears. I love you. The magic's in you my son. Dad. PS My father gave me these coins; I hope you can use them. The deed to the house is in my safety deposit box, along with the will.

Placing the note next to the coins, Ralph returned to the closet, and found a strong electric extension-cord. He tied one end to the clothes bar and the other around his neck. Muttering, "Forgive me," he relaxed his knees and went searching for Martha.

11

Jesus sat on the riverbank. He reckoned two days had passed judging from his sunburnt arms, but there were large gaps in his memory. No more watermelons for him. John Henry had explained the hair-of-the-dog concept, prompting another ride on the global merry-go-round. Did he get sick again? His last clear memory was an angry John Henry pouring out the remaining wine and telling him to get a blanking grip. Still, he cherished the time with the big man and felt much stronger in spirit, despite his growling stomach.

John Henry had already left. Probably a hot chess game with God. He smiled at the thought, John Henry sure could tell a whopper.

He spent part of the day waiting to see if he'd return, and then started home; it turned into late afternoon as his neighborhood came into sight. Passing the Bridger residence, he considered braving her wrath and checking on Maddie. But he felt it in his gut–she was gone.

Maddie's last words replayed in his mind. His face burned as he ran on toward his house.

It seemed unnaturally quiet as Jesus stepped inside the house, something felt different. Taking the stairs two at a time, he looked first in his mom's room, crossed the hall and then knocked at his dad's closed door.

He slowly turned the knob and peeked in; his father's bed was empty. He stepped inside, his eyes finding and locking onto his lifeless face. It appeared gray and waxy.

Picking him up, Jesus slipped the cord from around his neck. Carrying him to the bed he couldn't believe how light he felt. He gently closed his sad, staring eyes. A note on the desk caught his attention and he read it. Tears hit the paper in audible splats. "Yes, Dad, I know how it feels to be broken," mumbled Jesus. He stuffed the note into his pocket.

He went back downstairs and found a plastic garbage bag, returned, and grabbed a towel from the bathroom. Checking his father's pockets, he found family pictures in the shirt: in the first, Dad looked young, carefree, and incredibly happy with his arm around Mom. The second was an ugly, ratty school picture of himself.

Filling the bathtub, he removed his dad's soiled clothes, carried him to the water, and lowered him gently into the tub. He looked frail, pale and pitifully skinny.

The past few weeks had taken their toll on Dad, with Mom getting worse and then disappearing. He hummed a tune and shaved his face. Over the years, mental illness had ravaged him; but he loved this kind man, and no one would see him this way.

He sensed his father was now free, and that brought comfort to his heart. He washed and dried him, carried him back into the bedroom, and sat him in his overstuffed chair.

In the dresser, he found a nice pair of pajamas and dressed him. Kissing the picture of his parents, he placed both photographs in the shirt pocket, next to Dad's heart. Stripping the bed, he changed the linen. Filling the bag with dirty laundry, he tossed it over the banister.

Carrying his father back into bed, Jesus gently combed his hair, while repeating the nursery rhyme his mother had taught him. "Sleep tight in the angels light... " At the end, emotion overtook him so he whispered, "I love you, Dad." He wiped away tears, took one last look at his father and softly closed the bedroom door.

Jesus went downstairs into the kitchen, and opened the icebox door. It looked the same as his heart felt, small and empty, even his peanut butter jar was licked clean. Finding a piece of hard dry bread, he ate it, moved to the sink, stuck his head under the dripping faucet and sucked water from the tap to keep from choking.

In the basement, he searched his old room. Removing a loose board in the floor, he added the note his dad left to a few other treasures hidden there. Filling an old knapsack with clothes and the coins, he returned into the hallway. Not sure who to notify, he telephoned both an ambulance and the police.

Before leaving, he grabbed the dirty bedding and threw it in the trash. He took another long look at the house and moved to the front door. Now both his mom and dad were gone, and his best girl hated him. Somehow he must find Maddie. With no clear plan in mind, Jesus took a deep breath and stepped outside.

Suddenly the world looked lifeless; darker. The sun set in muted colors as shadows began creeping into his soul.

With a heavy spirit, he headed up the street.

Passing Maddie's house, Jesus could see a large black bird with angry red eyes perched atop her playhouse. It watched his passage in stony silence.

He moved fast until he arrived at the river where he last saw John Henry. Along the way, night crept in like a corrupt moneychanger, absconding with the twilight and leaving a mere nickel moon in change.

Moonlight gave the campsite a cold blue glow. He looked around, found a stand of rocks, put some coins in his pocket, stashed the rest in his knapsack, and hid that behind a large rock. The camp looked barren and unfriendly. Jesus stared into the empty night as hunger pains rumbled in his guts. How could one lost boy ever find his way in a world this hostile? Where was his mom? And where was Maddie Mae?

A cramping stomach became his sole company as he lay down on the cot. Right before falling asleep, fear grabbed him in a white-hot grip while his body convulsed on the bed.

12

Harlan Prophet was dispatched back to the home of Ralph and Martha. He felt content to get out of the office and away from the fat man. The street suited him. He pulled his cruiser into traffic and slipped on sunglasses to cut down reflective glare from the road.

Working around Poppelli grinded on him. It had to do with something other than his boastful demeanor. He could plainly see the chief was all talk, but some as yet hidden thing about the fat man didn't set well with him.

When he spotted the house, paramedics were already there.

The police had received a telephone call a few hours earlier and someone told the operator, "Daddy's sleeping with the angels," or something to that effect. Most suicides weren't hung and then found in bed, so his office got the call. Foul play needed to be ruled out. When they forwarded the message to homicide, he could still remember Poppelli's words. "Some people can't handle good news. Ralph probably freaked out about his wife. Silly bastard should have thrown a party instead."

The detective stopped his car and walked into the house.

Harlan's practiced eyes took in details as he climbed the stairs and went into the room. He could see the piece of cord the man used to hang himself. A pang of guilt hit as the earlier conversation replayed in his mind. He could still see the look on Ralph's face when the news about his wife hit.

Harlan half expected this. Take away the reason for life and death follows. He understood completely. His wife's own smiling face danced across his mind and he pushed it aside. From the corner of his eye, he noticed something under the bed. Reaching down, he picked up broken eyeglasses and placed them on the nightstand.

Harlan examined the dead man's fingernails and arms. No struggle. No defensive cuts and the nail beds were clean. The face looked peaceful. He always put credence in the facial expression; wrongful death stole serenity, the face always told him. He routinely ordered autopsies based solely on that last look.

Someone had cleaned the body and bed; Harlan believed he knew whom. The detective noticed a bulge in the pajama pocket and removed two photographs; they were a beautiful family. A dagger of pain shot through his heart as he imagined what happened to the wife. He wondered what became of the boy.

Harlan spoke to the coroner's office people. "Release the body. Suicide." The detective felt sadness for the man. He wondered if Martha could still be alive. Remembering the butchered foot, he hoped not.

He wanted this killer. For the past year and a half, his life had resembled a crusade; hating a system that catered to killers and perverts.

Over-paid lawyers finding legal loopholes to spring guilty clients and claiming justice served. Puss-sucking scum in designer suits. The sicker the client, the higher the celebrity in getting them set free. He could see it in their eyes, these attorneys knew they represented sadistic murders, and cared less. Egocentric seekers of fortune and fame.

Harlan believed this to be more damning than the actual killing; these inky-hearted protectors of crazed assassins were evil's vanguard. If there was a Hell, they would be the hot cobbles lining the fiery streets.

Inmate clients were released daily from crowded penal systems and mental hospitals. Their first order of business was to re-offend. Murderers walked in and out of State Hospitals as if they had revolving doors. Some got precious few miles before they slaughtered other innocents.

Harlan remembered a recent event from the Cottondale facility. The State psychiatrists pronounced a sociopath killer rehabilitated and cured. The killer's first act as a newly sane and free man was to steal a car and butcher the family who owned it. He killed five more people before they caught him, still driving the dead family's car.

The arresting officers frisked him and found three human ears in his pocket. One had been partially eaten. He sat there chewing away like a kid on bubblegum. When the officer told him to spit, he swallowed and smiled. The crazy bastard claimed that his voices told him to eat it and, besides, he found them crunchy. It seemed the high-powered psychiatrists missed reporting his proclivity for cannibalism.

When jailed, the killer bragged he'd get off again because, after all, he was mentally ill. Somehow, while the pervert awaited trial, someone left a door open and other inmates gave him a karmic killing. Poppelli made no secret about suspecting Harlan. But no proof, no case.

A fierce storm brewed just under the skin of the detective ever since... .

13

Jesus opened his eyes. The warm sun spread golden rays throughout the campsite and reminded him of John Henry. Having the big man around was the same as having sunshine in his face.

He looked at the cold fire pit and remembered their last conversations. He loved John Henry. However, this problem with Maddie felt personal. They were his words that ran her off and, somehow, he'd get her back. He wondered how many people wished they could take back something they didn't mean to say. He sure did.

Worrying about his mother brought additional pain, and not knowing her fate weighed heavy upon his heart. Jesus feared that his mom was dead, but not seeing her body left an unreal nightmare quality to this apprehension.

The scream and slap from their last meeting replayed in his dreams on a never-ending loop. His father's leaving didn't hurt as much. For years Dad barely lived in spasms, and just before his death, he started the process of slowly disappearing altogether. At least he wouldn't hurt anymore. And, hopefully, neither would Mom.

Moving to the river, Jesus took off his shirt and splashed cool water on his face and chest. It felt wonderful. The warm breeze, chirping birds, and blue sky refreshed his spirit, and the river's voice, as it traveled seaward, brought peace to his heart.

Locating his hiding place, Jesus used his shirt for a towel, dug out his knapsack and found a change of clothes. The freshly washed smell brought Maddie to mind. He swiped a tear from his cheek and dressed in a faded red T-shirt and frayed jeans. Transferring the coins from his dirty pants, he put the soiled clothes in the knapsack and hid it with the remaining silver back behind the rock. Carefully surveying the security of his treasure, he left camp.

It took a couple of hours to walk into town. On the outskirts, Jesus found a large building with a big neon sign that read, BIG BLACK FAT MOMMA'S PLACE.

He went inside and stood by the door while his eyes adjusted.

A deep melodic voice said, "Come in, child, if Big Momma doesn't have what you want then you probably don't need it."

Jesus looked at her. She seemed big for a woman, although beautiful. She had large expressive features with enormous dark eyes and eyelashes like black combs.

From behind the bar, she patted the bar-top indicating where she wanted him to sit. Her hands were much bigger than his were, but incredibly feminine, ending in long brightly polished nails. Everything about the woman came super-sized. Huge, sensual, cherry red lips set in a smiling chocolate face. She said, "Call me Big Momma, child. Unless you're whispering in my ear. Then use your imagination."

His eyes grew wide trying to process her enormous beauty.

She touched her breast with a hand and said, "Mercy, child. If you were any cuter you'd likely break Big Momma's heart. Come over here and sit down. Would you care for a coke?"

He climbed up on the bar stool and said, "Yes please." Digging into his pocket for the silver dollars.

"Now don't go pulling something out of there that's going to scare Big Momma. I might need to whisk you off upstairs." She lowered her eyelashes and gave him an intent look.

He smiled and pulled out a silver dollar.

"Hand that here, handsome boy. Mercy. If that's not rare money I ain't got good sugar. And, child, my lips put men into diabetic comas."

"What's rare, Big Momma?"

She gave him that look again. "I expect someone as sweet as you managing to stumble into my bar with all these cute questions is. But Momma's thinking you mayhap fell off some hay wagon. I believe I'll take you under my wing." She held the coin up inspecting it. "This here money is worth a bunch more than just a dollar. I'll put it away, and everything is paid for until I say it's not." She placed her hand softly on his arm and added. "I'm thinking you don't have anywhere to go, child. Am I right?"

He nodded his head.

"Well, I'll put food in that belly, a roof over your head and new clothes on your back. What do you say, child?"

He nodded again. Big Momma's kindness put a lump in his throat.

She said, "What's your name, young man?"

"Jesus."

She lightly touched his cheek. "Jesus. When you get tired of carrying all those miseries, come find Big Momma. Hear?"

He said, "Thanks, Big Momma," and took a drink of his coke, trying to keep a lid on the warm feelings flooding his heart. In all his life, only John Henry had treated him this nice.

He sipped his drink and looked around. Big Momma's place sprawled out before him, with tables ringing a huge dance floor. A raised stage with red satin curtains stood in simple beauty at the back of the bar. Sitting in elegant splendor on the platform was an enormous black piano with a raised lid. Jesus never imagined such a fine instrument. The soft hum of large swamp coolers and multi-colored lights gave the bar a peaceful feeling.

He looked up at the sound of people coming through the swinging doors. Around a dozen large men wearing identical sleeveless denim vests were entering. Each vest had a large white skull with the initials B. B. in red letters on the back.

The first man through the door moved with catlike grace belying his large frame. Red scars lashed a boyish face, with eyes seemingly poised on the brink of laughter. Muscles danced just under his skin as he walked. Wrapped up his arms were tattoos. The left had black chain-lengths starting at the back of his hand and circling up under his open vest; the right arm displayed the same pattern only in Barbed wire. His head was shaved and tanned.

A smile split the man's face once he saw Big Momma. He leaned over the bar and hugged her.

Jesus couldn't believe his eyes, a huge tattooed tarantula covered his bald head; it had a black body with red-banded legs. He smacked his knee. It was the strangest thing he'd ever blanking seen.

Big Momma guided the man over and placed her hand on Jesus' shoulder. "Bart, this is my good friend, Jesus." The biker extended a scared hand.

Jesus shook his hand and said, "There's a spider on your head, Bart."

"Well fuck me, Big Momma, the kid's a comedian." Bart gave him a good-natured smack on his arm. "So where in the funny papers did you come from?"

"That's sure a big spider."

"This thing has been known to crawl off my head while I'm drinking."

"Wow! Really? What does B. B. stand for, Bart?"

"That would be Bartholomew's Bitches. I considered Babes who Butt-fuck, but the guys got testy."

Jesus started giggling.

The biker pointed at him and said, "Hey, Big Momma. What the fuck did you put in this kid's coke?"

"Big Momma's brown sugar. Is that boy sweet or what?"

Bart looked at him. "I'm thinking or what. Can we keep him? I haven't had so much fun since I fell asleep on my Harley on the freeway."

He couldn't help but hold his stomach. Bart was a riot.

The biker elbowed Jesus, pointed at Big Momma and whispered into his ear. "I think some large hunk of dark chocolate has her eyes on you, kid."

"I r-really l-like Big Momma, Bart."

The big woman smiled as she moved up the bar.

Jesus pulled out his wallet and showed its lone contents to Bart.

"Who's this lovely girl?"

"That's my Maddie-Mae. I said something bad to her and she ran away. I need to find her, Bart."

The biker studied the photograph. "Well, kid, I can see why you're looking."

He handed Big Momma the picture. She looked it over and passed it to the assembled bikers. One man omitted a low wolf-whistle and said, "He may have a weird name but the chick's pretty."

Bart's eyes flashed. "I can fix that whistle for you. And if anyone wants to talk about names, start with mine." The offending biker handed the picture back with an apology. Bart raised his voice, "Anybody spots this girl, bring her here to Big Momma's."

With hope gleaming in his eyes Jesus said, "Thank you, Bart."

"Anything for a friend of Big Momma's, youngster; be careful though or she'll have you doing things you can't even pronounce."

Big Momma came over and slapped the bar with her hand. "Okay, Mr. Bart, keep talking that way and I'll see if I can't knock that spider clear off your head."

The biker raised his hands. "I'll be good, beautiful dark and sexy. But if you must hit me, I'd prefer a spanking."

She shook her head, batted her lashes, and moved back down the bar.

He looked at Bart, and said, "She-She's... " Panic locked Jesus tongue in his throat as he struggled for air, time gapped and his vision blurred.

When he could see again, Bart appeared not to have noticed; instead, he was talking with the man next to him.

Jesus had intended to say something else about Big Momma, but couldn't remember what. He looked around the bar, it looked as though no one had witnessed his attack, and he was very thankful.

Jesus finished his coke and started yawning. He looked up as Big Momma regarded him. She said. "Do you want to get a shower and see your room?"

He nodded his head, being cleaned up sounded good, and he felt tired.

Big Momma yelled, "Honey, get it in here."

From a door behind the bar sauntered a slim black girl. Her face came from the same cast that had molded her mother's beauty. Other than Maddie, Jesus had never seen a girl this lovely. She had a way of lowering her head and looking up through her eyelashes that seemed both bashful and sensual. By the way her eyes slowly traveled over his body, shyness seemed out of the question.

Big Momma pointed at Jesus and said, "Take this young man upstairs and put him in room six. Get him food and buy some clothes over at the department store."

The girl came around the bar and offered her hand. He took it and followed her up the stairs. Her mother's voice rumbled in the background. "Mind your manners, Honey girl."

On the way to the room, Jesus' body kept colliding with hers. He looked at his feet wondering what had happened to his walking ability. Maybe he was more tired than he thought. She opened the door and showed him the room.

Honey moved up close and lightly touched his chest with her small hands. In a husky voice she said, "I'm measuring you for new clothes." Jesus for sure didn't think she missed any dimensions. When she finished, her eyes did the head-to-toe thing again and she offered her small hand with fingers pointing down. He shook it the best he could. Honey said, "You were supposed to kiss it, baby boy." He blushed.

She said, "At first I thought you were a cute white boy. Now I'm thinking Indian." The girl stepped even closer. Jesus could feel heat radiating from her body. Honey said, "Do you think I'm pretty?" His eyes got big as he bobbed his head up and down.

She stepped against his body and held him. "I know you have a girl friend. I'll be your little sister." Her hands were lightly touching his backside; apparently taking the remaining measurements. She added, "At least I'll try." With her lips merely inches from his she whispered, "My name is Honey, as in melt in your mouth sweet." She had a bright smile, with big dimples.

"M-My name is... ."

Honey stopped him with a quick kiss. "Hush now lest I forget that you're my new brother." She turned and walked away. He couldn't help but notice that, for someone so small, Honey could certainly shake her bottom.

Jesus pushed the door shut after she left and went into the bathroom. Stripping off his clothes, he stepped into the shower.

He found some miniature soap wrapped in paper and began to wash. Abruptly, crippling fear shot through his body. He fell on the floor as the attack progressed. He felt powerless. Since around eleven-years-old these spells would come and never gave warning.

He believed that everyone in the bar would probably treat him much differently if they witnessed this. No one tolerated a sissy. In school, the larger boys said he was turning into a pulsating pussy and when he finished they would take turns fucking him. "Hey Sue, do the beaver-dance for us." Remembered voices tormented him. Normal people weren't afraid, especially men.

In his mind, he conjured up images of Bart and Big Momma spitting on him during an attack. Jesus saw a movie once where someone sold their soul to the Devil. If Satan could stop this fear he'd sign—and quick. Feeling miserable, he stumbled out of the shower, dried off, and found his way to the bed.

14

She hung from her wrists. Her clothes were gone. And she was past caring. Urine trickled down her leg.

Warm blood dripped on her face from ropes cutting deep into her wrists.

She dangled in some large cavernous building. The air carried a preternatural chill.

Her right foot oozed blood from being butchered by the maniac-thing. The former sharpness of pain now dulled, replaced instead by numbness, both in spirit and mind. Her body felt dead.

How did she end up in this weird place? Would she ever see Jesus again? Instead of answers, darkness cloaked her in blessed unconsciousness...

15

Daniel Saurian appeared ghostlike in the darkness of the antebellum mansion; a malevolent phosphorous shape seeming to float in inky blackness.

Three things still connected him with the outside world: running water, a telephone kept hidden and unplugged in a drawer, and the gas he used in the factory.

The entire manor was void of furniture, appliance, or bed. He ate mainly dried fruits, candies, and boxes of cereal. These items were horded in the un-plugged refrigerator, safe from rats.

He slept on the floor, using the same for his toilet, smearing feces on his body and marking territory wherever he went. He found the pungent smell of his stool intoxicating.

Large wharf rats were thick in the house. Sometimes he would feign sleep until one would get within distance, then grab it, bite the head off and drink its blood. Lately, few would venture near him. He enjoyed listening to them communicating in the dark. They spoke of him–their master. He loved the house. It reminded him of a black, fetid womb, birthing his transition.

Heading for and finding the back door by touch alone, he stepped into the factory and moved toward the tunnel.

He felt strong, unlike the weak mixed-sex being of his youth. His body pumped with rage, and that manifested in constant clenched muscles. Slowly, these maniacal isometrics produced inhuman strength. His claw-shaped hands could rip fleshy chunks. Overdeveloped jaw muscles, powered razor-sharp teeth, decapitating butter-soft finger joints with ease.

With his fingernail, he sliced his chest and watched the blood flow down his alabaster skin. Bait for the rats! Ah to kill. The word *he* crossed his awareness. Yes, he felt maleness. Like the too-daring alpha rat, after munching off his head, he dinned on its balls. Daniel felt energy from each new life he took. Clarity and focus in the coppery taste of blood.

He went down the tunnel toward the family crypt. He enjoyed these trips. He loved the perpetual twilight of his territory, his eyes becoming more and more suited for the nocturnal. Darkness cloaked his identity–and the past. This realm belonged to him. The cement floor shone dull gray in the dim light as he walked toward the metal chair bolted in place below the crypt. He kept the door to the outside closed.

When collecting offerings left in the chair, he used a wooden dolly with hard rubber wheels. The cart made an unusual sound from one wheel with a chunk missing. Thunk, thunk, thunk, he enjoyed the hypnotic spell it cast. His father had used the same cart years ago in his boat building business.

He carried tools. Keys for locks, chloroform to subdue victims, and a short ball-bat if needed. He also carried lengths of rope and was highly skilled in tying knots.

The manor connected to the factory, that in turn with an underground passageway, leading to a secret door under the crypt. The crypt door opened to stairs designed for quick escape during the civil war. The huge angel became a visual landmark in times of heavy fog.

Two things were especially useful in his work. The chain-hoists that slid on an overhead rail system and the huge vat marked *Ballast*. The vat stood full of shiny cold lead. However, in a short time span, the super-heated gas jets could turn the hard metal into a bubbling inferno.

One entire end of the boat factory was originally open and launch-ramps led down to the sea at the bottom of Cemetery Hill. He had long since sealed it. Few reminders of the original enterprise remained, except a huge skeletal boat keel stretching half the length of the building.

He turned back toward the factory.

Offerings arriving here were bound at the wrists and feet. If the noise from their mouths distracted him, he taped them. Saurian became a creature of ritual and habit. He gave important service to the world, purging sins from the tainted beings brought here. All who came here had black hearts. Their dirty sex organs bore perverse witness to misspent lives, and only he could offer absolution. Only the fire could restore balance. And he was the keeper of the flame.

A body hung from the chains now. It had a dirty pink slash between its legs; he hated that wet gash and the small chest tits. He punished this one. It kept repeating the name *Jesus* and he found it disturbing. Following the slow cutting, it mouthed sounds with the volume turned off. He found this more to his liking. Silence afforded proper ritual. He looked up at the face. Death seemed close. It always followed the pale blanching around the eyes. He must hurry.

Stepping up close he rested his face on its leg. Looking up at the hair-covered slit, he flicked out his tongue, tasted the salty flesh of its upper leg, and spit at the fuck thing. He fought back the instincts to rip at it, tear the hole open, crawl inside, and eat its guts.

He moved over to the vat and started the fire.

A metamorphosis was taking place under the skin of Daniel Saurian–a changing. He looked at his own chalk-white, hairless body. Small at five-foot-seven, with mixed sex, a small flap he urinated from covered his own stinky gash. Girlish breasts and effeminate hips with bitch legs, his father said he looked like half-baked pussy. His newfound muscles couldn't erase that heart breaking affirmation. His eyes clouded over as he remembered...

His mother died in childbirth and Dad said many things to remind him–all bad. "Wife killer," hurt terribly. It hurt more than the beatings and cigarettes put out on his skin. It hurt more than the repeated molesting, but much less than the way his dad looked at him. The revulsion in his father's face broke his heart. He could see his grotesque body reflected in the hate-filled eyes of his rapist daddy.

Afterward, Dad would always beg forgiveness and he would gladly try to give it. Those were the good times, cradling his sobbing father in his arms and telling him it would be all right. Then in mere hours, it would start again.

Somewhere at the beginning of these molestations, he had his first reoccurring dream. In the dream flew a huge, mighty wraith, wreaking vengeance on bad people. It looked like Daniel except it was half eagle. It had a razor-sharp flesh rending beak, and gripped a flaming sword in its talon shaped claw. Its name was Sole Taker.

At age seventeen, it happened. While working with the lead, his dad slipped and fell onto the floor. It knocked him out cold. Without hesitation, Danny tied his wrists together, inserted the chain-hoist hook between them, and effortless hoisted him off the floor with the pulley system.

While his father was still unconscious, he pulled off his shoes. Inspecting the bottoms of both feet, he found the telltale mark, a faint, red cross etched into the skin. In Danny's eyes, it glowed. Grabbing a sharp knife from the tool rack, he took his first sole.

He'd discovered the location by accident. In one of his infrequent days in school, the teacher talked about the foot, and how all the nerves ended at the sole. At last Daniel knew the location of the spiritual nature of humans, but which foot?

Embarrassed to raise his hand in class, he puzzled over making the correct choice. Taking off his shoes that night, he examined his own. The right one bore the mark, along with old scars from his father's cigarettes burns. Dad enjoyed hurting him in places that wouldn't show. He tucked the information away in his mind for a special day–a day of liberation. This day.

That first sole went into the vat; his dad was beyond redemption.

His father's body shook in the chains as consciousness returned. Stripping off the remaining clothes, he looked at his penis. Daniel hated it. With deadly purpose, he went to the molten vat. Grabbing a long handled ladle, he dipped it into the steaming metal. His father had barely opened his eyes when he tossed the fiery liquid. The hated organ disappeared as hot lead melted a smoking hole in his groin.

Daddy shrieked like an animal while he pushed his body over the vat and lowered him. One louder shriek left his mouth and then silence. Daniel let the vat burn for three days. The body incinerated within hours, but he worried that his father would somehow climb out and hurt him again.

He called the family attorneys and they in turn called the police. They officially listed his father as missing and launched a formal investigation. The detective in charge insisted young Danny be put into foster care until they found him, or he reached majority.

Tears were streaming down his snotty face as he pleaded, "Please, just leave me here." He kicked and bit at the officers and, as a result, was sent to the State Juvenile Detention Center.

The attorneys finally emancipated him, giving him control of his father's estate, but not before repeated raping by larger boys. They hated him and looked on him as a contagious disease. They made fun of his alabaster skin and girlish body, calling him "Ghost Pussy" and "Hershey." The boys took turns molesting him. They bragged about all the girls they had fucked and gave him a perverse crash course in sex education.

Daniel found one ray of light in his jail experience. A social worker named Grace paid multiple visits. She spoke of faith, extensive therapy, hormone treatments, and operations. She almost made him believe that, with forgiveness, prayer, hard work, and his family's vast resources, healing was possible. Forgiveness was the one thing he would not give. EVER.

Daniel thought it odd that Grace would always be there to comfort him after each abuse, seeming to appear magically in his cell. She even invaded his dreams until he willfully banished her.

Another, stronger call pulled at him. A winged nightmare wooed and raged under his skin, pumping blistering fire to his thoughts and fantasies; courting his bitter schemes and painting them a hot, vengeful, gore-splattered red.

Once released, he would no longer go outside. Daniel hated the world and every creature in it. Ever slowly, he killed his second person–himself. He murdered all memories of the misshapen boy/girl thing and started becoming something else on the evolutionary ladder. Something greater than humankind. The Sole Taker.

The past fell away as his eyes cleared...

Daniel looked at his hands. He squeezed them until veins bulged and muscles vibrated in his steel-cable arms. Loosing a screech of happiness, he turned to the woman in chains. He would kill soon.

16

Jesus awoke to find that his late nap lasted until dark. There was a sandwich by his bed, set on a small blue plate. Thick brown bread that smelled of wheat cut in spread opened halves. Looking inside, he found lettuce, tomatoes, and stuff he couldn't identify, but it sure looked good. Each half came neatly speared with decorative toothpicks and separated by potato chips. He even had his own napkin. Things were never this way at home–not at all. It tasted wonderful.

He spotted new clothing stacked on the dresser. Slipping into pants and shirt, he found that Honey was expert at measuring. Jesus could smell her musky fragrance lingering on the clothes. She seemed different from any girl he'd ever known, or women for that matter.

Jesus finished dressing and headed down the hall. As he neared the stairs, the sound of Big Momma's amplified voice reached him. She sang a slow bluesy song and it sounded beautiful.

He went into the bar toward the stage.

"Hey, Rip Van Winkle," said Bart, motioning from the booth he was sitting in. Jesus started walking over. The biker slapped the table and yelled, "Barkeep, a coke for my good buddy." Honey was delivering drinks nearby looking especially cute in her tight black dress and white frilly waitress apron.

"'Best be putting some please with that order, chrome-dome." She leveled her gaze at the biker.

"Pretty please, Honey-Girl, it's for Jesus."

She batted her eyes. "Tell him to keep his pants on. At least until I get there."

Jesus moved by her and she winked at him. He felt his face burn clear down his neck.

"I'm going to scalp me that Indian," said Honey.

Bart reached out and snatched him into the booth. His big arm held Jesus immobile while he messed up his hair. "What the hell are you doing to the women around here?" The biker released him and softly punched him on the arm.

Jesus felt something soft press against his cheek as Honey reached over his body with his coke. When it occurred to him what that something was, she'd already left.

Big Momma tapped the microphone and said, "Were going to take a short break. Give a big round of applause to the master of the bones, Mr. Ivory Keys." A tall, thin, graying piano player stood and bowed. Stage lights dimmed and both exited between the curtains.

The piano caught Jesus' eye. It glistened in the foot lights. He looked at the instrument and blue lights and music notes danced in his head. He didn't remember going onstage, or sitting behind the piano. Jesus became entirely emotion and sound, as his fingers struck the keys.

The composition expressed losing Maddie and making the biggest mistake of his life. In his mind, the bar, the people, and his body disappeared. Only music lived and it expressed itself through his fingers flying over the ivories. He felt melded with the keys, and they existed solely for his feather touch, seeming to leap up and meet his fingers traveling over the keyboard. The piano and Jesus became one.

When he finally stopped and looked around, people swayed in their chairs. Tears fell down the most hardened faces. Jesus felt anxiety short circuiting his brain with the realization that all eyes were upon him; he swallowed hard and tried to find his shaky legs.

Big Momma and Honey were holding their chests and weeping.

He started walked back toward his table. Big Momma hugged him and said, "That was wonderful, child. It felt as though you were inside my heart and yanking on the strings. I haven't cried this much in ages." He apologized in a shaky voice. The big woman continued, "No, child, those were good tears. If you ever want to play for a living, you come find Big Momma and I'll get you started." She released him and headed toward the bar.

Before he could move, a wet-faced Honey grabbed him. He self-consciously held her with her warm cheek pressing his. Music started playing from the jukebox and she began moving in his arms. Jesus stiffly tried shifting his body, wishing instead that he could sit down.

Honey said, "No, baby boy, this way." She placed her hands on his hips and guided him. She pulled him into her, lowered her hands to his butt and said, "Be loose. Feel me move and follow."

She moved her hips with the music. Despite his shot nerves, he began to feel the rhythm and followed her lead. She smiled at him. "Yes, baby boy. That's what I'm talking about. Shake that thing."

After the music ended, she held him, slowly rocking in his arms as another song started. Dancing with her became effortless. She rubbed her cheek against him and hotly breathed quiet, perfumed words into his ear, "That song gave me chills, baby boy. While you played the piano I felt the music deep inside my soul. I know you have a girl. But if...
."

Jesus said, "I think you're one of the most beautiful girls that I've ever seen, but when I played, it was about Maddie. The one good thing in my whole life has been her and I'm no good. I-I well... "

She placed her fingers on his mouth. "Hush, baby boy. Something is wrong with everyone. It's called life. We change what we can and live with the rest. I can tell that you love her and I respect that. But, don't think you're the only messed up person in the world. Take a look around. Everybody has problems. I see nothing but sweetness and light in you." Honey stopped dancing and looked him in the eyes. She reached up, kissed him softly on the mouth and then turned and left.

Jesus felt rooted to the spot with mortification.

Bart stood up and started to walk over. Without warning, he fell onto the floor and began to convulse. His eyes rolled up as foam oozed from clenched teeth and his Levis turned wet at the crotch. Bikers formed a ring around their leader, facing out toward the crowd.

Something about the attack brought panic back into Jesus' heart. He looked questioningly at Big Momma. She said, "He has seizures, child." Taking charge she spoke to the bikers. "Take him upstairs. Someone stay with him. He'll likely need to sleep for awhile."

Jesus watched the men carry Bart up the stairs. He felt an arm on his shoulder. Big Momma said, "He got hit over the head with a pipe last year. Ever since, he has these attacks. Sometimes two a day. It'd be best not to say anything about this to him. I've never heard him come out and say it. But I think he gets embarrassed."

Jesus felt the need to get away. He said, "I'm going outside and look around for a while."

The big woman said, "Be careful out there. Bad folks be moving about this time of night."

He put his arms around her and hugged her tightly. "I will. Thanks, ma'am."

She waved a finger at him. "Don't be aiming them madams at me. They could put a body's eyes out." She smiled at him as he went out the door.

Outside, Jesus looked around. Maddie crossed his mind and he said a silent prayer for her safety. He'd barely taken a couple steps when another panic-attack hit him. He went to his knees, placed a hand on the building and gasped for air.

He'd just started breathing normally again when a man walked up, and said. "I watched you play the piano through the window. Man that's good stuff. Ever consider making money at it?"

Jesus shook his head. The black man had a pleasant face and seemed nice. He had the greenest eyes, they seemed to sparkle. Jesus stuck his hand out and introduced himself.

The man acted as if they were old friends and took his offered hand into both of his and pumped warmly. "George

Jones is the name. Making dreams come true is my game. What was happening when I came up?"

"I get t-these attacks sometimes. I get fearful and I can't breathe until they pass." He briefly wondered why he told this to a total stranger. Something about the warmth of the man, he seemed trustworthy.

George said, "Hey, the same thing happens to me sometimes. I get so nervous that I think I might pass out." He reached in his pocket and produced two red capsules. "The Doctor gave me these. Take them and I promise the problem will go away."

Jesus grabbed the drugs and swallowed them without even thinking about water, he couldn't believe his luck, now he wouldn't live in fear. "Wow! Thanks George, you're the best friend ever."

"No problem. Come with me and we'll get some coffee. I'll even give you more magic drugs." The man started walking and Jesus skipped up next to him. Distant thunder rumbled in the night sky.

He felt happy. This was the absolute, O-boy-best moment of his life. The whole town seemed packed with nice people. He reached over and patted George on the shoulder. The green-eyed man smiled back at him knowingly. Jesus felt as though he floated on air. He glanced down at his boots and grinned, if only John Henry could see him now.

In about two blocks, they came to a small restaurant. George picked a spot in a back booth and motioned for the waitress as they sat down. A cute young girl came to their table with her pencil poised over her opened order pad. George said. "Bring me some coffee and whatever my friend here needs."

The restaurant had polished tables, with bright red booths, the friendly smell of coffee and food filled the air. Jesus said, "Hot chocolate, please."

She gave him a pretty grin and said, "Will there be anything else?"

George growled at her. "Fill the fucking order and leave the romance to us."

The waitress looked shocked and said, "Pardon me, sir. I'll bring the drinks right away."

Jesus wondered why his new friend got so mean with the woman. He seemed the perfect gentleman–until now.

George looked at him, and said, "Hey, man. I'm sorry. I didn't mean that. A young girl got brutally raped and I'm not over it yet." He lowered his eyes and placed a jeweled covered hand over his face. "I feel terrible. She was a good girl. Like my own daughter. There are some really bad people in the world. And one found her."

The waitress came back and he apologized profusely.

Jesus said, "I sure hope nothing happens to my girl. I hurt her feelings and she ran away from home. I wish I knew where she was." He pulled the picture from his wallet. Handing the photograph to George, he said, "This is Maddie."

George studied the photograph and handed it back, he grew quiet for a moment, pulled out his own wallet, flashed a bright silver badge, and said, "I'm a detective and finding people is what I do best." With a warm friendly look he inquired, "First time she's left home?"

He nodded.

"Tell me her last name and where she lives, and I'll locate her. I'll meet you back here in two days at eight PM. If I don't have her by then, I'll know where she's at."

Jesus was thrilled with the news. George would grant the one wish in his heart. He couldn't believe his good luck and gave the needed information. What a swell night, first help with the fear, and now someone smart enough to find Maddie.

George said, "I'll need some personal item from you so she'll believe me. Women are cautious. There are some monsters loose in the world. And I don't want to upset, or frighten her."

Jesus took off the golden ring. Twin green colored hearts clung to his finger, it seemed as though the ghost of the ring remained attached to his skin. His most valued treasure felt feather light in his hand. Reluctantly, he handed it to George and said, "She gave me this." He felt tears building behind his eyes. "Please tell her I'm sorry."

"Hey, no problem. Call me the man with the plan. That's your man working your plan." Reaching into his pocket, he produced a plastic bag filled with red capsules, tossed it across the table and smiled. Jesus could see two large diamonds stuck right smack in his front teeth.

"Well, blank me."

"Is your name really Jesus?

"Yes, sir, that's my name."

"That sucks. Why don't you change it?"

He felt his face go red. "It's the name my mother gave me, and I love my mother, George."

"I love my mother, too. But if the b... woman, named me something like that I'd k... ah ask her to change it."

Jesus shook his head and lowered his gaze.

George reached over and cuffed his chin. "Hey, what do I know? It's only a suggestion. My name sucks, too. Too bad people can't name themselves. I'd call myself, Mr. Ebony Allure."

Jesus appreciated the honesty of the diamond-toothed man. Most people avoided the subject or teased him. He'd been having problems with this issue ever since he could remember, but this was a gift from Mom, and he loved her with all his heart, and he'd keep the name she gave him.

George looked at his watch and said, "See you later, Jesus. Time is ticking. I'll meet you when I said. And I'll bring more red candy." The greasy-haired man got up and left the restaurant.

He watched as George walked away. He appeared injured or something; one leg dragged stiffly, his arm seemed uncoordinated, and he almost stuck his thumb in his butt.

Jesus waved goodbye and took another sip of hot chocolate. The waitress came back over to the table and he read her nametag. Jesus gave her a slow purposeful look up and down and said, "You're a sweet bunch of pretty woman, Rebecca."

She started to move away then turned back and said, "I don't know why I'm bothering. I thought you were a nice boy, at least before you opened your big mouth."

Jesus felt the same warm feeling that happened while drinking with John Henry. The drugs in the red capsules made his head buzz. However, this girl was confusing. He thought that women enjoyed having nice things said to them, he sure the blank did.

She continued; "Here's some free advice: the man that just left is bad. I've seen his type before."

Now he understood, the girl's feelings were still hurt. He said, "Mr. Jones is really a nice man. It's just that someone he loved was recently hurt and he feels bad about it. He didn't mean to say those things." Jesus fingered the plastic bag in his pocket. George Jones was the blanking best.

The girl raised her eyebrows. "It's more than what he said. It's how he says things and the way he looks at people. I know bad news when I see it."

He was feeling better and better as the warm buzz intensified. Talk about cool medication. Maybe this girl wasn't feeling well or something. He placed his hand over hers and squeezed while sliding his other hand up her arm. "You sure have pretty eyes, Rebecca."

She yanked her hand back. "You're a complete waste of time. Get your hands off me. You jerk."

Jesus left the restaurant.

The girl was puzzling. It was the same thing Big Momma did to him and it made him feel wonderful. Then he wondered why he did it in the first place. It had something to do with seeing how much he could get away with, but why would he do that? Maddie was his girl. Still, Rebecca both excited and confused him.

Jesus reached into his pocket and popped another capsule into his mouth. Women, go blanking figure...

He breathed in the warm night air. He loved the way the city sounded and smelled. Multihued lights with colorful people doing the exotic things colorful people surely did.

Neon-silver lightning flogged a defenseless earth as thunder threatened to split the heavens. A summer storm seemed possible.

Jesus headed for the river.

George deserved payment for finding his girl, and he couldn't forget Big Momma. The streets were dark and Jesus felt good. He lengthened his stride. The toe-guards on his boots flashed silver in the moonlight. He smiled. The boots were the thing all right, and he was just the blanking cowboy to wear them.

He recovered the silver dollars, returned to the bar, and went straight up to his room. Feeling more tired than usual, Jesus put the coins in the dresser, took off his clothes and, instead of turning on a night light, jumped in bed.

17

Jesus woke in the middle of the night. He couldn't make up his mind where the blank he was; everything seemed dreamy. Getting up, he went into the bathroom, found the pills, and tossed another capsule in his mouth. He didn't feel nervous—not in the least. His heart felt a warm glow for the miraculous wonder-drugs, and the marvelous black man who made dreams come true.

He returned to bed. Jesus felt rather than saw someone else in bed with him. Pulling back the covers, he could see Honey's face in the moonlight. She smiled up at him. He said, "Honey, what's going on?"

"Hush, baby boy, you'll wake up momma. Can you keep a secret?"

"Yes."

"I probably shouldn't be telling you this. But six months ago the Doctor's said that I have less than a year to live."

He felt sad for her.

She continued. "Some nights I wake up terrified. I guess dying alone scares me the most. Can I stay with you tonight?"

"I guess so." He thought how exceptionally sweet she was and how unfair her death would be. "But you're so young."

"I know. I still have trouble accepting it. I'll never get to do so many things in life. That's another reason I came in here. I've never even lain in bed with a boy before." She lowered her eyes, "At least not without my clothes on."

Jesus felt uncomfortable with the warmth of her nude body pressing against him. Rubbing something wet and incredibly hot against his leg was more accurate. But hearing her story filled his heart with sorrow. He pulled her close and patted her small back.

"Would it be okay for me to come in here now and then?" She asked.

"Sure, Honey."

He felt her hot thing getting hotter as she said, "This may sound dumb. But, I have a special wish before I die."

"What?"

"This is hard for me to say. I know you have a girl friend. And I wouldn't ask for sex or anything. But there's something we could do that would simply involve kissing. It's nothing bad or anything."

"I don't think... "

Have you heard of French-kissing?"

Jesus nodded his head and said, "Some girls mentioned it at school."

She grew excited, grabbed his hands and whispered, "Girls love it! And they don't stay with boys who don't know how to do it. Nor will they ask. They expect you to be sophisticated. Do you understand sophisticated?"

He barely nodded and felt color return to his cheeks. He didn't have a clue, but it sounded cool...

"Will you do it?"

"Honey, I-I'm not sure if this is right."

She pulled away from him with tear-filled eyes. "It's okay. It's only a dying girl's stupid dream."

He touched her shoulder. "I'm sorry, Honey. Show me what you want."

She threw off the covers and batted her eyes in the fashion of her mother. Her slender body looked lovely. "Relax and give me your hand," Honey said. She placed his hand on her sex. "Move your head down so you can see." She reached over and turned on the lamp.

He did as she asked. Wow! So this is what these things looked like.

She positioned his finger and said, "Don't move, that's the spot. Are you ready?"

He swallowed hard and nodded.

"I want you to lick and kiss it when I tell you."

He touched the spot experimentally and it seemed to respond. "Is this the right place?"

Her voice became husky. "Jesus! Yes! Yes, right there, that's the spot... Ooo it feels so-o-o good."

"Like that?"

She grabbed his head, pushing him down. Her voice became commanding. "Kiss it. Yes!' All right, ooh, yes, yes, that's what I'm talking about, baby boy."

He kept doing as directed in the general area of *the spot.* She provided verbal encouragement and tactile guidance with her hands tightly clutching his hair. Soon, her body started shaking similar to the fit Bart had earlier.

Recovering her composure, Honey said, "Thanks for making my dreams come true. You're the best." She switched off the light, winked, yawned, and rolled onto her side.

Granting her dying request made him happy. Honey had become very special to Jesus. And, apparently, she enjoyed his newfound sophistication, because she woke him up two more times that night. Before morning, he became excited. Now he knew how to French-kiss and he could hardly wait to tell Maddie. Maybe she would enjoy it, too. Grinning like a wino with a five-dollar-bill, he passed out...

***

Jesus woke up shielding his eyes from the bright sunlight streaming through the window, took more drugs, jumped in the shower, and put on new clothes. Looking at the nice garments reminded him of Honey and her secret. He felt terrible. He decided he would be especially nice whenever he saw her. Talk about a bum deal for such a sweetheart of a girl.

He recovered the money sack. Dumping the silver from the bag, he counted them, fifty-eight coins. Jesus kept eight, placed twenty into his pocket for Big Momma. The rest he put away for George. With all the self-importance of a new man of means, he went down the stairs, pulled the coins from his pocket and clunked them down on the bar, and said, "This silver's for the loveliest lady in town."

Big Momma took the money and placed it in the cash register. "Don't be giving me any more money. This will last for years. How's my handsome child?"

He gave her a slow wink and said, "I'm sweeter than maple syrup, gorgeous."

The big woman laughed and put her hand over her chest. "Mercy, I think my boy's gone and grown new body parts." She brought him a coke and lightly raked his arm with her long fingernails. Goosebumps leaped to the surface of his skin in the wake of her touch.

He gave her a slow smile and purposely let his eyes slide down her body. "Those new parts think entirely about you, pretty woman."

She gave him an intense look with her hands on her hips. "I don't know if I should change his diaper, or spank his butt. What's the verdict, Bart?"

The newly-arrived biker shook his head. "I'm all for a good spanking. But maybe pod-people got him while he slept last night. You know, like those body snatching aliens in the movie. Should I shoot this pod-person, Big Momma?"

Honey pinched Jesus' butt from behind. "Nobody messes with my brother." Jesus couldn't quiet figure out how she managed, but every time Honey got anywhere close, she bumped him in the face with her breast.

Big Momma gave her a stern look, "Best be getting about your business, young lady."

"Yes, ma'am." Honey said, and got in another pinch before moving away. That Honey. She was too blanking much. Jesus felt downright good about the new way people treated him.

Bart stood up and walked over. His vest fell open and Jesus' eyes got big. A large silver plated pistol with a pearl handle stuck from the waistband of his Levis. "Wow, Bart! Can I see your gun?"

The biker winked at Big Momma, "Well, it looks like he hasn't been totally possessed yet. "Ever fire a hand-cannon, kid?"

"Not blanking yet."

"Tomorrow we ride then." Turning, he winked at Big Momma and said, "I'll take the little alien out for some air."

She said, "Just don't be hurting that cute boy, at least not until I see what's in those diapers."

Jesus slapped himself on the leg. He sure loved his new friends and really looked forward to hanging out with Bart. If he could be like anybody, it would be the biker. In his entire life, and even in the movies, he'd never seen anyone as cool as Bart. And there were a bunch of cool people in the movies. Bart was one capital COOL dude.

18

After George left Jesus, he had little doubt where Maddie would be. He placed a call, waited until the next afternoon for his answer, and drove toward the house.

Usually runaways returned home, especially the first time. A few days in the reality of the world, and all thoughts of finding that wonderful knight in shining armor to rescue them dissipated, as someone put the moves on. Boy, girl, didn't matter, some freak-daddy ever waited to use, abuse, and warp their little minds. Candy would have eventually returned to her abusive stepfather, if not for skillful manipulation from the master. Thinking about his talents gave him reason to stroke the blacksnake a few licks.

Too fucking bad the killer didn't need new meat, but even without the big payday, money was in his pocket, just as sure as he was some sweet dark meat. And his mirror answered that one. Often. Exerting extreme willpower, he pulled his hand out of his pants and focused on the job at hand.

Parking the car, he smiled into the rearview mirror, time to work his magic. He got out and slid up the steps at 1008 Garden Street. George knocked on the door and checked the knob–locked.

The door opened with the security chain attached–peering out was the girl in the picture. "Is your mother home?"

"No."

He already knew that information. Bobby Bones had cased the house and called when her mother left.

George produced his badge. "I'm a detective." He could see the suspicion in her eyes, but working her would be fun. "Maddie, Jesus sent me."

Her face lit up as she hurried to take off the chain. "Where is he?"

"Not far. Come with me."

A troubled look crossed her face. "I'm on restriction and my mom will skin me if I left."

"Should I tell him no then?" He could see her hesitation, not quite ready to take the bait–yet.

"I'm not sure, Mr."

He wished he had more time to continue the game. It would be fun playing her with only words, but her mom might show up and spoil the whole thing. He took the ring from his pocket. "Jesus said you'd recognize this and to tell you that he didn't mean to hurt you. He's really sorry. All teary-eyed and shit." The girl's face changed into immediate trust.

George felt that special warmth in his heart from conning the mark. Maddie opened the door, turned her back, and went back inside. She disappeared into the house while saying, "Wait a minute, I need to leave my mom a note." The girl wore a blue dress and, from the way her ass moved, George suspected a fine body.

He quietly followed her in, and watched over her shoulder as she wrote. *Mom, a detective is taking me to Jesus.* Something he couldn't make out and... *Don't be mad, back soon, Maddie.* She put down the pencil, turned, and gasped. He put up his hands palms up and said, "Hey. I'm sorry. Only waiting for you to finish."

George saw a brief troubled look cross her face and quickly handed her the ring. She examined her prize as her face lit up with enormous brown eyes and a brilliant cheek-stretching smile. Ka-ching! The lovely sound of money filling his bank account. Anyone could be twisted with the right bait, and the master at the pole.

She locked the house and they walked out to the car.

After holding the door open for her, he slowly strutted around the hood, fully extending his neck, making sure she got the benefit of his be-so-fine profile and masterful moves. He got behind the wheel of the sedan furnished by Bobby.

He turned the rearview mirror and checked his do. Licking his fingers, he smoothed the hairs down, flicked out his tongue and moistened the ends of his thin mustache. Few things in the world fascinated George more than looking at his reflection. He was beautiful. No. If he got any better looking at all, he'd be fucking himself, and often, too. He blinked at his likeness. Damn! Talk about a fine…

George tore his eyes away from the mirror and checked on the girl. This one had that sexy little girl thing going on. He glanced at her hands folded over her crotch. *Oh please let her be virgin.* If so, the Cherry Auction would be in her immediate future, and the money deep off in his pocket. He flared his nostrils and sniffed the air. Could that be pussy in the wind? He steered with one hand and covertly tickled his cock with the other.

The girl asked him where Jesus was. He didn't answer until after reaching his destination and parking. George pointed upward and said, "Upstairs waiting." He thought she might jump from the car in her excitement. He suppressed laughter as they exited the vehicle, and led her to the same room that he had used earlier with Candy.

Keying the door, he motioned her inside. She turned with a frightened look on her face and said, "What's… ?" George hit her with a short punch under her chin. He immediately checked his hand for damage. A cut would wreck his day. Choking her would have been preferable but the look on her face preceded running. Damn timing anyway. He kissed his sore hand and then followed with a more meaningful kiss.

George picked Maddie up, dropped her on the bed, pulled up her dress and dropped her panties, would she be a virgin? Yes! The girl had a beautiful body with long shapely legs. He felt the blacksnake stir in his pants and pondered sneaking some booty. She'd probably wake up and snitch to Fat Tony–And the fat man didn't take kindly to booty bandits.

Having a hard cock, defenseless pussy, and no means of getting any hurt more than when he zipped his cock up in his slacks–and that fucking hurt. He considered chucking it in her mouth, a little wake up surprise, but this one might bite. She had that look.

George harbored a secret phobia. It absolutely terrified him to think that someone might bite his cock off. He thought their might be a medical term for this, maybe, Biteoffacockophobia.

He was psychically strong and all, but in none of the scenarios where he imagined this horrid thing happening to him could he prevail. Anyway, George looked at this he'd be fucked. If a bitch bit down on the blacksnake, it was curtains. Begging went against his motto, and if he smacked a bitch off while her teeth were clamped down, she'd take the end of his beloved cock with her, leaving him pretty much fucked with no other option than holding the severed stub. And against his every moral fiber, begging like a motherfucker for the cunt to spit it out, so he could maybe get it fixed. George shuddered. Thinking this way could really fuck a player's day up.

He looked again at the girl on the bed and grinned remembering his big payday.

George felt a great love stirring in his heart. People were but simple pawns and he the grandmaster. He found the syringe, gave the injection and redressed her. Fat Tony would furnish special clothes for the auction.

Before she woke up, he made the call. Moving back by the bed, he regarded her. Signs of consciousness were returning. He removed the ring from her finger and placed it in his pocket.

She moaned and opened her eyes. "What? Why did you... ?"

"It seemed like fun at the time."

"Where's Jesus?"

Her question totally shocked him. Most girls asked about their own fate or begged and pleaded for mercy. It turned him on... He was beginning to get pissed. He would gladly smack a decent amount of fear into her, and grudge-fuck the bitch, but her value lay in being unspoiled in either area. Therefore, he did the next best thing and went for her heart.

"Your boyfriend hates your guts, and wanted me to teach you a lesson."

"You're a, lying G-Goober... " Maddie's eyes were blazing, "... Big tall-haired poop-butt."

George almost reacted out and touched her up a bit, but changed his mind and said. "Jesus told me you were a virgin, and a prick-teasing bitch."

Glancing down at her dress, she looked confused. "I knew you were a nasty man, I knew it." She was hitting her leg with a closed fist.

"You knew, too? An educated bitch, imagine that. Now don't go hurting the merchandise. How's about I spank that sweet booty?" He made a false lunge at her.

She backed up against the wall with her shaking fist stuck out. The girl looked pathetic except for the burning look in her eyes, and that gave him pause.

He laughed at her. Someone knocked on the door. He moved to the door and opened it with the security chain still on. Satisfied, he let them in. George took the money again, and the same trio grabbed Maddie's arms, and led her forcefully out the door. The black woman turned and said, "Fat Tony will be pleasantly surprised."

He gave her his crooked, sexy smile. "Shit, girl. I always please... ." He slow blinked his eyes, licked his lips, and stared at her crotch. "Check me out sometime. Put some fire up in there, girl."

She turned and left. He grabbed his cock and shook it at her retreating form. Delilah wanted him. They all fucking did.

George smiled. Being the sexiest man alive had its moments.

19

Jesus had barely slept the night before; the morning of shooting Bart's gun seemed forever in coming. He showered, dressed, and bounded down the stairs two at a time. Before he could look for Bart, Honey put him to work helping her clean tables.

Finally a group of bikers came in. Bart hugged Big Momma, and waved for him to come. He hurried toward them, but not before Honey managed to squeeze his butt again.

He went out the door of Big Momma's with Bart and four bikers. Using his hand, he shaded his eyes from the sun. Jesus waited in front while two men went to get the car.

Soon, an old gray van pulled up. The hood was missing and a whooshing noise was coming from the engine, he could see three carburetors! What a cool machine!

Bart pointed at the passenger side and Jesus got in, while he went around the van, scooted the driver over and pulled away from the curb. A man in back said, "Feeling okay boss?"

"I think one of my spells is coming on," replied Bart.

Bart stepped on the gas and the van shot forward burning the tires. While the biker drove, he gave Jesus instructions. He pointed at the gas pedal. "See that thing? The important part is holding that sucker down." He jammed his foot on the brake bringing the vehicle to a screeching halt. "Pushing that really hard brings all the people in the back up front with us. This concludes your lesson."

Bart opened his door and walked around the van.

The biker next to Jesus said, "Fuck this," and started climbing over the seat. His friends in the back gave him an assist and he landed with a thud, and started laughing.

Jesus moved over behind the steering wheel. The bikers in the back were chugging on a whiskey bottle. Someone said, "We're fucked either way we look at it. The kid can't drive and Bart has fits."

Bart jumped in the passenger door, reached back for the whiskey, took a long drink, passed it to Jesus, and pointed down the road, "Let's away then, pod-person."

Jesus swigged enough liquor to fry his vocal cords. Mouthing the word, "here," he handed the bottle back, nailed the accelerator, and left the curb in a combination of lurches and spinning tires.

He found that when he kept the gas-pedal floored, the carburetors made nifty jet-engine sounds.

A man from the back said, "Fuck me, I'm getting whiplash."

Bart said, "Don't waste the momentum, kiss your ass goodbye, homeboy."

Several times while trying to figure the controls out, Jesus left the road. Laughter and nervous whoops were coming from the back. He reached into his pocket and popped a few capsules into his mouth. Grabbing the whiskey, he downed the drugs. The liquor tasted much smoother this time. He took an extra long gulp. Handing the bottle back, he brought the van up to speed and soon they were flying down the country road.

The steering wheel had a green knob sticking out with a picture of a nude woman on it. He was in the process of learning to steer the vehicle by holding it with one hand, the same way Bart did. One biker in the back referred to it as a, "suicide knob." Whatever it was, it made driving a swell experience for Jesus.

His first small error happened when taking a small hill at high speed. The van went airborne. The sounds of bumped heads and drunken screams issued from the back. Out of the blue, a corner appeared. Misjudging his speed and cranking hard on the knob, Jesus sent the van sideways and ended up in a cloud of dust beside the road. Someone opened a second whiskey bottle. Greedy hands grabbed for it in efforts to calm wrecked nerves.

Back on the road, all seemed well and Jesus felt he had the hang of driving–kind of fun overall. He settled back in the seat to enjoy himself.

He started getting that mellow feeling again and closed his eyes to enjoy it. Jesus could have sworn that he'd barely closed them… The next thing he knew, a tree came crashing into the van and his head hit the windshield.

Things seemed to happen in slow motion. He watched as Bart's knees jammed into the glove compartment and bikers flew over the front seat. He smelled broken glass and his head hissed like the ocean. He grinned. Too much blanking fun, thought Jesus.

Bart said, "Mother fucker, kid, I almost ended up a few feet shorter."

Words hadn't found their way through the painful waves cresting in Jesus' brain.

Bart found the whiskey bottle, took another drink, handed it to Jesus, and said, "Well, at least I wasn't straddling the floor shift."

"Blanking trees," said Jesus.

Once everyone crawled from the wreck, Bart told the other bikers to get some help.

Jesus and Bart sat on the roadside. Four men limped out in the road and flagged down the next vehicle. The car didn't appear to be stopping, then at the last minute the driver slammed on the brakes. The bikers jumped in and disappeared in the direction of town.

Jesus looked at Bart's tattoos. "Why did you get those?"

"It's a statement about man's freedom. The chain lengths remind me that I'm bound by societal mores. The Barbed wire is for when I think I've outrun them, slashing into my spirit with the sharpness of reality… or some shit." Bart added. "And before you ask, I fell asleep in the Tattoo Parlor and woke up with the spider."

"Really?"

"No, kid. Just screwing with your melon."

Bart looked at him and said, "Those burning questions aside., why are you acting so crazy?"

Jesus pulled the reds from his pocket and said, "Probably these capsules... I need them. They help me with fea... something."

Bart took two capsules from the bottle and tossed them into his mouth. "It's your life. But easy, my friend. These things are more deadly than driving a car into a telephone pole. Or tree in this case."

"I'm sorry about all this, Bart."

The biker thumped him on the back. "It'll take more than a tree attacking the van to mess up our friendship, kid."

"I love you, Bart."

The biker rubbed his spider. "Well, that's good I guess. Just don't tell the other guys." He handed Jesus a beer.

Jesus decided this was another hallmark day in his life; he would need to work on driving, but he sure as blank loved the biker.

Bart pulled out his pistol. "Here, kid. Point the long end at the telephone pole. And pull this thingy."

The weapon felt heavy. He tried holding it steady, but the target kept moving.

The big gun recoiled in his hand and dirt flew from somewhere behind the pole. Wow! This must be how cowboys in movies felt. With ringing ears, Jesus tapped Bart on his shoulder with the smoking barrel of the pistol. "Whacha think?"

Bart used his hand to aim the weapon away from his head. "You're a fucking natural, kid."

Jesus rubbed his head. Afterward, he looked at his red blood-soaked hand, "Holy bologna!"

Bart looked closely at his cut, and said, "We're starting to look like brothers. Between your gourd and my knees, we'll need stitches"

He smiled, he couldn't think of a finer thing than being Bart's brother.

Bart reached into his back pocket and swore. "Damn! Big Momma's gone and lifted my wallet again."

"Why?"

"She has a problem with taking things and enjoys practicing on me. I can never catch her at it. Do you have hospital insurance?"

"Nope."

"No problem. We'll use one of the guys' medical cards," Bart handed him a fresh beer and threw an empty across the road. "Try and hit it."

Jesus emptied the gun and never got close to the bottle.

Bart said, "Well, you've mastered driving and shooting. Maybe next I'll turn you loose on my bike."

A faint rumble preceded the returning motorcycles. As they came to a halt, Bart walked over, got on behind one biker, and pointed at another cycle. Jesus got up and jumped on behind that man.

At the county hospital, he got eleven stitches over his eye and the biker received a similar number on both knees. Riding back from the hospital, Jesus felt the pain returning over his eye and his legs felt numb.

Arriving at the bar, swerving motorcycles parked and crashed as men limped, fell off, or both. A bunch of cussing, stiff-legged bikers made their way inside. Big Momma watched them come in, tossed Bart his wallet, then blew on her finger tips. Bart frowned, shook his head, and put it back in his pocket.

Looking at Jesus, Big Momma said, "I suspect the driving lesson went well."

He gave her a wink and hobbled up the stairs toward his room. Closing the door, he fell across the bed and passed out.

20

Harlan Prophet responded to a call from Faith Bridger. Her daughter was missing and under suspicious circumstances. Behind him in a van were crime scene investigators. He felt uneasy. Seldom did things occur this close together and were not related. Anytime a location involved in a homicide showed unusual activity, his office was notified. The abduction and probable killing of Ralph's wife established location. A kidnaper posing as a police official grossly surpassed unusual activity.

He clinched his fist and banged the dashboard. Today, he sat helpless as a child-killer walked away free because of a Miranda violation. Often the system failed. Too damn often.

Harlan wiped a tear from his eye as unbidden memories of his daughter replayed in his mind. First came her laughing face and goofy sense of humor. She was remarkably like her mother; beautiful and in love with the world around her.

He hated what always followed. Brief unwanted flashbacks of blood-splattered walls and feelings of helplessness. Awaking to inhuman screams ringing out in the middle of night–his. Harlan's eyes would snap open with sweat pouring off his body and rage far into morning. Empty arms rigid and reverberating like a tuning fork; beating clubbed fists against empty air; tearing open stitches in the ever gaping hole in his soul; cursing God for allowing perverts to roam the world; and babbling apologies to his baby girl for not being there.

And his soul mate. Loosing her was the mortal blow in a life sucking one-two punch combination. His reason for living. For breathing. She always knew what he was thinking just by looking at him and communicated clearly with a raised eye brow, or quick to pout bottom lip her every mood.

He loved her fresh-soap smell and the way she insisted on sleeping in the curve of his arm at night. Now he dreaded sleep and his arm stayed tombstone-cold. Each morning, in the semi-conscious state before waking, he'd smell her fragrance, happily reach out, find her gone, then remember...

Harlan stopped the car. Muscles in his forearms quivered in vein-bulging contraction. Anger-clenched hands caused the steering wheel to protest in a tortured grating sound.

Composing himself, he drove on to the Bridger house, parked, slammed the door, walked up, and rang the bell. He could hear movement inside. The curtains slightly parted and a muffled voice from within asked, "Are you the detective I talked with?"

He pulled out his badge and held it up. "Yes. I am." The sliding of the security chain forewarned the door opening. Out stepped an older white woman, maybe mid-fifties, gray hair braided, and pulled back so tight that she looked Oriental. She stared at him with an odd light in her eyes; he'd seen it before. This woman was insane.

She extended a sheet of paper with a shaky hand and said, "Here's the note she left me."

Harlan took the note. The Bridger woman's voice had a harsh ring. He imagined a life strictly structured from the necessity of raising a child alone. Maybe that's what drove this poor soul over the edge. Glancing down, he saw a small black Bible clutched in her hands. It was engraved with her name in gold letters. She would need her faith in the days to come–all of it. He requested permission to fingerprint the downstairs and front porch area.

She held her Bible across her chest as though it were a shield and said, "Anything you need to catch whoever took my Maddie." In a deeper, husky sounding voice she added, *"Beware the beast that walks as a man–but is not."*

His neck hairs stood on end. Partly because of her weird tone, and partly because he'd seen this evil occupying human form, hidden beneath the guise of normalcy. How could someone sink into that putrid state? What drew the spirit into such darkness that black deeds fed the soul like maggots sucking fetid meat? Another flashback hit him and he pushed it away.

He said, "Seen Jesus?"

Seemingly close to tears she answered, "I-I saw him around the time of Ralph's suicide. I think the police were here right after. He lit out carrying a backpack. I told him to stay away from my daughter." Her eyes narrowed, hardened. "She has her father's willful nature. *Each wayward child is another thorn on Christ's brow.*"

Harlan wished she'd can the voice thing.

A lone tear fell slowly down her cheek. Swiping at the tear, her cold blue eyes bored into his. "Jesus is a bastard child and almost grown to man. I told Maddie about men—wicked fornicators, all." Her eyes lowered and Harlan thought she blushed, but when she again sought eye contact, he could see the burning hate. "Maddie thinks she loves him. But she's sick, too." Now color flushed in the Bridger woman's cheeks, apparently from giving too much information, her voice trailed off and she ended with, "I pray that Jehovah God will forgive Jesus. But if you see that abomination, tell him to stay away from my Maddie."

Harlan nodded, wishing he could slip some Thorazine into her drinking water, a few quarts maybe. He asked for and received a picture of the girl, tried comforting the woman, and dug a card from his wallet. Handing it to her, Harlan wished that he could offer more hope. But, in reality, her daughter probably already had her foot butchered and soon would be mercifully dead.

He turned and walked back toward his cruiser. Sweat dripped down his face. It was more about flashbacks than the hot day.

21

Maddie was sandwiched between the two men. Her feet hardly touched the ground as they swept her down the hallway and out of the sleazy hotel.

A knife poked her ribs on one side and a gun on the other. The black woman walked in front. Maddie's wrists felt as if they would snap under pressure exerted by the meaty hands dug into her flesh. Horror welled up inside her.

She felt certain that any move to run or scream out would be followed by death.

They dragged her onto the sidewalk. The woman opened a rear car door. One goon shoved Maddie inside while still holding her arm. The second man got in the other side, and the woman jumped in front and started the engine.

She watched helplessly as they pulled away from the curb. Maddie felt green goober-snot sure that things were bad. Her jaw hurt and she felt sleepy. Even in this horrible situation a nap seemed tempting. The ideas almost made her laugh—or cry, maybe pee her pants. It was hard to tell; something didn't seem quite right with her thinking. *My brain's like a train that gets rusty in the rain.* With that thought she became fairly certain that either she fried a circuit, or popped the old noggin-noodle cork.

She realized that these people intended to hurt her, but the reality seemed vague and dreamy.

Since her journey through town, evil people were popping up like Jiffypop. This reminded her of the men in the city. The picture her mom had painted all her life was turning out to be real. She felt tears sting her eyes. If this represented the stinky world, she wanted no part of it. Thinking about her mother unearthed another gem buried in her subconscious: *"The wayward child reaches for the devil's hand."*

A chill in Maddie's heart overpowered her sleepy feelings. Somewhere downtown, the car stopped.

Once more, the knife pushed into her ribs as the goons hauled her into a huge modern building with dark, tinted windows. It filled the entire block. There were uniformed men standing by the doors and guys wearing new suits with brightly-polished shoes. They grinned and acted as though dragging a girl against her will was common occurrence.

Maddie dug her heels in at every opportunity. It felt as if her captors were snatching her baldheaded. A small inner voice assured her they wouldn't cut her, but their strong hands really hurt. She also reasoned they wouldn't rub her out with all these other people around, but most seemed the same sort as the ruffians holding her. And the others... well... they had double super-duper yucky looks in their eyes.

The men gawked and leered. And she was triple slimy-snot certain that she didn't want to know why. It felt the same as being undressed with their eyes. Her brain started the rhyme thingy again; *The boy's all stare, when on a dare Maddie shucked her underwear.* All of a sudden, she couldn't decide what frightened her most, the situation or these weird thoughts. She looked once more at the drool-dripping faces. The situation–definitely.

Shoving her into an elevator, one thug reached to push a button. The movement exposed a pistol in his belt. Maddie briefly considered grabbing it. But her good sense won the day, especially, once she imagined the doors sliding open... In her fantasy, she stood there with a hot-barreled semiautomatic in her hand and a cigarette dangling from her lips. Gunsmoke swirling around her knees and dead bodies littering the floor. *Hit girl Maddie snatched the gun and plugged them all one by one.*

Reality returned with a ding as the elevator stopped and the doors opened. The hoodlums half dragged and pulled her down a red-carpeted hall. She donated more hair as the gangsters yanked her kicking body into a large room and left her with the black woman. The men laughed, exchanged knowing glances, elbowed each other, and hurried off. She heard another door open and close near by.

The woman said, "Take off your dress or I'll call the guy's back and they'll do it."

She felt tears well up in her eyes. "Why are you doing this to me?"

"Honey, they kidnapped me around your age, too. I really don't enjoy doing this. But you'd hate what would happen if I didn't. My name is Delilah. What's yours?"

"Maddie. How come I have to take off my clothes?"

Delilah looked sad. "Because you look so young. There will be a virgin auction." The woman looked away. "Everyday for a week, you'll be brought here in this room. Behind the mirrors are men. Only a few today. But when word gets out, many more will come. Most are rich and they will bid against each other for you—your virginity."

Maddie's eyes were pleading.

"Last chance. Take off the dress or I'll call them," said Delilah in a commanding voice.

She woodenly obeyed and stood there in panties and bra. *"Wear clean underpants Maddie. You never know when you'll wind up in the hospital."* Would Mom's voice ever stop?

Delilah said, "Now comes the hard part, I have to pose you, it will be easier if you pretend you're somewhere else." The woman patted her on the shoulder. Maddie resigned herself and stood there trembling.

Delilah's hand slowly pulled the small brassiere partially off one breast. Maddie's nipple popped out and she could feel her burning face match its color.

The woman twirled her. She could hear muffled groans from behind the glass as tears sprang into her eyes.

Delilah cupped her breast and squeezed it. Holy freaking moly! A girl touching her unmentionables and perverts were watching! Maddie felt sick. The woman put two fingers at the top of her white panties. Slowly she pulled them down in front. Maddie kept her blushing face straight ahead, but she felt a breeze down there.

The unseen spectators were making a racket, and her stomach felt queasy as she realized where the two goons had gone in such a hurry. She felt Delilah's hand on her sex and began shaking uncontrollably. Maddie felt her face screwing up for a good bawling. "P-Please move your hand."

"I'm sorry, sweetie. We're almost done."

Maddie had never wanted to punch someone in the face more than now. Things became unreal. She could feel her panties being pulled down from behind, but it was hazy. Her body felt stiff. It seemed that in a far away dream the woman knelt down and opened her legs. Did she look inside? As soon as the idea of kicking Delilah in her lying mouth occurred, she felt her dress being slipped back on. She experienced the napping sensation again. *Someone emptied out my head and filled it up with mush instead.*

They half carried her into another room. Her eyes kept shutting. *Now I lay me down to...* Delilah handed her two red capsules.

"Nope. Thanks anyway. Not hungry."

Delilah had the sad look in her eyes again. "Believe me, they'll help. You'll just feel sleepy. Don't try and walk through this nightmare wide awake." Her eyes hardened. "Take them, Maddie, or the men will give you an injection."

She returned Delilah's hard look as she swallowed the drugs and said, "You're nasty chicken's droppings." Fresh guilt welled up inside her. *"Each curse word spoken by a child, removes another chain that binds Satan."*

Maddie looked at her surroundings. The place looked very much a luxurious hotel suite with two notable exceptions: The door was locked with a big fat key and chicken breath had it in her pocket.

Maybe she could pick up something and give Delilah a good smack over her frizzy head. As if reading her mind, the woman pointed to a mirror and said, "This room is monitored. There's one in the bathroom, too. Do anything stupid and the men will join us." Delilah turned her back to the mirror and whispered, "Please. I don't want you getting hurt anymore, honey. I hate this, too."

Maddie decided that her voice sounded sincere. However, after the black man with the big hair, she wouldn't be buying any. Nope. Thanks all the same. She'd never met so many slick-talking liars. She also knew a better place for those diamond teeth.... . A place he sat on. These people were as trustworthy as weasels babysitting fresh-hatched chicks.

Someone knocked on the door and Delilah opened it.

A fat swarthy man dressed in a purple silk suit entered the room. He walked like a girl. The initials F. T. were embossed in gold on the pink handkerchief in his pocket. He flourished the handkerchief with a diamond-studded hand. Dabbing it to his forehead with his pinky finger pointing skyward, he said, "They call me 'The T,' or 'Fat Tony.' Maybe I'll let you call me daddy. But show respect, least I arrange for bedtime with the fishes. *Capisce*?"

Maddie decided this guy looked remarkably similar to the short fat cigar-chewing man from the gangster movies that always said, "Yea", and "See?" He even talked the same. She said, "K-what mister?"

The fat man smiled and said. "You're a cute split-tail. Mind your manners and good things are in your future. But let The T down, and I'll bust a cap in your butt. Do what you're told and live the good life. Be a pain and I give you misery. If you were a sweet boy, I'd take you under my wing and show you a fun time. But hey, sometimes you win and the next... Well... I think you get my drift. Little split-tails like you get to enjoy my auction. Later, maybe we talk about those sugar cakes."

Goober snot-sucking gross! What was a split-tail? For the first time Maddie fully appreciated being a girl and she for sure didn't want any cake either. The men behind the glass were scary, but she couldn't see them. The look in this man's eyes was somewhere past scary. Actually, that word did not quite express her meaning and nowhere in her vocabulary could she find one. Fat Tony was that evil thing that made her momma clutch her Bible so tight.

The gangster and Delilah walked out, followed by the sound of the key turning the lock.

Maddie ran into the bathroom and began scrubbing her hands. She chanted the words, *"I wash my soul free from sin, scrub and rub then scrub again."* The soapsuds turned pink from blood. She stopped. Holy bloody moly! This habit was old, and she needed to change it. She threw the soap down, and adjusted the water to cold. The water soothed her burning hands. Something didn't make sense anymore about the way she viewed guilt. Gently drying her hands, she left the bathroom and sat on the bed.

The keying of the door startled her. Delilah walked in with a food tray, set it down, came over, and grabbed her hands. Forcing them open she said, "Why the hell are you doing this?"

The question brought a fresh surge of guilt. "The men and this place, I feel nasty."

"You don't look stupid, Maddie. Do you really believe that?"

"It's what the preacher said about sin. I think nasty things."

"About the men watching you?"

"Yuck! Holy puking maggot guts. No! I'm not sure exactly. It's mostly about my boyfriend, and the urges I have."

Delilah frowned and said, "Well, honey, if you can't see what's wrong with that thinking, then go ahead and scour until all you have left is little white bones."

She watched her leave and reflected on the conversation. Looked at her hands and wriggled them. She could almost envision bleached skeletal fingers. Old Delilah certainly had a way with words.

Maddie's reasons certainly sounded different in her mind than when she talked about them. Now they sounded stupid. Not that she trusted the woman, but the concern in Delilah's voice sounded genuine. For now, she pushed the thoughts aside.

Her thoughts touched on the events preceding her mom's relating Ralph's suicide. She was running the last few blocks to her house, happy to survive her scary adventure in Cottondale and ran right into the arms of a big uniformed police officer. His prophetic words were, "I don't know what you're running from, but I know where you're going. Someone's going to get hurt, young lady." The cop took her to his cruiser, clear back into town and called her mom to come and get her. Talk about a mean goober-snot.

Her mom never said a word all the way home. Then as Maddie stepped inside the front door she got snatched by the hair and pulled to her knees. As Mom descended like a flapping, screaming, prayer-spitting harpy, with her pious voice rising to the heavens and anyone not completely deaf within a zillion miles.

Being sent to her room on restriction for two days without food was a comparative blessing. Getting her window boarded up and her door padlocked at least gave her privacy.

During restriction, she told her mom that she loved Jesus and would never stop seeing him. A beating followed. Later, Maddie overheard Mom at the front door telling him that she wasn't home.

Only then did the lock matter, she could tell by his voice that he was in pain. She smacked her head into the door until her mom came with a fresh hickory switch and threats of another beating. For the first time in Maddie's life she stood her ground with clenched fists and screamed in her mom's face. "LIAR!"

Dropping the switch her mom replied. "My daughter NEVER came home, just some hell bent harlot with Hell's own fire in her britches."

Upon Maddie's release, Mom launched into a tirade about God's will for wayward daughters, suicide, and mortal sin during forced Bible study in the kitchen. Sending her bolting for her room with fingers stuck in her ears... Leaving a vivid picture burned into her mind regarding her place in Hell alongside Ralph... And a sore head. After all that, the double dealing phony baloney detective kidnapped her.

Her jaw muscles bunched in anger.

She lay back on the bed. Staring at the ceiling, her eyes glazed over in other memories. Her brow crinkled. She wondered about what George had said in the sleazy hotel and decided that Jesus would never say such a thing.

Thinking about Jesus brought Maddie comfort. Something was wrong with him. It had to do with his shiny pink feet and notched toes. According to her mom, Martha caused them, but she didn't know how, or when. They were that way for as long as she could recall. The burn scars connected to something deep inside his soul. And it refused to heal.

Maddie intuitively felt that dragging this thing into the light would help. However, every effort to discuss them was always met with resistance. Jesus would walk away or quit talking and, usually, be more nervous for the next few days. She wished her thoughts weren't working so slowly. There was some connection between his injury and why he became so frightened. The last words he spoke to her were unlike him. And, if she hadn't been totally shocked, he wouldn't have gotten away with them. Not one bit.

On the other hand, maybe he did hate her. Well, this sucked snot. If she *hadn't* ran away and *didn't* open the door... *Stop freaking yourself out, Maddie Mae!* Evoking her middle name brought some sanity back... Looking around her prison they called a room scared her silly again. In her mind, she imagined what terrible things were going to happen next. And she had a super-duper imagination...

Jeepers. This thinking needed to stop. As she closed her eyes to sleep, she felt the spark of hope flicker and fade. There were so many people to get away from and, right now, she felt too small. She fell into a restless sleep...

In a dream, Maddie saw a yellow butterfly with torn, blood-stained wings, hopelessly trapped in a spiders silver web.

22

Upon awakening, Jesus went to the dresser and removed the remaining silver dollars. He found a large bandana that Honey had bought for him, carefully wrapped the coins, and tied them around his ankle. He would see George soon and could hardly wait to pay him. Jesus felt certain the news would be good. Detectives found people all the time and his new best friend would surely find Maddie. He felt blessed.

Whistling a snappy tune, he went down the stairs to help Honey work the bar.

Jesus spent most of the day being teased by Honey. He'd either find her breast in his face or her fingers pinching his butt.

Day drifted into night and Big Momma began singing on stage. Jesus was sitting in a booth waiting for Bart to get back, and enjoying the song.

Honey began dancing with some guy from a group that came in earlier. Her voice rose in anger. "Let me go! You jerk. My brother knows Kung Fu."

Jesus could see that the man was making her dance. He walked over, tapped him on his shoulder, and said, "Let her go, mister."

Things happened fast. The guy turned and said, "Mind your own fucking business." Jesus reached for the man and suddenly found himself on the floor with a sore head. Luckily, the guy didn't hit his stitches. Just as it occurred to him to get up, the same man made the trip to the floor beside him with blood spurting from his nose.

Bart reached down, grabbed the guy and said, "All right, prick. Don't come back. Next time no one walks out." His friends were already scrambling for the exit as the biker tossed him out the door to join them.

Bart returned, helped him up and yelled at Big Momma, "Hey, beautiful, can we use the back room?"

She replied, "Yes, but don't be hurting my sweet boy."

Jesus followed Bart into a storage room. A mirror hung from the back wall and a gym mat covered the floor. From an overhead pipe hung a punching bag. Bart said, "Sometimes I come in here and work off tension. I watched the fight. Show me how you throw a punch."

"I never have."

"Could've fooled me. Pretend that you have."

Jesus clenched his fist and held it over his head like a club.

Bart said, "Fair enough, little man. But doing that to someone will get you hurt. The object is to strike fast without warning. Don't wind up or give it away. Punch straight from your shoulder. Try hitting me. I'll let you know what gives you away."

As soon as Jesus thought about throwing his fist, Bart grabbed his wrist. "Your eyes widened." He tried looking away and hitting the biker. This time Bart deflected his arm. "Shoulder. Cute trick, but keep your eyes on target." Bart told him to look into the mirror, and said. "Try touching your reflection and watch your eyes and shoulders. Remember, speed and accuracy"

Jesus didn't know how he was supposed to watch both things at once but gave it a shot. "Well, blank me." He could see his own eyes widen, or his shoulder flinch each time he started to move his hand. Before long, he could strike without his eyes widening but his shoulders still gave him away. A few more minutes practicing and he became better. He turned with the confidence of a world class boxer, and thumbed his nose like a fighter.

Bart put a cigarette behind his ear and said, "Once you get fast enough to grab this, you've got the idea."

Jesus pointed at the door and said, "Look, Bart." The biker turned his head, and Jesus made a grab for the smoke. His wrist was grabbed well short.... .

Bart said. "Not bad all in all. What it lacked in sophistication was gained by your shrewd imagination. Keep practicing. I need a drink. Several actually."

He left and Jesus turned back toward the mirror. Jesus pretended to be a cowboy with six-guns and put his hands down by his sides. "I'm going to burn you down, hombre. On the count of three... . One... " *Thunk*... He flicked out his hand and hit the glass–hard. "Blank."

After twenty-some minutes of practicing in the mirror, Jesus felt satisfied. He reached into his pocket and popped two red wonder-capsules in his mouth. Then it dawned on him that even though he'd been beat up again, fear wasn't there. He could thank Mr. George Jones for his change in good fortune. He decided to check his boot after being knocked down. Taking the left one off, he examined the handkerchief tied around his ankle holding the coins. Present and accounted for.

Looking up, he spotted pipes running along the high ceiling. He jumped up and dangled from one. Back on the floor, he removed his boots for a better grip. Leaping back into the air, he gripped the pipe, flipped his body, and hooked his toes under his hands. Letting go, he dangled from his toes.

Jesus smiled. He'd done this since childhood. The grip in his toes was exceedingly strong. Maddie called him bat-baby. He enjoyed hanging from both his feet and hands. He got away from more than one bully by pulling himself up into a tree, hand-over-hand and dangling there until the kid gave up and left.

Feeling his face turn beet-red from his inverted acrobatics, he flipped in the air, dropped down, and put his boots back on.

The door opened. Honey entered, and locked the door behind her. He could see tears in her eyes and asked, "What's wrong?"

She fell into his arms and buried her face into his chest. "B-Boys think I'm ugly."

Jesus sat on the mat and tried rocking her. "Honey, you're a beautiful young girl. And someday... ." He felt her stiffen as the realization hit him. He'd said the wrong thing. There may not be many days left for her.

"I found a new lump," said Honey. She took his hand and placed it under her blouse.

Jesus tried to conduct a proper doctor-like examination. He deduced that her breast felt soft and warm except for the nipple and it was hard. "Is it in the nipple, Honey?"

She said. "No. Try the other one."

He felt sure that he'd already diagnosed the culprit, but followed direction. Still no sign of lumps but, ironically, this nipple was hard as well.

"Maybe you can see it," said Honey.

Opening her blouse as instructed, he looked, touched, poked, and prodded. Her breast reminded him of coffee with extra cream. Funny though, the tips kept getting larger and stiffer to the touch... Forgetting all about his clinical objectivity, he started rubbing one and then the other, trying to determine which would get the biggest. Talk about fun!

Jesus felt her hand on his crotch and said, "Honey, I don't think you should be doing that."

She pulled back and looked at him. "You're probably right, Jesus, no one wants to touch a stupid, ugly girl. Especially one that's dying soon." A tear formed and fell down her face as her hand found its way back into his lap. This time he didn't say anything. She blinked her eyes at him again in the fashion of her mother, and said. "Remember when you did the French-kissing thing for me?"

He gulped and nodded.

"If you would do it one more time, I think I could face the end and be happy."

He couldn't find it in his heart to say no... Before he said anything, she slipped off her pants and pulled at his head. She whispered rushed instructions, "This time more softly. And when I tap you on the shoulder kiss it really hard."

He did as requested.

She took longer this time, although she touched him on the shoulder on several occasions and had multiple spasm attacks.

Afterwards, she came into his arms and said. "I'll be good now. From now on I'll be the perfect little sister. By the way, you're getting really good at that." Honey jumped back into her pants, headed for the door, unlocked it, turned back and said. "Some girl's in for a special treat. Just don't forget who trained you, baby boy." She winked and left.

Jesus sat reflecting. Girls were complicated but wonderful... .

He decided to see the man with the greasy hair. He left the storage room and walked toward the front door. Big Momma said, "You bring back that nice young white boy, hear?"

Bart chimed in, "Don't hurt anybody out there," and patted him on the back.

He whirled and snatched for the cigarette behind the biker's ear. Bart caught him but he got closer.

Jesus laughed and went outside.

The warm night air smelled of cars, food, and city life. He filled his lungs. Everywhere he looked, things were happening. Scantly-clad women prowled the street corners. He turned and started walking. A woman stepped out from the shadows, looked him up and down, and gave a low wolf whistle. Jesus bowed, tipped an imaginary hat, and moved on toward the restaurant. He'd observed how Bart walked and was in the process of developing his own swagger.

Gunshots boomed in the alley. Jesus smiled. Fear no longer concerned him; he welcomed it.

Up ahead he could see George sitting in the same window seat as before. He took another capsule before going in to calm his nerves. His heart thudded with excitement, he could barely wait to hear the good news. He loved Big Momma and Bart, but Maddie was as elemental as the air in his lungs.

He walked in the door and sat across from George. Reaching down into his sock Jesus untied the bandana and tossed the silver to him. George quickly put the coins away, and said. "It took considerable investigating but I found her." He handed the ring back and then his eyes took on a sad look. George added, "She told me that she never wanted to see you again." Jesus felt dizzy. George continued, "She said to stay away from her."

Jesus looked at the ring, it looked smaller and tarnished. "Did you tell her that I didn't mean what I said?"

George nodded and spread his hands indicating helplessness. Jesus' stomach felt sick and his ears stung as if he'd just been slapped. George added, "If you want I can keep trying. But I know women and that one can't stand you."

Jesus shook his head. Who cared anyway? He was a no good stinking loser and she had the right idea. He'd always suspected that he wasn't good enough for her. He didn't know how, but he was determined to erase Maddie Mae from his mind. The black man tossed him another large pill bag. He pocketed them.

George said, "Look, women come and go. It's a sad part of life. But if you ever want to make some money, get in touch with me. If one thing doesn't work, we can find another. I know places where a handsome young man can make a fortune by doing hardly anything. With my help of course. I could dress you in fine clothes, and set you up with some rich and influential people. Consider me your closest friend and business manager." George handed him a card, patted him on the shoulder and said, "That's my phone number. Call me."

George pulled a small mirror from his shirt pocket, looked at himself, smiled, and said, "Later man," then walked out the door.

Before the waitress could make her way over, Jesus left. Pain welled up like dark vomit from his soul. He staggered into the alleyway. Lurching against the wall, he surrendered to body-racking sobs. Finally the tears subsided as coldness settled over him. Reaching into his pocket, he found the ring and hurled it far into the darkness.

Swiping tears away from his eyes he took several more capsules. He stepped into the night walking aimlessly, without care. Once, his heart rose slightly as he thought he glimpsed John Henry. The person turned out to be someone else.

Jesus felt that this was his one great mistake; his eternal burden for the unforgivable words he'd spoken, forever damning him to painful isolation; killing hopes, dreams, and any reason for living. Loosing Maddie Mae to a scum sucking, coward's tongue. The city looked as desolate and empty as his heart, except for the pain, and it consumed him. He walked woodenly. Unanimated. A string-less puppet without purpose or direction.

23

Martha opened her eyes as warm blood trickled down her arms and dripped in audible splats on the floor beneath her. Drip, drip, drip... Draining, tiring echoes beating fatal cadence to flickering, hissing flames dancing blue-red under a large vat. She repeated her first question. How did she end up in this weird place?

Then she remembered...

Walking the streets she spotted a black man. She walked up and put her hands on each side of his face. Looking into his beautiful green eyes she instinctively knew he was the one; the chosen one to reunite her with Angel. He introduced himself and led her away.

He helped her to his car. On the trip, he kept touching her in bad places. Her voices instructed her to ignore this behavior. The car made its final stop. In the fog-shrouded night, headlight beams sliced an eerie tunnel, illuminating a marble building with a great angel on top. Martha jumped out and tried running to the angel but he caught her and dragged her unresisting body down cement stairs.

Tying her to a chair he left.

Noise caught her attention. A shape appeared in the distant hallway. Coming toward her was, by any account, a monster. Ghost white with pink, lidless eyes. No words were needed to convey the message glaring from them; ear-shattering in its silent, frenzied intensity. It opened its mouth. But Martha already knew the sound. Roaring, screaming, rage! It penetrated the core of her being.

It grabbed a club and struck her over the head. In the twilight between conscious states, Martha observed it carry her off. Wet throbbing ooze dripped into her eyes as the monsters rough handling flung bloody patterns onto the cement. The abstract art of a madman creating original prints with each swing of her body. So this was the final betrayal from her internal voices, and the answer to her twice asked question.

Martha felt more shocked than surprised. Living with her disease meant waking up repeatedly in strange places and never feeling integrated. Voices screamed in her head, confusing the simplest task. She could start out intending to go to the store and wind up on some crazed journey; the malignant commands guaranteed a bizarre reality.

Martha experienced five different internal voices, three male and two female. All were malevolent save one. Angel. She was blessed with Angel's presence once early on in her illness. Martha walked with the winged beauty across golden flowered meadows in complete rapture. Angel's soothing voice mended every tear in her shredded soul. Ever since, she experienced a longing; a vacuous soul sucking ache. The remaining voices gave neither compassion nor quarter.

Once, her voices sent her into a motel room and she was not allowed to flush the toilet. She stayed there for five days, staring into the porcelain bowl filled with waste. They repeatedly called her a piece of shit and commanded her to eat the excrement. Finally, Martha believed; she took a bite. You are what you eat.

The monster had all but done her in. She kept regaining consciousness, repeating her son's name and speaking words she didn't understand; foreign-sounding expressions in a high pitched fluid stream. It felt as though she was possessed by some gibberish-spitting harpy. This angered the pale ghoul. It stabbed her with sharpened sticks. Her body bristled with them. She felt death coming and welcomed it, loathing a lifetime filled with delusions, voices, and hallucinations.

Even in remission, she could go into a crowded store and be overwhelmed by the noise of people. It seemed as though her fragile filters were incapable of separating her thoughts from theirs. She would have to rush out or risk activating her demonic voices. Did demons lurk among the words of people? Slithering over egg shaped skull tops, searching for cracked noggins to invade and scramble, leaving victims clucking like a lost, sick hens? Martha thought so.

Everything was wonderful in the beginning; a beautiful bride with a dashing groom and the world seemingly at her feet. Then her parents died, and she learned that mental illness was in her family. Her grandmother had it. The disease waited a full generation before it took her. Weeks would pass without symptoms. Then one nagging idea could suck her down into a whirlpool that would spit her up on the banks of some nightmare.

To not fit in the world and know it; the awareness killed her. Hated and shunned in biblical proportions, labeled, "Crazy Martha," by her peers and even being called that to her face.

She remembered before her son was born. During a breakdown, she regained clarity while being raped by construction workers. The voices in her head said to beg for more. She did and got it. The same source named her baby and assured her that his seed did not come from earth. Her beautiful son. Naming him Jesus snapped Ralph like a twig.

Martha loved her child. It seemed ironic, loving so deeply, yet hating the responsibility. More specifically, she hated herself. Only a mother of circumstance, the smallest things overwhelmed her. Diapers were often left half done or forgotten altogether.

She recalled Jesus playing the piano. Something about the haunting rhapsody caused her voices to stop and she could see inside her son's mind; a profound loneliness locked in a beautiful heart overflowing with love. That whole day she remained lucid. It was the single worse day of her life, knowing just how badly she'd hurt him.

The horrible accident; she remembered how it began. The urge to do something special for her husband crossed her awareness. Ralph had been trying so hard at his job. She started preparing chicken dinner, humming as she moved about in the kitchen with happy thoughts of her surprise, playing with Jesus and changing his soiled diaper.

Tickling his pudgy face while preparing meat for the deep-fat fryer. Coochie coochie coo! He always smiled for her. Dimpled elastic lips, stretching into silent, body wiggling, gummy laughter. Ejecting honeyed puffs of milky breath. Saucer blue, trust-filled eyes watching every move. Small hands reaching...

Suddenly it changed. Whispering demons re-breached the crack and jumbled her thoughts, leaving Martha muttering, clucking and turning in blind twisted confusion... Voices snatched her awareness. They yelled in her head and told her to run from the house. Lost in tortured, tormented confusion, she had no idea of where she went or for how long, until the police picked her up and rushed her to the hospital.

They showed her Jesus' poor legs. How could that many days pass as one? That's all she could remember. Any chance for redemption was lost, wrapped in the burned decaying flesh around his small feet. Her sweet child. The doctors assured her that, due to his hideous abuse, he would never be sane. She'd robbed him of any chance of normalcy.

This became her mortal sin, and she was immensely sorry–every waking moment of her life.

And in her last moment with her son, she slapped him. How could she?

The monster returned, disrupting her thoughts. At first when it talked, she couldn't understand. Its voice pitched to shrieking intensity slurring words together. Again the question, "Confess your sins?"

With clarity, the horror of what happened to Jesus settled on Martha. She screamed with hurricane force, "Yes. I burned my baby."

It scurried over and took a long metal rod from under the steaming vat. The end glowed red hot. Its pink eyes fixed on her sex. Martha could see the hate burning in them. Saliva sprayed on her body as it said, "This fire purify sins."

Martha felt searing pain for only a millisecond as the metal plunged inside her. It sounded as though her skin itself cried out in a frying whine of scorching molecules. Her awareness fled.

From up above, she watched her body as it slid into the vat and burst into flames.

A familiar voice spoke. Martha turned, found Angel's embrace and absolute joy...

24

Jesus walked aimlessly down Main Street in the ever-darkening night.

He looked down. A cigarette butt floated in the gutter. He watched it flow down a drain and out of sight. Somewhere inside him, his dreams took a similar course falling into some dark abyss, forever lost.

For reasons not clear, he felt partial relief that Maddie no longer wanted him in her life. Even without fear, he lacked something. He didn't know what, but he realized that, without it, life was empty and without meaning. Still, his heart hurt. A bigger part of him clung doggedly to the fantasy of being with Maddie. He struggled hard to shove the eternal dreamer off a cliff and out of his life.

He heard screaming coming from up the street. Jesus looked ahead and saw a tall, thin, white man with a hawk nose set in a long cadaverous face, wearing a striped fur coat that reached down to the sidewalk. Parked on the curb sat a bright red Cadillac convertible.

The man had his fingers wrapped around a black girl's neck bending her back against the car. Her eyes bulged out. All the while, a blonde-haired white girl kept hitting him over the head with her high-heeled shoe. Both women were dressed in tight-fitting short, sequined gowns, and both were beautiful. The one wielding the shoe yelled, "Let go, Jimmy, you fuck, you're killing her."

Jesus' vision clouded red. He ran over, grabbed an empty bottle lying on the curb, and busted it over the man's head. Things went strangely hazy. The guy reached for a gun, Jesus grabbed it first and kept hitting. He continued striking after the man fell. In his imagination, he saw his own face and wanted nothing more than to erase it and smash the gory remainder into oblivion.

The girls pulled him off. Bloody bubbles were coming from the thin man's nose in wet, snoring sounds. Jesus stared with no feeling at the now crushed face and a certainty settled over him; without the women's intervention, he wouldn't have stopped. He dropped the gun in the street as sirens sounded in the distance.

The blonde with her shoe now back on, said, "Come on, darling, let's get you somewhere safe." She opened the car door and Jesus jumped in. She got behind the wheel, the black girl jumped in the passenger side, and he sat between them.

Both women raised clenched fists and yelled into the night as the car burned rubber from the curb. The driver said, "My name's Shady and this is my sister, Smoke. Do you prefer creamy vanilla or hot chocolate for dessert, darling?" The girl's snapped fingers in unison, laughed, hiked their dresses up and tossed their shoes in the back.

Shady said, "You're barely a baby. Did you escape from the Orphanage?" Before he could answer she added, "What do you think, Smoke, shall we adopt him?"

Smoke rested her head on his shoulder looking him in the eyes and said, "Hell yes, girl. Finders keepers."

"Snap!" They yelled the word together.

Shady leveled green eyes at him, "I'd say that you may have just rubbed-out Jimmy the Nose."

"What kind of name is that?"

"Did you see the beak on the man?"

"Yes."

"Well?" She studied him then added, "Pinocchio took back stage to that fucking clown. Now people can call him, 'Jimmy the Scar.' Come to think about it, now the inner man matches the outer." Shady laughed at her own joke, reached over and kissed his cheek, then turned her attention back to driving.

Smoke began tickling his neck with long finger nails. She said, "What's a sweet hunk of white sugar like you called?"

"Jesus."

"Save me, Jesus."

He lowered his head, and said, "Please don't joke about my name."

Smoke picked up his chin and looked him in the eyes, placing soft hands on each side of his cheeks, and said. "You just saved my life, Jesus. And, baby, there ain't nothing wrong with your name, or that big heart. I joke about everything."

The women exchanged looks and Shady put her hand on his leg squeezed it and said. "Jimmy's a made man. We were put on the streets by his uncle" She looked at Jesus, "It's a long story, but my sister hated the bastard. He was nothing but a fucking woman beater. There may be trouble, but I'm never going back with that big nosed prick."

"Double snap!" hearing them say the words in unison amazed Jesus.

Shady continued, "Whatever happens, we'll watch out for you." She moved her hand up his leg and squeezed. "But first, we're taking you home. You can take a nice hot shower and we can get better acquainted." She began rubbing his knee, sending delicious shock waves up his thigh.

Jesus looked down at her legs and noticed a small pistol attached to her thigh. She watched him and said, "I've never shot anyone, but if you hadn't show up I would have. Nobody messes with my girl like that."

"Double Snap!"

Smoke pulled up her own dress exposing another pistol. It looked identical to the first one.

Shady took his hand and placed it on her thigh. "If you can't find what you're looking for. Ask directions." Both ladies were caressing him and Jesus felt pretty darn good. He put an arm around each woman and squeezed their breasts, trying to decide which one felt the best while the shiny convertible flew through the night.

They left the city behind and drove into the country. Finally, Shady pulled the car up a narrow lane, parked, and said, "Come inside, darling. This is our place away from town." He walked in beside the women. Shady guided him into a back room and pointed out the shower. "While you clean up, can I get you a drink?"

"Some Watermelon please," said Jesus.

"We'll eat later, darling, I'll get you a screwdriver."

"It doesn't need stirred."

"Don't make me spank you," said Shady. "I think somebody's pulling on my fine and shapely leg." She came back into the bathroom and looked at his nude body. "My, my, darling, aren't we a big boy." She reached between his legs and squeezed. "This girl's open for business–the monkey type." Shady started walking out the door and added, "Soap the parts you want kissed."

"*Snap.*" Followed by giggles echoed from the bedroom.

Jesus felt the heat of a blush coming on and something else quite different; the invisible pump. He jumped in the shower to cover his embarrassment from the reaction between his legs, and turned on the water. There were various bottles of soap and shampoo. He took off different lids smelling each fragrance and, finding the one he liked best, squirted it all over his body. Soon, he looked foamier than a Saint Bernard with Rabies.

Smoke came in and opened the glass door. "My-O-my, sugar, all I can see is candy for days." She wore lace panties with matching bra and neither left much room for imagination. She had a lovely body. "We're fixing dinner. You can help when you're done."

Smoke placed some men's silk boxers on the commode. "These are for you. Toss your old clothes in the trash and we'll get new ones tomorrow. 'Can't be having our man looking anything but fine," she said, giving him a slow wink.

Jesus reached out and gave her a soapy kiss.

Smoke ran slender fingers over her groin. "Now you did it! Set fire to my young ass."

He dried off, tossed dirty clothing in the trash, placed the capsules on the dresser, and threw his boots in a corner. He put on the shorts, and quickly pulled on a pair of socks before the girls returned. Shady came back into the room, also wearing panties and bra. She looked like a model. He gave her a long look...

She locked eyes with him and batted her eyelashes. "This is how we dress at home. I hope it doesn't bother you." She spotted the drugs, walked over and examined the capsules.

Before she could speak, he said, "I r-really need those. Can you get more?" He felt shaky with the sudden thought of his drug supply running low.

Shady said. "Yes, darling, I'll get more." She held up a finger. "On one condition." She stood close, her eyes searching his. "Consider quitting. I've seen these ruin people." She stepped forward into his arms and whispered, "Promise me you'll think about it. Okay?"

He said that he would and marveled at how soft she felt in his arms. His ear still tingled from her warm breath. She stood on her toes and kissed him.

Shady skipped back toward the kitchen. He smelled food cooking. Popping another capsule into his mouth, he walked in and joined them. Smoke stood by the stove frying chicken. Shady looked up from mixing salad and said, "You can butter the bread."

Jesus made his way over to the counter. He finished buttering the second piece of bread when he felt dizzy. Before he could support himself, everything went dark, his knees buckled, and he woke up on the floor. The same thing happened when he had the car wreck. All seemed to be going well, then up jumped the tree, or in this case, the floor.

The girls helped him up. Smoke left the room and came back with some small white pills. "These will help you stay awake," she said. The pills looked so tiny that he took three. He just tossed them in his mouth and swallowed.

Smoke looked at Shady, rolled her eyes, shook her head, and said, "How do white people do that? Give this girl some water, honey."

They sat down at the table and Smoke poured coffee. Dinner was excellent. Somewhere before the dishes were cleared off, Jesus' mood started shifting. It felt as if ideas came into his head faster than he could speak. He also had the uncomfortable feeling of wanting to do several things at once. Talk about feeling super—where the bleep have those little pills been all my life–good.

Jesus felt someone's toes sliding up his leg from under the table. He reached down and captured the ankle. He slid down his chair and began tickling her tummy. Shady screamed and ran laughing into the bedroom. He turned on Smoke. She began kicking and shrieking. He played her ribs like a crazed pianist until a dark spot appeared on her panties. She bolted for the bathroom cussing all the way.

He heard the shower start. What a swell blanking time! He walked in the bathroom and stuck his head in to apologize, Smoke said, "Boy, keep them bony fingers off my ribs. Don't make me pop a cap in your fine ass." In a soft voice she added, "I'll be giving you a chance to make up for that later tonight."

Shady grabbed his crotch from behind. He felt his excitement grow. She stuck her head into the shower and said, "Hey, Smoke, I think we have a problem on our hands. A hard one."

"I bet if we use our heads we can work it out," answered Smoke.

"Snap!" More good natured laughter as both women grabbed at him.

He tried squirming away. It felt too good. Their wriggling fingers were driving him nuts. They wound up in the bedroom, three bodies tangled on the large poster bed.

Together the women yanked off his clothes and slipped a rubber tube over his penis; he'd never seen anything that compared to it, except covering sausages.

Hours passed like minutes but nothing happened. Something weird was wrong with his thingy. It wouldn't go off, or down.

Smoke finally called it quits and went to sleep. He continued messing around with Shady, and felt strangely torn between cleaning the kitchen and telling her his life story. She said, "What happened to your feet? Why do your toes look chewed?"

His face burning with embarrassment, he slid his feet under the covers. "I-I don't remember," Jesus said, and started asking her questions... Near morning, his mood shifted. He felt sad. Shady was curled up on his chest. She touched his cheek with her hand and said, "What's wrong, darling?"

He said, "I lost my girl... " It all seemed so long ago. As far back as he could remember, there was one lone bright spot in his life and now only a dark vacuum remained.

Shady snuggled closer and began talking. "I know the feeling. They kidnapped me after my fourteenth birthday. At first they forced me to work from a building in town. That's where I met Smoke. Around eighteen months ago, Fat Tony gave me to Jimmy... " Tears fell down her cheeks, "You see we both have bad memories... I remember when a cute boy loved me. So long ago, it feels like another lifetime."

Jesus said, "Why didn't you run?"

"I suppose I could have. These guys never stop looking, but still I could have tried. This is hard to explain. Prostitution is the only life I've ever known. I'm used goods, darling. Along with the abduction, something inside was taken from me. Or maybe I just gave up. I'm not sure. But I feel broken. I won't leave Smoke though. We stick together. She's my family." Shady stopped and took his hand. "I don't think change is possible now. But I miss that cute boy. Being loved is all I've ever wanted; someone's special girl."

He pulled her into his arms and said, "I don't have any love to give. My heart is dead and I'm no blanking good. But you're a special girl, Shady–just as sure as the moon is silver." Before daylight, he finally fell into troubled asleep, the uppers and downers making a bizarre circus of his dreams. A winged Maddie tangled in a spider web. John Henry bound and gagged trying his best say something...

25

Jesus woke late the next afternoon and struggled to open his eyes. Sleep patterns had become erratic and sticky cobwebs seemed wrapped around his brain, holding it in paralyzed inactivity. His initial thoughts were about drugs; they were automatic, almost compulsive. Anything to deaden his reality.

He couldn't find his clothes and didn't remember throwing them away. Looking around, he spotted a new silk shirt and expensive-looking slacks draped over a chair. A brushed suede wallet, fat with money lay on the dresser. Classy brown leather shoes sat under the chair. Supplies of both the red capsules, and tiny white pills were in abundance. A golden box had been filled with each. He downed some drugs and started dressing.

Not that it mattered, but he made sure Maddie's picture was inside the new wallet before putting it into his pocket then, at the last moment, he scrounged his old wallet from the trash and transferred everything back into it. Some changes he just wasn't ready for. He hid the new wallet in the bottom of the trashcan so he wouldn't upset the girls.

The clothes felt whisper-soft against his skin, and the silk boxers felt strangely erotic. Ignoring the shoes, he found his boots and put them on.

He walked into the kitchen.

Both women were drinking coffee at the table. As one, they gave wolf-whistles. Smoke looked at his feet and said, "Sugar, why you wearing those ugly things?"

He looked down and said, "Because my best friend gave them to me. They have sentimental value."

Smoke retorted, "So'd my first doll. But I tossed its natty ass away years ago." She laughed and looked at Shady. "We done got us a fine dressed man with hobo shoes, girl." She rolled her eyes and added, "But, baby girl, he screwed me straight into a coma last night."

"*Double snap!*" With synchronized finger accompaniment.

He looked at the women. Shady wore a white skirt with a yellow top and Smoke wore the same combination in reversed colors. Both appeared around his age. He kissed each on the cheek and said, "How're my good-looking ladies?"

They looked at each other and laughed. Smoke said, "Did you hear that? I may to drag him back to bed. He made me wet again."

"*Snap.*"

Jesus looked at her crotch. He didn't much care for the way she got when she peed her pants. He remembered the question that slipped his mind. "Why's there money in my wallet?"

Shady answered, "Simply a small present from your women." She added, "Want to go somewhere?"

"Thank you." Her question sunk in and his eyes got big. "Let's go to Big Momma's." The words came from his mouth almost without thought. He missed everyone at the bar. He poured himself a drink while the girls gathered their stuff.

Shady walked up and handed him the keys. She squeezed his butt and said, "I love your tight ass, darling."

He pulled her close. Sliding his hands over her round bottom he said, "And I think these are nice." Wow! Was she wearing panties? Before completely loosing his train of thought, he added, "Thanks for the clothes, drugs, and nifty box."

She said, "Thank me later. The pillbox is so you can throw everything away if we ever get stopped by the cops." She wagged her finger. "And don't forget your promise." She pulled away and moved toward the door.

Smoke kissed him on the cheek and said, "If you feel sleepy, holler. I hear windshield-therapy sucks."

"Double snap!"

Shady locked the door, turned and yelled, "Last one to the car picks their nose and eats it."

All three ran for the car. In a flat out race, they giggled and pushed each other. No one opened a door as they all vaulted into the Cadillac without a clear winner. Jesus punched the gas pedal and smoked the tires. Birds scattered for trees and children ran looking for their mommies. Both women laughed and placed their hands on the windshield. Pulling themselves up, they stuck their heads over and yelled into the cool air.

The setting sun painted rose-colored hues on a baby blue sky.

With the bennies kicking in, Jesus felt wide awake and the drive was uneventful, except for scaring several pedestrians and earning some well deserved honks from other drivers. The Cadillac's horn made a cool sound. He drove to the bar and tried parking between two large motorcycles. The back bumper of the car struck the bike behind him. It rocked but didn't fall over.

Everyone exited the car the same way they'd gotten in. With a woman on each arm Jesus walked inside.

Honey smiled from behind the bar. Stopping in the middle of serving a drink, she gave him a slow wink and pointed at the bandstand.

Bart yelled, "Hey, pod-kid, over here." Several bikers moved to make room. Bart stood for the women. Jesus took the opportunity to embrace the biker. Bart shook his head, looked at the women, and said. "Kind of grows on you, doesn't he?"

Shady said, "We found him. Now he's ours."

Smoke suggestively touched her breast and added, "Besides we done opened his eyes, sugar."

"Snap!"

The biker gave the women a concerned look and said, "Well, he's probably imprinted then. Now he'll never leave."

Turning to Jesus he said, "Looks as if your luck has changed, kid. By the way, I'm throwing a party down by the river in a couple of days. Want to come?"

"You damn bet, Bart."

Bart said, "First you show up with strange women and now the d-word. What's next?"

They all turned to the sound of Big Momma tapping the mike. "Ladies and whatever those guys with you are, just a reminder that next month will be my fourth annual concert at the fairgrounds."

The crowd stood and applauded. Big Momma held her hand up, "Don't be working me for drinks now." A chorus of boos started. "Remember we're showcasing local talent, and speaking of that, put your hands together for our very own, Jesus of Cottondale."

Shady swatted Jesus on the butt and said, "Tear it up, darling."

He went up and embraced the big woman.

The spotlight hit the grand piano. Jesus made a big production of walking over and seating himself, similar to great pianists he'd seen on television. He suspended his hands over the instrument and waited until the crowd started booing. Then winked at the girls and began. He let fly with the boogie-woogie.

Halfway through the melody, Jesus used his legs to push the bench back. Half-standing, he started shaking his butt in time with the beat. His hands were a blur as the crowd stood and cheered. He held one hand in the air and play like hell with the other. He threw in riffs he invented on the spot, and gyrated like a madman.

The playing was crisp and gifted, but it lacked its former magic. Something had been lost. The notes were colorless, no longer originating from his soul. Still, the crowd clapped and stomped their feet in wild abandon.

He started an encore. The girls jumped onto the stage and began dancing with each other. They spun like ballerinas, turned and rubbed their butts together in time with the music.

Jesus watched the two incredibly beautiful women, moving with complete abandon.

They glided next to him and began bumping hips with him while he finished the song. Soon, everyone in the bar stood and yelled for more.

They bowed in preparation to leave the stage.

Jesus noticed half dozen men in suits and derby hats sitting at the bar. All but one dressed in pinstripes. Bart had moved over by the men. The man closest to the biker pointed at the stage with one hand and had the other stuck inside his suit coat.

Bart opened his shirt and rested his hand on his pistol. Other bikers formed a ring around the group. Bart looked angry. The bar grew quiet as another man reached for his gun.

The heavy metallic clicking of hammers introduced Honey, leveling a sawed-off double barrel shot gun from behind the bar. Looking capable, sincere, and confident she said, "Nobody messes with my brother. Let's see if you spaghetti suckers can hit the door before I drop these hammers"

The man formerly doing all the talking tipped his hat at Honey, and the group filed out.

Bart walked up to Jesus and said, "What's this about you putting a gangster in the hospital?"

"I only wanted him to stop. I really didn't mean to hurt him."

"Fat Tony has requested a meeting."

"Is that bad?"

"Not if I can help it. Come by here tomorrow and we'll take care of this." He smiled, "Don't worry, kid. We'll face this monkey straight up, before it turns gorilla."

The girls came up and hugged Jesus. Shady said, "Darling, if that prick hurts a hair on your head, I'm popping caps in his ass."

Smoke added, "That's right, sugar. If you need us we'll go with you."

He kissed both women and assured them it would be better if they didn't.

He went over and thanked Honey. She winked at him and said, "No problem. Besides, I have far too much training invested in you, baby boy." He reached over the bar and hugged her.

Bart winked at Honey and said, "Tactile little fellow ain't he?"

"You have no idea," she replied.

Bart raised his eyebrows and said. "Is someone terminal again?"

With a hand on her hip Honey wagged a finger, "Mind your business, spider-head, and I'll mind mine."

Jesus felt a tap on his shoulder. "Come here to Big Momma, child." He buried his face in the softness of her breasts and they danced out onto the floor. Looking over her shoulder, he could see Smoke curling her finger and Bart willingly following her gyrating body.

He enjoyed the dance and the big woman's warmth. After, she pushed him back at arms length and said, "I love you, son. But I wish you'd bring back the big-eyed young man who first walked in here." Jesus didn't answer, wondering instead what she'd think after witnessing one of his panic-attacks. Probably hate his guts.

She continued, "Remember, when it comes time for the talking, find Big Momma." He reached up and kissed her softly on the cheek. She laughed, "Boy! What's a woman to do with you?" Jesus held her in a long hug well after the song had ended.

He watched Big Momma walk back behind the bar to help Honey. Big Momma made his heart warm in a way that no woman had ever done before. It comforted something deep inside; something lost, something dying. What she said bothered him; he wished he could please her, but his course was set. He would bury the fear at any cost.

Reaching into his pocket, he produced the golden box and tossed several capsules and pills into his mouth. Any memories of life before now were fading, replaced by the now familiar haze. He had barely put away the box when Shady came up and said, "Time to shake it loose, darling. Smoke and I have business." Jesus waved goodbye to his friends and they left.

26

George received a call from the white fright. For the past few days he'd been holed up at a house in the city. The bitch who'd been on the receiving end of some good black boning had just left. He didn't particularly care for the house-mouse routine, but it provided a viable address, phone number, and no questions asked about whatever scam he was working. She did make one small inquiry early on in their relationship. A quick pop in the eye cured her inquisitive nature and restored her to sanity.

Time to make money. His thoughts returned to Garden Street. The old woman would probably be suspicious by now, but her isolated location and the constant construction noise would be perfect cover. Besides, an extended vacation by the mother would take heat off her missing daughter, and if his charm didn't convince her, there were other methods. Maybe if he explained to her that she'd won to die for tickets at a killer resort. Killer resort! Ha! He cracked himself up. If all else failed a sharp knife stuck into someone's belly did wonders in promoting obedience.

He called Bobby and told him to score a ride and make it fucking snappy. George hesitated before bringing the dice-man into this job, but he might need help. Coming up short in something this illegal could park his ass in the penitentiary until wrinkles adorned his handsome face. The idea repulsed him. He pulled out his pocket mirror and smiled; the reflection told the story...

He slid a hand inside his shirt and felt rock hard abs, moved his hand farther down and felt an erection starting. With supreme effort, George pulled his hand away and concentrated.

He didn't think Bobby would just jump up and snitch; he was simply too weak and therefore an excellent candidate for some detective playing the bad-cop routine. George had a small tattoo over his heart depicting a devils head. The inscription under it read, *"La mort avant le deshonneur."* He figured that his own strange eye color guaranteed a Frenchman in the old woodpile before his birth. Thus, this tribute to his heritage. According to the French-Biker tattoo artists the words roughly translated to, "Kill me before I bitch up;" Words a blood could live by. He would bring the dice-man, snatch the cunt, and drop off Mr. Bones before doing the deed.

A horn sounded outside. George left the house and walked slowly around the car. Acutely aware that Bobby followed his every step, George stuck out his chin and exaggerated his arm swing, while he slid with perfection. Talk about a super fine mother fucker! He knew that Bobby envied his moves–everyone did.

Getting in the passenger side, George gave directions. Watching Bobby drive, the thought occurred to him that soon he'd have to retire the dice-man. Bobby knew too much. George said, "Play the cop role and go easy. Charm, not force."

They parked at the curb in front. He put his fingers to his lips, indicating that the dice-man should shut the door softly.

Exiting the car, they made their way up the sidewalk. Bobby knocked on the door. George heard the woman coming and stepped to the side leaving Bobby standing alone.

The curtains parted. Mrs. Bridger's high-pitched voice questioned, "What is it?"

George watched as his associate held up a badge and went into his routine. "We've located your daughter, ma'am," said Bobby.

"Where is she?" Her voice raised in excitement.

"Please open the door, Mrs. Bridger," replied The Dice Man.

The door opened with the security chain attached. George grinned. If he wanted, he could rip the door open but he enjoyed playing the mark. She said, "Hand me your badge, young man." Bobby passed it inside and it grew quiet while the woman contemplated removing the lock. Bobby added, "She's in the hospital, ma'am. And I'm afraid she's been hurt."

The old woman snapped at the bait like a starving rat on welfare cheese. The chain slid off and George forced his way inside. She looked at him with knowing eyes and said, "You're the agent of Satan that took my Maddie."

He returned her stare. "I'm your worst fucking nightmare, bitch."

The old woman slapped him hard across the face. He returned the favor, busted her mouth, and said, "If you've cut my face, I'll slice you into sandwich-sized pieces." Pulling out his mirror, he examined the damage. Satisfied, he put it away and hit her again, this time a short punch to her ribs.

The old lady doubled over and made a wheezing sound as she fought for air. Her face reflected a properly administered attitude adjustment.

George said, "Here's the drill, bitch. I'm taking you to your daughter. But we need to make a little stop first." He pulled out his knife and pressed it into her side. A dark stain testified to the blade's sharpness.

He enjoyed the slow walk to the car; her walking all stiff and him step-sliding all the way. The woman's eyes said it all. Horror; such a wonderful tool when properly applied.

Faith Bridger said, "Get thee behind me, Satan."

"Butt fucking sounds fun and all, but save the sweet talk for the next guy, lady. He's just your type. Now shut the fuck up before you wreck my good mood," replied George.

He marveled at how incredibly stupid people could get. The bitch walked to his car with a knife held to her body, and she didn't have the fucking sense to yell. Once she got in, life as she knew it ended. Only the formality of death waited.

He opened the door and, without so much as a peep, she primly climbed in. George drove with the woman between them. Stopping at Bobby's, he told him to get out and he would return the car later. The dice-man did as directed.

George conked her over the head with his pistol. She fell against the window, lips sliding down glass in a gooey farewell kiss. He pulled her body close, placed his arm around her, and drove away like a high-school kid on a prom date. He found some tunes on the radio and settled back in the seat. For the hell of it, he slid his hand up her leg and inside her panties.

She started moaning as they pulled up to the crypt. Kicking the door open, he pulled her out of the car by her tits and hauled her semi-awake body inside. He half carried and half dragged her down the stairs, placed her in the chair, and secured the chains. She opened her eyes and said, "The eternal fires of hell await thee, evil sinner."

He slapped her again, ripped off her skirt and panties just to fuck with her head and said, "Wait and see what awaits you, bitch." He leered at her body. Not fucking bad for an old Bible thumper, thought George. He couldn't resist the temptation and unzipped his pants. "Care for a suck before the fun starts, Mrs. Bridger?" Winking at her horror-filled face, George kept the blacksnake well out of snapping range, zipped it, and left.

27

Maddie Mae flushed the toilet, watched the drugs swirl out of sight, and went back into the other room. For the past few days, she'd been hiding capsules under her tongue. She wanted to escape.

Nothing missed her scrutiny. She inspected the supposedly two-way-mirror. It looked heavy, but didn't resemble the one in the viewing room; she had no doubt about that mirror and the people on the other side. It had uneven colors and occasional glimpsed shadows of movement, besides the all-too-obvious sounds.

This one looked ordinary. Maddie found a small gap where she could see partially behind it. The wall looked solid. Her final test came after Delilah gave her medication. She waited until the woman left, stood in front of the mirror, and stuck her tongue out with the drugs still un-swallowed. She knew that she took a big chance, but she wanted out.

Maddie would not succumb to this lifestyle. A hot fire burned in her chest and the will to fight--somehow. There must be something to help her; a key or an unguarded door, but she needed more time to make a plan.

Everyday she exercised, trying to keep her muscles strong. She did push ups and sprinted the length of the room until her body ached.

When they rode up in the elevator, she'd noticed the light stop on the fourth floor indicator. Her entire world had shrunk to this floor. She sought to memorize it in detail. If an opportunity should present itself, she must be ready.

Maddie made small talk with Delilah and told the older woman her fears. She could tell by answers to her questions that her captor cared about her. She'd taken to hugging Delilah and thanking her for being so nice. Her efforts were paying off and she could sense an ever-deepening rapport developing. Delilah had even left a bottle of hand lotion on her last visit.

A knock sounded at the door. Delilah walked in with another food tray and a shopping bag. While she placed the meal on a small table Maddie said, "Why do the men behind the glass want my clothes half pulled down?"

Delilah shook her head in disbelief, "Because, Maddie, it excites them, and this creates the bidding. If you were naked it wouldn't be as effective. Perverts enjoy being teased. The more you turn them on, the higher the price goes."

"But I'm a young girl."

"Bingo! It's the only reason you haven't been raped." Delilah put her arm around her and added, "If I could change this, I would."

Maddie's voice became nervous as she asked, "How long before... you know?"

"These virgin auctions don't happen often. Usually the bidding is over in a week, but I've seen one go on for ten days."

Maddie sensed a way to buy time, and asked, "Why did it take longer?"

"This cute young girl drove up the price by the way she acted," said Delilah.

"What way?"

"Maddie, these men are sexual deviants and this girl did things to excite them. This is what I tried to explain about partial nudity, if you combine that with flirting the way the girl did, it drives them nuts. Some say the girl behaved naturally. Others say she was too young to be sexually aware, but she whipped them into frenzies. I have my own thoughts about her motives."

Delilah's words brought a strong surge of fear into her heart, she begged, "Please help me get away."

Delilah embraced her. "I would if I dared. I care about you. However, the truth remains they'd kill me in a second. I'm responsible for you and, even though I hate what's happening, I'm afraid of dying. Please forgive me, Maddie."

Tears fell onto her cheeks as Delilah added, "It's time for the viewing room again." Opening the bag, she pulled out some pink baby-doll pajamas and watched while Maddie put them on.

A decision hit Maddie. Striking in her chest, it settled on her with certainty; a steely fear-erasing resolve: if they wanted a show, she'd give them one. She desperately needed extra time. She asked, "Is it okay if I pull down my own clothes?"

"All right, sweetie, but take things off slowly."

They walked down the hall and into the room. Maddie stood on the viewing platform looking at her shoes and settled on a plan. Thinking a quick prayer she willed her shaking knees to still and began.

She pretended that Jesus stood behind the glass. In her imagination he had his big eyed goofy look that he'd get whenever she'd tease him. *How do you like me now, circus boy?* She slowly looked up, blew a kiss, and, little-by-little, exposed one breast, stopping right after the nipple. Next, she stuck out her lower lip as though she might cry.

She jerked from sudden muffled applause. *"Lust is the first of seven keys to Hell."* With great effort, Maddie ignored the mommy voice and covered her nudity. She needed to get through this and that meant concentrating; pushing away this inconceivable reality and focusing on fantasy.

Turning away from the mirror and looking back over her shoulder, she batted her eyes and cupped one cheek of her butt with her hand. Sliding her hand up, Maddie caught her thumb under the elastic and pulled her baby-doll bottoms down on one side, then bent over pretending to pick up something. While still bent over she stuck her bare rump out and gave it a little shake. The clapping grew louder.

Maddie hurriedly adjusted her clothes and turned to face the mirror again. Chills formed icy goose bumps as she realized who must be watching. Regaining her focus, she tried to figure out what to do next.

A picture floated into her mind. Whenever Mom scolded her as a child, she would stick her finger in her mouth and stare at her feet. *Check this out, my blue-eyed boy!* With one hand, she hooked her thumb in the front of her bottoms, and pulled them down exposing half her sex. While looking down, she sucked on her finger and added just the hint of a smile. The floor shook with a noisy explosion! A thoroughly frightened Maddie jumped into Delilah's arms.

She clung to the older woman all the way down the hall. Her body trembled with a guilty, stomach wrenching realization of what she'd done. They went back into her room and Delilah said, "Sweetie, I admire your style. You've got guts. If I could think of any way possible, I'd help you get away."

Maddie saw honesty in her eyes as they embraced. She reached up, kissed her on the cheek, and said, "I'm glad I've got someone as nice as you to help me through this." Delilah kissed her back and left the room.

Maddie fell onto the bed and started feeling sick. *"The wages of sin... "* She stopped the thought before it finished. She smiled. This was possibly the first time she had ever been able to stop one of her mother's admonitions.

Still, she didn't feel good about what she'd done. It felt nasty. The urge to wash her hands overwhelmed her. Running into the bathroom, she turned on the hot water. Grabbing the soap Maddie began the ritual. *"I wash my soul... "* Dropping the soap bar before scrubbing she turned off the water. She would beat this–she would.

Returning to the bedroom, she rubbed her hands softly with lotion. Maddie held her hands up, looked at them, and beamed with happiness.

She dropped on her knees beside the bed, said a silent prayer for forgiveness, and quickly added a second one for escape. Above all, she wanted out, and she was goober snot-sucking sure about that. Climbing back into bed, she felt hope rekindle in her chest.

Turning her thoughts back to a peaceful time, she remembered being with Jesus before all this happened. Her heart flooded with warmth and she whispered, "Star light star bright... ."

Drifting into sleep Maddie's face became attentive. She cocked her head as if listening and, ever-slowly, a peaceful smile spread onto her lips. Maddie's dreams were about porcelain hands caressing a golden haired boy, and bright yellow butterflies cavorting through rainbow slashed skies.

28

Jesus squinted in the bright afternoon sun and tried his best not to run over any more motorcycles. They surrounded the bar. Parking, even under the best circumstances, was difficult for him, but Shady's hot tongue in his ear presented an extra challenge. He brought the Cadillac to a jerky halt, reached over and squeezed her breast in retaliation.

"Do me, darling," said Shady.

Bart stood on the curb shaking his head, and said, "I'm glad no one's lost any sleep over this."

"I'm calming him down," replied Shady.

Everyone jumped out and crowded around the biker. Smoke pressed her body against him, rubbing first his shoulders then, looking up at his tattoo, she said, "I can think of some fun stuff we could do with that spider. Does it glow in the dark?"

Bart said, "We'll have to let it crawl on your stomach some night and see."

"Yum, I love nasty boys," Smoke replied and sucked her finger suggestively into her mouth. She popped her wet finger out, pointed it a Bart, and added, "I'm holding you to that with both hands. Make me cum, white boy, and I'll make that spider quiver."

"Until your knees buckle, sweet thing."

She grabbed her crotch. "Now you've done it. My panties are ablaze." Wolf-whistles came from the collective bikers.

Bart held his hand up for silence and addressed them. "Easy, girls. Here's the plan: the kid and I go inside alone. In a show of force, take slow runs past the gangster's place. If we're not out in thirty minutes, come find us." He turned to the women. "We'll see what's up and be back before you know it."

Shady grabbed Jesus, stuck her hand down the back of his pants, and squeezed. "Bring your sweet ass back, darling, we have unfinished business. If you haven't returned in an hour, I'll come looking."

"Double snap!"

He hugged both women and turned to go with the biker.

Jesus walked to a parked car and got in the back with Bart. Two large gang members were in front. They drove downtown and stopped beside an enormous office building.

Exiting the car, Bart told the men to wait. An endless line of motorcycles paraded past them, revving engines.

Jesus and Bart went inside. Everywhere Jesus looked, men wore suits. Some looked similar to the kind of people who came to Big Momma's. The rest looked impressively rich.

Waiters passed with trays of drinks in fancy glasses. The lobby was huge and exceptionally ornate. A big man with no neck motioned for them to follow. They moved toward the elevator. The guy wore an expensive-looking pinstriped suit with an obvious bulge under his arm. He looked at Bart and said, "Hey why'd you tattoo a fucking spider on your head?"

Bart stared back for a long moment then replied, "Why do you work for a greaser butt-freak?"

Jesus felt certain that something bad would happen next. The atmosphere crackled with tension.

They stepped into the elevator. No-neck appeared thoughtful and then said, "I'll let the greaser bit slide. I don't care for the booty thing either. It puts a bad light on everybody. It's hard to be taken seriously as businessmen when the boss plays drop the soap."

The gangster pushed a button, the door slid shut, and the sinking feeling in Jesus' stomach marked their ascent. They rode in silence with only the faint humming of the elevator. Jesus watched the numbers light up. They stopped and number four stayed lit on the panel.

The door opened. They followed no-neck across a large carpeted expanse and stopped in front of double red doors. The gangster held one open and Jesus went inside alone.

A fat man sat behind the desk smoking a big cigar. Jesus stopped and stood well back from the desk. The gangster stared at him; he felt uncomfortable with this intense appraisal. The man spent a lot of time looking below his waist. When finished, the fat man said, "So you're the pup that retired Jimmy the Nose."

Jesus still felt shame regarding the event. "I-I wanted him to stop hurting the women, sir."

"You got respect, son, and Fat Tony appreciates that. As for the Nose, he was beginning to embarrass certain people—a nameless uncle." He spread his meaty hands. "Now Jimmy's gonna need a new occupation, maybe mathematics." Fat Tony's big lips curled up, and he added, "Hey, I'm kidding already. The Nose can't remember to tie his own fucking shoes." He twirled a finger around his ear. "Like talking to a fucking cabbage."

Jesus felt his face burn with guilt. The fat man slapped the table with his palm. "Here's the deal, kid. Leave a dollar and I'll buy the Nose a coloring book. Not a problem. But, the girls report back to me before two more weeks pass, capisce?"

Jesus took a dollar from his wallet and tossed it on the desk. "I don't think the girls want to come back, sir."

The big man clutched his chest. "On my mothers honor, kid, it really hurts a sensitive guy like me when I get that kind of rejection. But tell them anyway, okay?"

"Okay," said Jesus.

The gangster pulled a pink silk scarf from his pocket and waved it in dismissal. "And pick up the Washington, kid. Fat Tony made a joke, already. But, now that were on the subject, come back sometime and maybe I'll buy you something nice."

Jesus felt increasingly self-conscious with the way the fat man continued to stare at him; he grabbed his money and backed toward the door, bumping into the door before his trembling hand found the knob. The fat man blew him a kiss as he turned and left.

Bart and no-neck stood waiting in the hallway. They reversed their steps and started back toward the elevator.

Gangsters stared as the trio passed and Bart returned their extended looks. The biker moved with his normal unhurried ease.

The plush carpeted floor was patterned in deep reds with golden trim. A waiter dressed in white with thin gold stripes on his pants passed by them carrying a drink tray. The glasses were tall-stemmed, filled with clear liquid, and each had a red cherry in it. He proceeded to ornate double doors, and two large, uniformed men wearing white gloves pulled on golden handles giving him entrance. As the doors opened, loud applause could be heard.

Jesus said, "What's going on in there?"

No-neck replied. "It's called The Cherry Auction. Rich men are bidding on some new tight ass. I haven't seen her yet, but everyone says she's a real sweet piece. You want we should take a look?"

Jesus shook his head and fingered the pillbox in his pocket. His nerves were shot, from being around the pervert; he needed to get out of here. He didn't have time for watching some stupid girl parading around and putting on a sex show.

The elevator door opened, and Jesus thought he heard John Henry's voice. He turned expecting to see his friend, and saw nothing but strange faces in a stranger place. With a sad heart, he went with Bart down the lift and out the door. Until that very second, he never realized how much he missed his big friend and... .

29

Chief Poppelli sat behind his desk, hands laced behind his head, chomping on a cigar, deep in thought. For the past hour, he'd been on the phone with the FBI. He found the information down fucking right disturbing. He pushed a button on the intercom, "Send Prophet in."

While waiting, he reflected on the conversation. Harlan had family in Oklahoma. A wife, 15-year-old daughter, and a ten-year-old son. By all accounts, he was the perfect family man. He married his childhood sweetheart and became a devoted husband and father. They attended Church weekly and were never seen one without the other.

The story Poppelli got was: the detective returned home from work and found blood smeared all over his front door. Inside, he found his wife's disemboweled body posed with her legs spread on the bed. She had been raped. On the wall were the words, *pig pussy,* written in her blood. The same words were in his missing daughter's room. She was found two weeks later with her limbs hacked off after repeated raping.

The local police apprehended the suspect during a routine traffic stop. A blood-stained hatchet stuck out from under the car's front seat and the girl's panties were in his pocket. He came from a local rich family; the same man Harlan had busted for the brutal murder of an eight-year-old boy. In that trial the sentenced was reduced to 'not guilty by reason of insanity.' Serving only 18 months, the doctors pronounced him cured and he walked back into society.

The single bright spot in this grim horror was that Harlan's little boy had spent the night with his sister.

The agent relating the story said that Harlan turned into a friendless introvert, disappearing for days when not working, seldom talking to anyone, including his partner.

At trial, the same insanity plea was entered and accepted by the court. As the defendant was being led away to the psychiatric holding unit, he sneered in the direction of Harlan. Then things went sour. Before his transfer to the State hospital, police found the man with his sex organs sliced off and his throat cut so deep that his head was almost detached. The missing organs weren't found until autopsy. They were in the victim's rectum.

Harlan became the prime suspect, but no evidence supported the theory, and no one could place him anywhere around the crime scene. Nevertheless, with pressure from the rich family's political connections, the police commissioner gave him the choice to transfer or retire. Leaving his son with his sister, Harlan came to Cottondale.

Poppelli didn't care for the way this sounded. Harlan was up to shit and he knew it. Too many suspicious accidents had already taken place around the big Okie. He found it tragic and all that, but shit happened and there would be no crazed crusaders in his department. The last fucking thing he needed was a bunch of Fed's sniffing around. A knock interrupted his thoughts. "Come in, it's fucking open."

"You called?"

"Yeah, Harlan, I just got off the phone with the Feds and I have one important question. Did you kill that guy?" He watched as the detective's eyes flashed. Seldom in his life had Poppelli felt uneasy, but he did now and, more than anything, he wished that he'd never opened his mouth. The ensuing silence became unbearable. Suddenly, the need for control was the farthest thing from his mind. "How's working here been for you, Harlan?"

"Forget the condom. What's up?"

"There's talk about another investigation."

Harlan's lips curled up. "So?"

He noticed that, even while smiling, the detective looked deadly. He felt his balls shrivel up and wanted nothing more than to get this maniac out of his office. He said, "Fuck the sick bastard. Someone did the world a favor. I just wanted to give you the heads up."

"That's all?"

He nodded and Harlan left. Poppelli felt as though a great weight lifted with the big detective's departure. Looking at his hand, he discovered that it was shaking. He slid the offending hand under his desk and out of sight. He would keep an eye on Harlan, but from a safer distance.

Opening his drawer, he took a long swig of straight whiskey. Never in his life had he felt so threatened over so few words. Somehow, he needed to rid himself of Harlan. Now if he could only find a reason to transfer the detective, his world would be a better place.

Poppelli briefly considered working the situation from another angle, then discarded the idea as the booze took effect.

30

The Sole Taker moved in the darkness. No longer feeling any link or relation with humanity, rather, a manifestation of wickedness that's walked the black alley-ways of mankind's existence since the beginning.

He let his foot drag. Not from pain or injury, instead, seeking connection with that dark, scrabbling thing lurking in the universal subconscious, waiting for the moment when depravity crossed over into pure evil.

He relished torture and killing, swelling with each dark scream; each fear-filled death. Like a monster kneading the teat of nightmares, he suckled the brackish puss in an attempt to fill the bottomless void in his life form; happily cursed in being anything other than what he once was—humanity's joke. Only ritual and murder brought respite from his memories, and each reprieve was shorter than the last.

Compulsive walks throughout the compound ensured no breach in his security. He hated the day. Hot molten sunlight waited to burn his pigmentless skin. Pushing these thoughts away, he lurched on.

A young boy now filled his meager requests from the outside world. Once a week, he would come and collect the envelope with money and instructions on the front step, then return and leave needed supplies.

The Sole Taker paid well for these services and his anonymity. In the beginning he'd asked the black man. He could still recall his indignant reply; "Leave the kidnapping to him and get a bitch for the housework." The big Negro did, however, agree to mail the soles, but not without complaint: "Postal-punking will cost you extra. Five-hundred-clams a pop."

Soon the black man would be needed to deliver again. The Sole Taker found it important that the police knew and respected his power.

He slowly made his way under the thing hanging by its arms. This one omitted a constant high pitched sound stream. A singsong chanting with its eyes staring upward. Usually he ignored these creatures. But this clatter got on his nerves, even more than her predecessor. He found the noise offensive.

Taking a long metal bar from the forge, he advanced on the clamoring thing. It seemed not to notice. He stuck the red glowing end close to the ever-moving mouth–no change. A quick thrust and the fiery tip plunged into the babbling orifice.

He pulled the blazing, hissing brand back. Now smoke poured from the wound, and bloody bubbles of frothy sound issued through the nose. The entire mouth and neck area ballooned into a red swollen mass. Eyes rolled up and the head fell limply forward. Bloody drool trickled down its cracked, blackened lips.

He poked at the unconscious body. Its breathing seemed slow and jerky. Anxiety grabbed at him, this one might die before absolution, and wreck the ritual. Turning on the cold water, he sprayed it with the hose. He could only see the smallest flicker of life. In his loudest voice he screeched, "Do you confess your sins?"

It made a low moan. Close enough. Grabbing another glowing piece of hot steel from the forge, he thrust it into the nasty-hole. Metal seared flash-frying flesh. One last explosion of sound as blood flew from its nose. With a skinning knife, the Sole Taker expertly cut the bottom from its right foot. Ritual complete. He lowered the remains into molten liquid. The corpse burst into flames.

Contented humming sounds came from his lips as he hosed body eliminations down the industrial drain in the floor. The Sole Taker felt complete.

31

Jesus and Bart walked into Big Momma's Place. Both Shady and Smoke ran up and embraced him. Shady had tears in her eyes. She said, "I missed you, darling. I was ready to come shoot that fat fucker."

"Double snap!"

He hugged both women and relayed the message from Fat Tony.

Smoke grabbed her pistol and said, "He's not taking me back. Not without a fight. I hate that bastard." She swiped tears from her eyes.

"Double snap!"

Bart said, "You can count me in, ladies. He's got to get through me first."

Smoke replaced her pistol, ran over, jumped up, and wrapped her legs around Bart. With her arms around his neck, she said, "Can I have this one, Jesus?"

"Ask him, Smokey girl."

Bart held her up over his head, spun her around and said, "Well, I'm not really sure. Are you saddle broke?"

She started laughing and twisting in his grip. "Hell no. It'd take some big spurs to calm this filly down." She gave him a sexy look. "Be a good boy and I'll teach you things you've only heard about in rumors."

Bart laughed. "Take me to school, sweet girl." He lowered her and they danced out onto the floor.

Jesus felt good. Before coming inside, he'd stuffed his face with a handful of uppers and downers, with a resulting hyper-relaxed feeling. Too bad he didn't write down the dosage. Talk about a super cool mix.

Shady pulled him in the direction of the dance-floor, saying, "Come on, darling. Your sugar momma wants to shake her young and lovely thing." She let him go and backed up, pulling her skirt above her knees, curling her fingers in a come here motion while undulating her hips.

He glided up next to her and fell into the same easy rhythm. Hands at his side, he moved his hips into hers and coordinated with her movements. He marveled at the silky hotness radiating from her loins. Jesus loved dancing, shaking his booty, and was having an absolute blast.

Abruptly, someone jerked him away. A huge biker took his place. Shady pushed the man back and punched him in the mouth. The biker laughed at her, then turned to Jesus and said, "Hey, cunt, if you scratch my Harley again. I'm breaking your bitch neck."

Jesus started to apologize for hitting the motorcycle. Then the words sunk in. Instead he pretended the biker had a cigarette in his nose and went for it. At the last moment he remembered to close his fist. When the punch landed, his arm went numb clear up to the elbow.

His perception changed. It felt as though the entire scene played in slow motion and nothing existed but a tunnel with the biker at the end of it. A drop of bright red blood formed at the end of the man's nostril. He felt transfixed as he watched the brilliant drop fall...

Jesus woke up on the floor. His vision blurred and his head felt full of angry bees. The biker reached for him with murderous eyes. Bart pulled the man back and said, "Fight's over, Mace."

Mace said, "I'm getting damn tired of the way you treat this bitch-boy." He slapped off Bart's hands and continued reaching for Jesus. Bart's speed and ferocity were amazing; Mace now lay on the floor beside him. Jesus burst into laughter. The downed biker got up and gave him a dirty look and stalked toward the door.

Between giggles, Jesus said, "Fuck you and your ugly bike."

Bart extended a hand and said, "Now you've taken up swearing! What's next? Shooting people?" Shaking his head he added, "Looks like you'll need to learn the two cigarette trick." After being pulled from the floor, Bart clasped him on the shoulder and said, "Not bad, little man. Got him right in the snot locker." For the rest of the night, Jesus felt as though he walked on air.

At closing time, with his arms around Shady and Smoke, he said goodbye to his friends and left.

***

Jesus felt the bedcovers move as his eyes opened to the sunlit room. "Wake up, Shady girl."

She opened her eyes and regarded him. "Are you still missing her?"

"Yes."

A brief look of sadness crossed her face, and then she noticed he was still wearing socks. She pointed and said, "You don't need to wear them all the time. I've seen your feet and they're not that bad."

He looked down and acted as though she had never spoken.

Shady came into his arms and started goosing him with educated fingers. He squirmed like a monkey in the grip of a triple coiled python, unable to escape her probing digits. She finally let him go and he scrambled off the bed. She turned and began tickling Smoke. "Let's get showered, girl, the river waits," said Shady.

Smoke came to life with a stream of cussing. "Mother fucker! Is making a sister pee her pants the only cock-sucking talent you white people have?" He watched her storm into the shower with another wet spot on her panties.

Shady grinned ear to ear as she held her hand over her mouth to keep from laughing, then her eyes softened and she went after Smoke. He heard her apologizing. In minutes, both women were laughing. They walked from the bathroom hand in hand. Jesus could see they were the best of friends. He could also see that they loved each other very much. He envied their closeness.

32

Afternoon began gearing up for the heat to come. The sun was bright and warm as one lone puffy white cloud broke up an expansive blue sky, like a silent message from unseen Indians.

Jesus drove the convertible according to directions given by Bart. They were to drive five miles past the end of his first driving lesson. Harleys in groups of three or more were occasionally roaring past them.

Shady whispered in Smoke's ear, and both jumped into the back seat. Leaning out over the trunk, the girl's motioned the next set of bikes close. As they got near the car, they pulled down their halter-tops.

Motorcycles swerved. The women stood, dropped their shorts, then turned and mooned the men. Harleys left the road in a giant dust cloud! When the dirt cleared, he could see bikers lying beside their Harleys. Both girls were on the seat hugging and laughing.

About two miles from the river, a bright red Harley pulled alongside the car. With his fat face contorted in rage, Mace shook a meaty fist. His bike caromed against Jesus' door as he yelled and flipped his middle finger.

Without giving the situation thought, Jesus cranked the steering wheel hard left, and the red bike shot off the road in another dusty cloud. He tried returning the finger gesture at the downed biker, but couldn't master the technique.

Smoke said, "Watch out for that maniac. He'll be coming for you."

"Double snap." Their voices sounded grave.

Jesus didn't comment. He was developing a strong dislike for the overgrown biker. Cresting a hill, he could see numerous motorcycles parked next to the river. He turned the car down a dirt road toward the water. As they slowly drove through people, Bart appeared and jumped onto the driver's door. He mimed a kiss at Smoke. She pretended to catch it and stuff in down the front of her shorts.

Jesus said, "Some bikers crashed back there."

"Those idiots can't drive," replied Bart.

Shady stuck her bottom lip out, squeezed her breast while batting her eyes, and said, "I'm afraid we distracted them, Mr. Bart."

"Two track minds, bikes and b... " Bart stopped. "I started to say, and wonderfully unique ladies."

Smoke said, "All that flattery's getting me hard again. School time, biker boy." She pulled a non-protesting Bart into the back seat, and kissed him.

Jesus parked and Bart took Smoke for a ride on his bike.

Jesus grabbed Shady's hand and ran into the river. The slow current and cool water felt nice. They swam together into the center. He wrapped his arms around her and floated. The feel of her warm body in his arms took him back to another place; a place filled with the wonder and spontaneous antics of a dark-haired girl. He felt a glow fill his heart. Memories flooded his being; memories from back in the current of time. Without thinking he said, "Mad... I-I mean, Shady, can... ?" His words ended as her body stiffened.

She turned, looked at him with tear-filled eyes and said, "You can't stop what's in your heart, darling. I already knew." She kissed him, half-smiled, and started swimming toward the bank.

He watched her return to shore while he floated in the green water. He never intended to hurt her feelings, he cared for Shady, but his emotions were dead. He shook his head trying to clear the memories.

He closed his eyes. Abruptly, hands snatched him under. He finally broke loose and resurfaced, barely managing ducking a fist thrown by Mace. Jesus punched him in the nose and submerged to escape.

Swimming downward, he could hear the biker thrashing above. He spotted a rock on the murky bottom and clung to it. For some reason, it occurred to him that, with Mace's incredibly fat head, hitting him was easy.

The idea struck him so funny that he barely made it back to the surface before he laughed and, when he did, the biker hit him. Stars exploded in his head. Mace had an evil gleam in his eyes. He said, "Your ass is mine now, funny girl."

Gunfire erupted from the bank. Shady stood holding her smoking pistol in both hands. Arms stiff, legs spread in a shooter's stance, with a deadly serious look on her face, she sad, "Get your ass away from my man. Pig-faced cocksucker."

Jesus started laughing and said, "Take that, fathead."

Bullets whined by like angry wasps. Shady ejected the clip and was reaching for another when a just-returned Bart talked her into stopping. Raising his voice so Mace could hear he said, "Don't waste ammunition, Shady. If he acts up anymore, I'll see how he swims tied to that bike he loves so much."

Mace climbed out on the opposite bank, did the middle finger trick again, and disappeared into the crowd.

Jesus swam over and lay down with Shady as she reloaded her pistol. He said, "Thanks, Shady girl."

She scooted over, cradled his head on her lap, and said, "I told you. No one messes with my man." Her eyes traveled to his feet. "People don't usually swim in their socks, darling." He pointed at the bikers. Some wore boots in the water. Kissing his cheek and running her fingers through his hair, she added, "I said *people,* not these mutated monkeys."

He gave her a let's-change-the-subject look and closed his eyes. Remembering the drugs in her purse, he rolled over and grabbed another handful. Maybe taking more would erase his memories. She started pulling at him. Moving a short distance away from her, he tried relaxing and waiting for the now-comfortable buzz. Every time he started getting sleepy, she started back in. She kept tickling him between the legs with her toes. "Stop it, Shady!" She seemed bent on driving him nuts.

She said, "All the gunfire has gotten me horny. Take me over behind those bushes and show me what a thankful man does for his best girl." She straddled him and rained kisses on his face. "Please, please, darling. Your woman needs you. Haven't I been a good girl?"

He started getting up when Smoke ran by, sprayed beer on Shady, and dove in the river. With Shady in hot pursuit, Jesus turned to see Bart idling up on his Harley.

Jesus had never seen Bart's motorcycle up close. It was a beautiful machine. Bart motioned for him to get on. "Come, pod-person, let's ride." Throwing his leg over the bike, he got on behind the biker. The motorcycle started moving. To keep from falling off the back, he grabbed Bart's butt.

"Hey! Let go of my ass, we're not that close," yelled Bart.

Jesus laughed. He was having the best time and he was fucking sure of it. Nearing the highway, Bart said, "I haven't been riding because of the seizures."

"Like the one after I played the piano?"

"Yeah, and speaking of that, I haven't had one since. By the way, that song you played made me feel all tingly and weird."

He apologized.

"No, kid, sometimes weird is good. Like you." Before they went onto the road, Bart turned and said, "Speaking of bitch-fits. If we're going really fast and I have one, it's important not to embarrass me if I wet my pants."

Bart gunned the engine and took off in a screaming roar of smoldering, smoking rubber. Jesus tried picturing the biker falling off during a fit going this fast. In his estimation, if anybody peed on themselves, it would be him. He tightened his grip.

When they returned, a large bonfire burned by the river's edge. Jesus went over and grabbed some beer from an ice-filled tub. Spotting the blanket, he sat down and opened a can. He popped the top and watched suds appear. Jesus loved beer. It rather amazed him. At first, he didn't care for the taste and now, he couldn't get enough. He slurped the suds off, shook the can, and slurped some more. Suds were the fucking coolest.

Shady came walking up with her head down and a pout on her face. She opened his knees and squeezed in. Leaning back on him and finding his free hand, she placed it around herself. She laid her head back and sighed. "I'm feeling lonely, darling." He thought she sounded drunk. They'd been drinking most of the afternoon, and he believed that he saw her take some capsules from the bag in her purse.

She seemed different today, clinging to him more. He didn't know how he felt about that. He enjoyed being around her, but his heart felt hollow. He would never be able to return her obvious affection. He sensed she needed more, but it was something he wasn't capable of giving. He hoped someone would come along for Shady. At the same time, he wanted things as they were; keeping the focus off the past.

Jesus dozed off and woke up having a nightmare. In the dream, a small blue sock burst into flame and he felt as thought he was buried in a consuming blackness full of red-eyed, flesh-eating monsters. Fear coursed through his body. Opening his eyes he focused on the campfire and looked quickly away. The air coming into his lungs came in short gasps. Shady turned and looked at him. "Are you all right?"

"I'm fine."

She kissed him softly. "We have to get back, the sun's starting to go down." Putting two fingers into her mouth, she whistled for Smoke.

Jesus got up and started walking toward the car. He offered to drive and then fell, hitting his head on the side of the car. "Damn! I tripped over something."

"I'd say that something would be all the drugs in your system," replied Shady. She hugged him and added, "jump in the back and rest, darling."

He dove over the back seat and passed out before the car ever left.

The terrible impact and sound of breaking glass woke him. He was flung into the floorboard. The pressure felt as though it would mash his body. The wreck seemed unending.

Mashing, smashing, bending, and twisting as excruciating G forces pinned him to the floor. It ended with dead silence. His head spun so badly that he couldn't get free. When the world turned upright once more, Jesus stumbled out of what only slightly resembled a car and went looking for the girls.

The Cadillac had hit a telephone pole. Oily black fire poured from a contorted engine compartment. Twin holes punched through the windshield. He saw Smoke and didn't stop. Her head was twisted clear around backward. Lifeless eyes stared into oblivion. He moved on to Shady and fell to his knees beside her. She looked at him with eyes dulled by shock. He said, "you'll be okay."

She had difficulty replying, "N-Not this time, darling." Her breath became shallow and rapid, then uneven as she gasped for air. She grabbed his hand and fought to get words out, "I-I never got to be anybody's girl."

His eyes felt wet. "You're my Shady girl."

"I'll take the lie, darling."

She started making a rattling sound in her throat, and said, "H-Hold me."

Jesus lay down beside her and gently placed his cheek next to hers. "I have you, Shady."

"T-That's all I ever wanted, darling."

He felt her breath falter and stop. Tears fell hot from his eyes, as the warmth from her cheeks grew cool. He lay there for what seemed forever... sirens sounded in the distance. He kissed her forehead one last time and said, "sleep tight in the light... " His voice trailed off and he added, "Shady girl." Jesus walked away as the first shadows of night covered her like a shroud.

33

Following the funeral, Jesus became progressively despondent. He cared little about his appearance, and less about food. Mostly, he sat in a back booth and ignored any efforts at conversation. Waking up with his face covered in drool became common occurrence.

His only effort at social interaction was bribing a biker to score a large quantity of Seconal, and stashing his booty like a deranged pirate hoarding gold; frequently slipping off with suspicious, darting eyes to inspect his treasure's security, filling both his pockets and mouth with brain-numbing swag.

Memories of the memorial service were blurred. He did remember stumbling repeatedly, and probably would have fallen in after the coffin if Bart hadn't grabbed him—something about his balance. He banished emotions and feelings. Jesus felt that, if he could just stop thinking, then just maybe the dam wouldn't burst and drown him in sorrow.

Big Momma and Bart handled the arrangements. Jesus could barely manage dressing. And that wouldn't have happened without Honey guiding him around by the arm, helping with everything. She said, "Hey, sad boy, you need to pull out of this, at least eat and stay clean. I can't be having my handsome brother turning into a drunken bum."

He looked at her.

Honey's eyes became wet and she grabbed his shoulders, shaking him. Stepping back, she pummeled him on the chest with her fist. "Don't do this to me, Jesus."

He lowered his eyes. Nothing mattered anymore, except the drug habit and it consumed him.

***

Days passed in a blur. Honey gave up and avoided him. Jesus tried to disappear inside himself. He started drinking whiskey and usually had a small bottle in his back pocket. He slipped in and out of awareness. Bar sounds would come and go.

Loud laughter rang out. Looking around, Jesus saw Mace sitting with some other men. He believed that the fat biker was making fun of him. Rage welled up in inside him. He grabbed a beer bottle and threw it. Somehow, Mace ducked and the whistling missile broke the window.

Things happened fast after that. Big Momma came over and said, "I've been trying to let you work through this thing, but there comes a time when help becomes crippling. And I won't allow that." She took him by the arm and led him out the door. Before letting go, she hugged him in a bone-crunching embrace. With wet eyes she said, "I love you the same as my own son, Jesus. Get over this and come back home." He saw tears flowing down her face as he left the bar and walked into darkness.

However, the picture still burning in Jesus' mind belonged to a winking Mace, with his lower lip stuck out in an exaggerated pout, big body quaking, and fat finger knuckles twisting beside squinted eyes mimicking crying, while Big Momma had hugged him goodbye.

Walking over to Mace's bike, he pushed it onto the side street. He wanted a good view of this. Taking off his left sock, Jesus opened the gas tank and lowered half inside. Pulling it back out, he switched ends and replaced the gas cap, leaving the wet end dangling. Realizing that he didn't have matches, he started looking inside saddlebags. After trying three different motorcycles, he found some. Before lighting the sock, he ran halfway down the block and pulled the lid half off a manhole cover. Steam wafted up from underground. Walking back, he lit the fuse.

The sock burst into flames! He barely managed running back and pulling the cover almost closed before the block rocked with explosive concussion! A giant fireball lit up the night sky!

Jesus screeched with maniacal laughter.

His eyes reflected the blast. He kept switching from crying to fits of laughter, holding a hand over his mouth to stifle the noise while Mace fell on his knees and began weeping beside his scorched Harley. Jesus hid until the crowd finally dispersed and the burned motorcycle was hauled away. The initial event with Mace was all but forgotten in the cold, charred, unfulfilling aftermath.

He looked down into the dark abyss. Some invisible force seemed to pull at him; dark, immoral, and without reason, very much akin to what he was becoming. It took all his will power not to crawl down into the hole and seek out this fetid thing. At least he would truly belong–somewhere.

He pushed the lid aside, climbed out, and glared at the hole... not yet. Looking toward Big Momma's place, his eyes flashed once more. Not there either. Jesus turned and went searching for the darker side of town.

He walked the streets aimlessly, giving little thought to shadowed faces in murky corners, watching his progress from darkened, hollowed eyes. Up ahead a black woman stepped from a doorway. She was around his mother's age, with the same good looks. She said, "hey, sweetheart. Whatever you're needing Miss Betty can get it for you."

Jesus introduced himself and said, "More of these." He pulled the remainder of his drug supply from his pocket.

The woman took his hand and said, "Come with me. I'll take you somewhere safe and score the drugs." Betty pulled on his arm and added, "I can get you a jar of each for two hundred dollars. Just show me the money, honey."

He pulled out his wallet, opened it, and showed her. A fat sheath of hundred dollar bills stuck out.

She pushed his hand down and looked around. "Never flash money out here, Jesus." She reached inside her purse. "I may have to shoot somebody."

He laughed. He couldn't see anyone within sight, but Betty reminded him of someone filed under people and things best unremembered; nameless faces and events stuffed into the attic of forget.

He followed her into a sleazy hotel. A man sitting inside a smudged Plexiglas booth slid a key out of an oval slot and she grabbed it, nodding as they passed.

Betty led him up rickety stairs, down a lime green hall with smudged walls, and into a small room. Once inside, she said, "Give me the money and I'll score." He gave her a handful of bills and watched her leave.

Sitting on the dingy bed, he stared four feet into the bathroom. Between the two rooms was a cigarette-burned coffee table and a stuffed chair with holes torn in the arms. These were the only furnishings. Paint peeled from stained walls and a bare light bulb hung from a plain electric socket that dangled from the ceiling. Cockroaches scurried across the floor and disappeared into a large hole in the baseboard. A new looking mousetrap, set and baited, was by the entrance.

It seemed but a minute when she returned. Betty carried a large grocery sack. From it, she tossed two plastic baggies containing drugs. Digging deeper, she pulled out a six-pack of Budweiser and set it on the table. She opened one, sat down in the chair and regarded him.

With a heavy conscience, Jesus ignored the drugs and opted for beer instead. He took a long drink, and locked eyes with the black woman. Repressed emotions slid up his neck like foam from the beer.

Jesus began talking. It felt as though a dam broke inside him, releasing a flood of misery and memories, the death of dreams, and the dream-like reality of death. At the last, he mentioned the worst part: losing Maddie. Betty moved to the bed and held him to her breast. She rubbed his brow and stroked his hair. He clung to her while grief racked his body. Somewhere in the night, sleep took him.

***

In the predawn hours, Jesus had a dream. It felt twisted, distorted, mirroring his life on drugs. He lay at the edge of a bottomless pit and held a dangling Maddie by her wrists. She looked up from the black hole with terror in her eyes. Mist swirled and, when he could see her again, their positions had shifted and he dangled in the pit. His weight began pulling her over the side and into the abyss with him. He remembered looking into her eyes, saying, "Forgive me," and letting go...

He woke up sweating and shaking the next morning. Betty had left, and his empty wallet lay open on the table. Nervously, he looked inside. Once his fingers touched Maddie's picture, he felt relief.

Something about the picture re-triggered last night's dream. Chills accompanied the memories. He felt a growing sickness at the very core of his being; a dark, light-consuming cancer eating away at any claim of goodness left in his heart.

Jesus looked up and noticed a dead mouse. Its eyes were bugged out and glazed from the trap that had snapped its neck. He felt that his life was headed for a far worse death. His future and every hope was terminally failing. The magic capsules turned out to be the same dark bait that the mouse had took. They were a curse.

He could hardly believe all the things that he'd done. The horrid problem now was he needed drugs; needed them to feel normal, and this *norm* was as damning as the metal pinning the mouse to infinity. His thoughts turned to his father. Jesus looked into the closet and stared at the clothes bar. No. Not that. Not now. Not ever.

Movement caught his eye. Another mouse appeared and sniffed at the one in the trap. It paid little attention to Jesus and climbed over the body, apparently trying to figure out the problem with its friend. It stood on its hind legs, made a high-pitched squeaking sound and then tried chewing the wire. It climbed back around, nose to nose with the dead one. It seemed to say goodbye, and returned the way it came.

Jesus rose with new determination, walked over, opened the trap, and gently placed the dead mouse by the hole.

He picked up the drugs and dumped them into the toilet bowl. Remembering the pillbox, he pulled it out of his pocket and threw it in the trash. It looked worn and tarnished. Taking a last look around, he grabbed the trap and broke it into pieces. Turning the doorknob with a shaky hand, he left the room.

He retraced his steps to Big Momma's, then turned and headed for the river. He paid little attention to the sunny day; harsh and glaring, cutting at his eyes like sharp glass.

He felt the first hard cravings from drug withdrawal, shoved his hands deep in his pockets, and balled them into fists. His shoulders were slumped forward as he focused on the road ahead with singular intent. Jesus gathered courage to face alone the single most important battle of his young life.

He'd walked about two blocks past the bar when a motorcycle idled up alongside him. Bart said, "Someone roasted a Harley last night. I ran all over the place and couldn't find a marshmallow."

Jesus felt tears sting his eyes. "Bart, I'm going to the river, I have to get off these drugs."

Bart looked at him and softened his voice. "Get on, kid. I'll drive you there."

He climbed on, gave directions, and they rode to the spot John Henry had showed him. He said, "I'm sorry, Bart."

"We all go through shit, Jesus. You're like a brother to me, and blowing up half the block doesn't change that." He added, "It'll do Mace good to walk for a while. And nothing's done that can't be put right." They came to a stop by the old campsite.

He got off, reached, and hugged the biker. Bart smacked him on the back and said, "I'll be checking on you," then rode off. Jesus removed the boots and placed them on top of the camper. Dizziness almost took him before he reached the cot and fell into darkness.

34

Time was running out. The auction had been extended to a record-setting eighteen days. Dressed in a butt ugly, little-girl dress with a short frilly skirt, Maddie crossed her eyes when Delilah began slipping shiny black and white saddle shoes on her feet. Maddie said, "Hanna holy banana, these are dorky children shoes."

"Pretend you're wearing the latest style."

"Easy for you to say. I'm the one who looks like a Dorkasaurus." Concentrating on the shoes kept Maddie's impending horror in check.

Over the past few days, she'd managed not to scrub her hands. She held them up and looked. For the first time ever, her fingernails were starting to grow out. She even used lotion regularly. Dancing for the perverts felt nasty. However, awareness of her need to stall for time made the mommy voice a mere whisper. It still came, but her reactions were improving.

Her bond with Delilah continued to grow. She could sense the woman wanted to help her, but something told her that, if any help was forthcoming, it must come from within. Still, she felt too small for the task.

Delilah fixed her hair into side-mounted ponytails. Maddie said, "What's next, a diaper?"

"Shhhhh. Try and be calm, Maddie. Think of it as a game."

"I don't want to play."

"Do you want more drugs?" Before Maddie could answer, Delilah reached out and hugged her. "I'm sorry, sweetheart. This is breaking my heart, too."

She looked at the pain in Delilah's eyes. Impulsively, Maddie reached up and hugged her and patted the now crying woman on her back. "I know you'd let me go if you could... I love you, Delilah." Then she asked the burning question. "When's it going to happen?"

"In a few minutes, I will take you to a place called 'the play room'. All you have to do is climb on the bed and wait. Whoever won the bidding will come and explain what he wants."

"Will it hurt?"

"Yes, Maddie. It will hurt a lot."

"Double-gooey green woolly-boogers."

The woman rubbed her shoulders. "Remember, you can't control what happens in there; only the reaction."

Maddie was searching her brain for something just as stupid to say back when they heard knocking.

The two goons came in and her three captors escorted her down the hallway past the viewing room. Delilah keyed a large brass lock set in a blood-red door. *Double yuck,* thought Maddie. She felt hands shoving her forward and heard the lock reengage. It sounded deafening! Her stomach felt sick. The reality felt much more terrifying than how she'd imagined this day.

Racing around the room, she looked for a weapon, and found none. Her breath came in ragged gasps. She mumbled every prayer that she could remember, and made up new ones as she searched. Someone had to be coming– and soon.

She focused her thoughts. There had to be some way to fight back.

She ran to the bed, pulled back red-satin covers, took a cushion off a chair, and placed it on the bed along with four pillows. She replaced the bedspread and decided that it looked as though someone lay there. *Someone built like a gigantic marshmallow with a big square butt,* thought Maddie.

She walked over and stood beside the door. Taking off one shoe, she held it by the toe, pulled it back over her head, and prepared to hit the fiend with the heavy heel.

Her heart beat so loud that she felt certain it would give her away. Gritting her teeth, she stood poised with her weapon. After what seemed forever, there came a tapping at the door. Maddie heard a key shoved into the lock and as it turned someone said, "Yoo-hoo, sweetie. It's time for some fun and games, and, if you guess what's in my hands, I'll let you kiss it."

Maddie could hear his ragged breathing even before he came in. The man advanced on the shape in the bed. As he passed, his impossibly huge penis led the way like a pulsating salami. He wrapped his hand around the base and started smacking it into his open palm like a cop with a billy club. He reminded her of a larger Fat Tony. He said, "Here comes the fun guy, honey, and I'm bringing Mr. Doodle Dandy. We can't wait to meet you."

She hit him with the shoe as hard as she could. *Kerr-Thunk!* The shoe caught him in the temple. It must have shocked him because he grabbed his chest and his face turned red. He fell onto the bed and gasped, "P-Please g-get m-my pills," indicating a bottle that must have fallen out of his pocket and now lay on the floor.

Maddie ran over, smacked him again with the shoe, and said, "Get Mr. Doodle Dandy to get them, you nasty snot-sucker." He fell off the bed making grunting sounds, holding his seemingly paralyzed left arm at his side while trying to crawl to the pill bottle.

She slipped on her shoe and made a dash for the door. The pervert hadn't bothered to lock it. Panic erupted into full blown terror as she ran.

Spotting some double doors that she hoped led to the stairs, she burst through. As soon as she cleared them, something hit her in the face. She went sprawling.

Maddie looked up and saw the cigar-smoking gangster still attired in a purple suit. "So, you gonna break the rules on Fat Tony, eh? First, maybe I teach you a lesson. Then, we check on why the rabbit act."

"P-Please, Mr., don't."

He grabbed her in a surprisingly strong grip and dragged her over to a desk. Wrapping his meaty hand in her hair, he slid her face down over the hard wood. Her flesh made a low rubbing sound.

Tears stung Maddie's eyes. She was helplessly pinned with her butt in the air. Using his free hand, he yanked down her panties. "For being a bad girl, I'll show you what the T does to sweet little boys. He started breathing fast. My goodness, but that's fine ass. Be quiet so I can pretend."

She heard a zipping sound and felt a blunt hardness pressing against her butt. Maddie screamed in pain and flailed her arms on the desktop. It felt as though she was being split apart with a fence post.

Her eyes focused on a small jeweled pistol on the desk-top. Maddie grabbed it, tried to strike over her shoulder and hit him in the head. She heard a loud bang as the gun recoiled and flew from her hand.

It sounded deafening and smelled as if something burned; a smell that stung her nose and made her eyes water. The gangster let go of her. She turned and looked. He stood there with a surprised look on his face, still holding his thing, and said, "Hey, why'd you go and do that to old Fat Tony?"

Her immediate answer to his question was throwing up on him. Then she saw a small black hole between his eyes. The slight wisp of smoke curling from the hole mesmerized her, just as the fat gangster seemed overly fixated with cleaning her puke off his suit with delicate dabs from his handkerchief.

His eyes rolled up and he fell with a thud.

She vomited again. The sickness passed, and she reached to pull up her underwear. A drop of bright red blood fell into her panties. Cold realization hit Maddie like a punch in her gut. If someone caught her now, she'd be *bloody-red dead.*

She opened the door and peeked into the hall. No one in sight. Her ears still rang from the gunshot.

She ran to the elevator and pushed the button, hopping from one foot to the other in nervous anticipation. Finally, the door opened and she jumped inside the empty car. Standing inside the small space reminded her of being pinned by the fat man. She punched the L button and, when the door opened, she was crouched; coiled spring-tight.

A large gangster stood with his back to the door. Beefy hands clasped behind him twiddling his fat thumbs.

Mimicking a rabbit she'd once seen at a dog racing track, she shot between his legs. The large front doors were her singular fixation. Several arms reached for her but she dodged them all. Thanks but no thanks. By some miracle, she made it outside and rushed into the street.

Maddie heard the honking squeal of tires, but didn't see the car that hit her...

35

Jesus opened his eyes. Time kept getting away from him. Days and nights melded together in a profusion of sweat and hallucinations. The sun came and went like a hyper child playing with a cosmic light switch.

Something else was happening as well, akin to a giant vacuum sucking at his soul; drawing him back into the past and that terrible event from childhood. This pulling sensation was intermixed with convulsions, fever, and diarrhea.

He regained consciousness and saw John Henry, who said, "How's it going, sonny boy?"

A smile crossed his face. "I missed you, John Henry."

"I missed you too, Jesus, but we can talk about that later. Want some jerky?"

He shook his head.

"Then get the blank up and drink some water."

Jesus staggered down to the river, stuck his face in, and drank the cool, sweet water. He splashed some on his head. Half-crawling back to the cot, he noticed John Henry had left. Shaking his head, Jesus fell back into the vortex...

He lay on the kitchen table. The comforting sound of his mother moving around was the singular focus of his being. She picked him up and started to change his diaper. His body shook with laughter as she tickled him. Jesus loved the sound of her voice.

Suddenly it changed. It became fearful. Abruptly, she let him fall back onto the table. The shock of the blow almost winded him.

Terror started to churn in his stomach. His mother picked him up again and suspended him over the stove. He stared in fascination as bright flame danced in the burners; stunning, dancing, blue jets with pulses of orange and red. Jesus watched his small, blue, covered foot touch the fire and burst into colors. Then sharp pain.

His spirit separated from horrendous pain. It seemed as though he'd traveled somewhere else; a place away from his mom holding him over the fire; no longer a participant but an observer. His sock burned away from his foot and fell in an exaggerated slow spiral onto the stovetop.

His mother made gasping high-pitched sounds. Jesus sensed her agitation and confusion. She gently placed him back onto the table, then, whining in extreme anxiety, picked him up once more. Shockingly cold water hit his skin, sucking him partially back into his body, as she dangled him by his arms in the kitchen sink and roughly scrubbed his skin.

She moved over and poised him above beautiful golden bubbles. His feet hit the grease and his eyes snapped shut. All physical awareness fled. The terrible intensity of this new pain threatened to snatch him from the secret place where he hid.

On the cot, Jesus felt the full impact of the horrific burns. He screamed until his lungs were sore. He got up and made his way back to the river, eyes half open and half locked in remembering the sadistic experience. Drinking from the river, he vomited, cleaned his face, and drank again. Slowly, on tired wobbly legs, he made his way back to the cot and more of the journey...

His mother placed him back on the table and wrapped him in a blanket. This time with gentleness and cooing, intermixed with nervous chanting. Her tears rained down, hot and salty on his face. She picked him up, moved across the floor, and placed him on the floor of the closet. Waving bye-bye, she shut the door.

Each event resembled a still frame on a roll of film, slowly unwinding before his eyes. Each missing sight, sensation, and smell, all there in lurid detail, waiting for this moment in time to be re-experienced in horrific specificity.

Jesus screamed again. He snapped his head from side to side on the cot. His face contorted in unbearable pain, consciously felt for the first time in his life. Then, from the core of his soul, came FEAR; the crippling demon that haunted his childhood, blasted through the fabric of his being like a point blank discharge from some horrid cosmic shotgun.

Here was the root of his anxieties: Speaking in public, confrontation, responsibility, and, worst of all, being with Maddie Mae.

Next, a hot feeling took him. It felt new and traveled inside his body like a blazing inferno. He fought to identify this sensation. It resembled the feeling he experienced with Mace when he torched his motorcycle, but intensified. It was RAGE. The focus, if any, was the bizarre circumstance and the crippling of both his mother and himself. For hours, his body was ravaged by this blazing conflagration, followed by chills, only to switch back to the fire.

Repressed emotions loosed in his being, compounded by years of denial, now raced free and unchecked; unstoppable fires, burning through the fabric of his psyche, driven by the blazing winds of memory.

Jesus popped out of the nightmares drenched in sweat. With fierce concentration, he fought his way back in. Back to red-eyed monsters waiting in the dark closet and the rest...

Blackness came with the door shutting. Lying on the floor, Jesus couldn't tell where he ended and darkness began. Gradually, his eyes adjusted to the narrow crack of light emitted under the door. After a time, rats came and bit his feet. Repeatedly, they came; dim fiery-eyed demons from the dark.

Every being knows when they have reached the end and it was no different for Jesus. Music came to him. It danced in blue notes in and around his head; soothing life-giving melodies. Of its own accord, the music rose in pitch and bathed the closet in blue light. It seemed as though the rats disappeared and the next frame on the slide show was his dad picking him up and looking into his eyes.

He re-experienced the same emotion as when his father opened the closet door and let in the wonderful light. His heart swelled with love. Lying on the cot, tears made twin trails down his cheeks.

Here, at last the broken... hated thing inside... just a helpless baby; a victim of his poor mother's crippling disease. He curled into a ball and convulsed in soul-racking sobs. For the first time in his life, love filled his heart, for himself, his mother, and the lost baby of his youth.

Emotions subsiding, he walked back to the river, searched the tall grass and found it: the bar of soap.

He stripped naked, slid into the water, and washed repeatedly. Each time, his body felt cleaner and his spirit stronger. It was almost magical! As he scrubbed off dirt and sweat, toxic residue dissipated from his psyche.

The fragmented boy slowly fell away as Jesus moved toward manhood. He just made it back into his clothes and onto the cot as John Henry reappeared. The big man's eyes were filled with love and tears. He said, "Well son of a blank. You did it."

"John Henry, I ... "

John Henry raised a hand to stop him. "I know, sonny boy, I know. Remarkable journey. But we don't have much time and I have a lot to say."

He reached for John Henry's hand and it vanished, "What the hell?"

"Careful with the cussing, youngster. I can still kick your blank." He swiped an unfelt hand through Jesus' hair and continued. "I'm called a *seeker*, Jesus. Certain souls are damaged so badly that they need special guidance. I'm yours. Most folks don't believe in my kind. But older cultures have known and welcomed seekers by other names since the beginning. People in this modern, so-called educated new world are unbelievers. Take them big-city brain doctors. They'd call me an alter-ego, hallucination, or some other such thing. But I've been called worse. And by smarter blankers than them."

John Henry sat close to him. "My job was to help you start your journey. Once the path is chosen, everyone must find their own destiny. I expect that after today, you won't need me anymore."

"But, John Henry... "

"I love you too, Jesus. But you've reached a point in life where answers will come without my help." He smiled. "It's a good thing, sonny boy. Soon you'll grow into man. I want you to know how proud I am. Few regain the light once it's been lost; most are lost to darkness. It took guts to come here and do what's been done."

Jesus said. "But... I've made so many mistakes, John Henry."

"Wait a blankin' minute, Jesus. I believe that the human condition guarantees mistakes." John Henry mimicked unrolling an invisible scroll. "Yep, that's what I thought. Says right here that, in life, you get two guarantees: The first is you'll mess up. And the second is you'll repeat the first."

Jesus thought about the one lie he wished he could change.

John Henry reached over, pulled his ear and said, "Yesterday must be forgiven to enjoy the gift of today. It's been an honor to know you, sonny boy. Don't get so caught up in the past that you forget to watch where you're going. Might get hit by a blanking bus."

"I love you, John Henry."

"And I love you, Jesus."

He watched as John Henry stood up, waved goodbye, and, like a television going off, fade then disappear. He felt terribly confused; his best friend in the entire world had vanished, but he would never leave his heart–ever.

Jesus heard the deep rumble of a motorcycle coming into camp. Bart stopped, got off, and carried a bag over and handed it to him. "Big Momma sent you some clothes and stuff to eat."

"Thanks, Bart."

The biker punched him lightly on the arm. "Well, Jesus, guess you turned out human after all."

"I love you, Bart."

Bart kicked a rock with his boot, and said, "Look, you shouldn't go around telling other men... " He stopped abruptly and gave him a hug. "To hell with it, Jesus, I love you too. Big Momma wants you to come back and play in her concert. And Honey says hello."

He smiled at the thought of his friends.

"I've taken care of the situation with Mace. He's decided to find another hobby, but someday, you'll need to square the debt for his new motorcycle."

Jesus started to speak.

Bart held up his hand. "All that can wait. You kicked the drugs. When you're ready, come back home. Family's waiting."

A memory fragment of Bart giving him food, water, and a red capsule flashed across his mind, he said, "Did you give me drugs?"

"Only one capsule. You were going into convulsions. Going off Seconal cold turkey can be fatal. And, even though you've kicked the habit, your nerves will be shot for a while."

"Thanks, Bart."

"You bet."

Bart turned and walked away.

Tears fell in streaks down Jesus' face. He felt weak and nervous, but, most of all, he felt loved.

Glancing up at the camper shell, he saw his old tennis shoes. He smiled. John Henry must have guessed that he wanted them back. He went over and carried them to the cot.

He stripped off all his old clothes, ran to the river, and dove in. Spotting the soap on the bank, he retrieved it and bathed again. Then the strangest thing, he didn't drop it; suddenly the soap was just gone! What a weird day.

He climbed out and carried the bag to a spot in the sun. He glanced down at his feet, seemingly for the first time. They looked strange, as if someone had painted them bright pink. Without thought, he slid his right toe under his other foot. He didn't want to think about that right now.

He opened the bag. On top of the clothes wrapped in plastic was absolutely the best looking sandwich–ever. 'Matter of fact, the best looking anything ever. To his delight, he found chips, soft drink, cup cake, and a note from Big Momma and Honey, saying they missed him and come home soon. At the bottom, Honey added, *'Or, I'll come beat your ass.'* Jesus smiled.

While he ate, the loud chirping of birds caught his attention. Looking up, he could see a nest in the oak tree, almost at the top, on a weak-looking branch. He watched two adult blue-birds coaxing their fledgling. The small bird looked over the edge, began to tremble, and backed away from the precipice. One adult flew into the nest and nudged it.

On shaking, trembling legs, the tiny bird walked onto the edge, and, with little hesitation, opened its wings and stepped into space. Jesus watched as the flight morphed from clumsy thrashing into winged acrobatics.

Soon, all three birds landed and filled the morning air with song.

He dressed in new Levis and a soft blue cotton T-shirt, took Maddie's picture from his wallet and kissed it before putting it away again. Feeling drained, he lay back down on the cot for one more rest before heading back to the bar.

36

Delilah sat looking at the roll of hundred dollar bills in her hands. Get out of jail free cards, yet she remained a willing prisoner, not quite institutionalized, but one with a brand new conscience. And growing ethics at this late date may very well kill her.

Something felt wrong. It was about the young man named Jesus in the hotel room. Robbing him didn't bother her. If she hadn't of, someone else would have. Besides, he held a reserved slot on an express elevator ride to Hell. All the earmarks were there: drugs, not caring about his appearance, that haunted look, and, worst of all, regret.

She spotted it a block off in his wooden gait, bent, world-bearing shoulders, and hollow eyes. He regurgitated his story in heaving, stinking, steaming, waves of emotion, and, after he finished, the sickness remained and would until he found absolution—if not death.

Delilah noticed his clothes were soiled but expensive. All except for the rattiest, holey tennis shoes she'd ever seen, that seemed to go nicely with one soiled sock.

When he passed out, she would have left him without a backwards glance, until the picture dropped from his wallet. This was the young man that Maddie loved.

She tried hard not to care for the girl, but there was something about her; something warm and alive in a place of darkness. She shook her head in wonder. Maddie was truly beautiful and it started from within. She was a small soul with queen-sized courage. A gutsy fighter; overmatched against corrupt and deadly ring-wise professionals.

Delilah realized that she loved this girl, and that under-standing bound her as tightly as chains to this moral nightmare.

Maddie's escape assured her death warrant. Fat Tony was dead and his brother was recovering from a heart attack brought on by Maddie. When he got well, if he hadn't already, people would die. The absolute minimum in that equation would be her and Maddie.

Once a made man died, so did any and everybody in their proximity. To save face, bloody examples were sprinkled about like gruesome calling cards.

Her dilemma with Maddie had roots it the past; Delilah's past. Once upon a long weary time ago, she set the original record at the Cherry Auction. However, unlike Maddie's acting sensual to buy time, Delilah learned early on in foster homes how incredibly easy men could be controlled by sex. She had barely turned sixteen when someone snatched her off the streets and brought her into the family. There were smaller buildings in a different location, but the faces were the same.

Delilah bartered her sex before puberty. Some long forgotten insult drove her; a childish succubus on the prowl. She could spot a male sex-addict in a crowd. It was that extra look, lasting mere seconds and overlooked by the sharpest-eyed mother. But it never missed her attention.

She would guide greedy eyes with her hands in snake-charmer fashion, taking them down the turn of her leg, and casually flashing her inner thigh, then slamming the trap shut with the man's sudden intake of air, and widening eyes when she pulled aside her panties.

From there, she would either work him into masturbation while looking at her nudity. Or oral sex. Spit, not swallow, and no penetration; she had standards for Christ's sake. For the killing stroke, she'd remind the pervert that she was just a little girl and what had he done to her. She extracted money and favors like some erotic dentist with the most effective pliers in the world–guilt.

Back when she danced, there were only sheer curtains. She tried playing every trick in the room. But, in the end, the only person played was her.

Virginity ripped. Lost in one, bludgeoning, tearing stroke by an uncaring, fat, whiskey-breathed, sweaty-skinned pervert.

Popular with the men for a brief while, then discarded in favor of newer, fresher meat: lost somewhere along the way, was any claim to the innocence of childhood; she went from a child-like temptress to worn-out woman with an ancient, withered heart, pumping icy-red despair.

Delilah rose to the pinnacle of her profession. She became a handler; the one who calmed new girls and prepared them for their dark ride down the twisted roads of desolation. She had freedom to come and go and a flashy new apartment in town.

A brand new car and the finest clothes were hers. Somehow, even though she kept her apartment spotless, it looked soiled. New dresses became old before they left the racks. And she never felt free—not even in sleep.

Now, Delilah sensed some distant chance at redemption. However, it all revolved around helping Maddie. Seemingly, any future left for her involved with taking a chance. She never believed in grace or God, but felt if she did the right thing, it might help her redeem her soul.

She fingered the money again, sighed, and dropped it back into her purse.

She remembered Jesus mentioned a local bar. Delilah left the hotel and walked in that direction. Maybe the hand of fate would be kind, and she could set something right in a lifetime pockmarked with wrongs.

37

The girl remembered a screeching sound, then waking up in the hospital a few days ago and being told that she had been in a coma for eight days. She'd peeked under the white bandage on her forehead and found a curved jagged scar about two inches long. The stitches were removed today.

Since then, she'd been eating everything in sight and attempting to answer some exceptionally stupid questions. The doctor wanted to know if she had been to a costume party just before admission. Did someone try to molest her? Did she run away from home? Could she remember her name?

Did he flunk medical school? Did he have a brain? Could he be more stupid? As sure as puppies smelled sweet, her name was… Oops! She couldn't quite remember.

Did she have a puppy? Where did she keep him? What was its name? This seemed the oddest thing. Her name kept bubbling up in the old think tank, floating around just out of reach in wherever it was that her brain kept these little informational tidbits. "Hello, brain, what's my name?" She startled herself by speaking out loud.

She left the room to roam the halls. Thinking about all this was giving her another headache. Maybe she was some rich young woman hiding from her movie star husband, or some dangerous bank robber on the lamb from her last heist.

Feeling somewhat better about her fate, she explored the hallways. The nurse had explained that a specialist would be here tomorrow to see her.

A rather peculiar thing kept happening whenever she went outside her room. Men in suits were usually conspicuously close. Either she was a total nut case or these men were following her, but why? Several times, she would duck in this or that stairway, and say, "Boo," as they walked by.

Whoever these guys were, they possessed minimal senses of humor. Always acting as if they couldn't care less when they found her. Who did they think they were kidding? They obviously enjoyed following her. And, even though she liked the game, her curiosity got the best of her.

Returning to her room, she resolved to find out. When the nurse came around that afternoon, she asked how come there were so many dressed up men hanging around this floor. The nurse replied, "They're detectives. The Chief of Police's a patient here. He's in room one-sixty-sixty, and gets discharged today."

She waved goodbye as the nurse left and decided to check it out. He certainly sounded important.

She went into the hall and looked above her door. One-fifty-two, so that meant Mr. Chief High Mucky Muck would be on the bottom floor as well. Skipping down the hall in her white gown and bare feet, she looked at the numbers. Reaching the magic figure, she glanced into the room.

The weirdest thing happened. Her mind reacted in some sort of delay; she smiled and waved at the man as she passed. His face blushed red and he picked up the phone by his bed.

She turned back for her own room and then the past came rushing painfully back like brain freeze from too much ice cream, leaving her mind aching from sensory overload. The man was the pervert who wanted to introduce her to 'Mr. Doodle Dandy.' It took all her courage not to break and run.

Maddie made her way back to her room in as close to normal movement as her shaky legs could manage. Shutting the door, she dressed in the little girl clothes in the closet, and, to her immediate dismay, she couldn't locate her panties.

Who would swipe her underwear? Tugging her dress down, she again donned the hospital gown.

Maddie stepped into the hall. Two goons were coming her way. She turned and tried to walk normally around the corner. She could feel her legs trembling all the way. If this kept up, she would have bruises on her knocking knees. As soon as she lost sight of the men, she ducked into another patient's room.

Maddie closed the door softly. On the bed, a bushy gray-haired man lay hidden behind a mask with an array of tubes sticking out. She dashed in and hid under the side of his bed away from the door. While there, she peeled off her bandage and chucked it on the floor.

The door opened and man with a deep voice spoke, "She's not in here."

Someone answered, "We should have smothered the little bitch in her sleep."

She felt goose bumps stand up and parade single file with cold, wet, webby-feet down her spine. Maddie waited mere seconds after the door shut. The old guy in the bed gave her the willies. His metallic breathing belonged in a black masked, light saber wielding science-fiction movie.

Stepping back into the hall, Maddie scurried for the exit. Her body tightened with the expectation of someone yelling at her. In her mind, she could picture herself jumping clear out of her skin and running; a glistening red-muscled body with bulging eyes like the one pictured in her anatomy book: a toothy hole in a skinless face mouthing silent screams.

The hallway looked endless. Her nurse passed her and didn't look up; she was preoccupied with some papers in her hands.

Maddie tried smiling, but her mouth felt dry. The spit was missing. Her top lip stuck to her teeth in the attempt, leaving her to manually erase a petrified sneer.

Nearing the exit, she anticipated the door being locked, or someone running her down at the last second. But somehow, against all odds, she stepped out the door and into the late afternoon.

Leaving the hospital in a fast walk that evolved into jerky skips and hops, she fought to maintain control. Maddie crossed the parking lot, rounded a corner, tore off the gown, and broke into a run.

To her immediate dismay, the wind blew directly on her private parts. She dashed several blocks while trying to hold the impossibly short dress down and crossed another street. Then déjà vu: another car screeched to a halt.

Maddie felt the second car almost hit her in mid stride. It felt like a bizarre slow-motion wreck. Using her hands, she flipped onto the hood, and slid off the other side, her bare butt making a farting sound on the warm metal.

It seemed as if her feet never missed stride as she landed on the street and continued to run. Fear sent her flying down the road even before whoever yelled, "hey, are you okay?"

She didn't turn to look back. The question sounded ridiculous and it was funny in some sick, repetitious way. Did everyone in this town ask the same question? Maddie's heart raced as she flew across another street. *"Never cross the street unless you've looked both ways, then look again."*

The image of the woolly-booger flattened by the child's tricycle crossed her mind, but instead of a caterpillar, it was her small body that oozed yellow-green goop. She turned in the direction of home and stretched out into a leggy run, damning the dress, her undies, and the breeze up her butt, as her kiddy shoes became a blur of motion. After what she'd heard and seen at the hospital, the world felt far from safe.

Maddie's thoughts turned to her mother. Even her strictness would be welcome now. Being put on restriction until the angelic septet jammed the final rendition of taps would be no big deal in her estimation. The world was a yucky place and color that gooey goober-snot yellow.

The events that happened in Fat Tony's office replayed in her mind. *Little Maddie's sinful plan, to shake that thing and kill a man.* She pushed out the unwanted words. There'd be no scrubbing her hands. Not this time. Nope. Her bottom still smarted from what the dirty gangster tried to do. He could stick that nasty thing in the brand new hole in his pig head.

Maddie shuddered and ran on toward her house. She flew up the sidewalk and onto the porch, her shoes making clopping sounds as she found the front door unlocked.

Looking for her mom, she stepped inside. Even a few bars of Ivory soap would go good right now.

***

Everything looked the same as always, except for a strange quiet. Maddie said, "Mom, I'm home."

She searched the house and then called Clair on the telephone. Without asking, her mom's busybody friend gave her the lowdown on every person in the neighborhood.

Clair had to be the only person in the world that was absolutely interruption-proof. Once she launched into gossip, nothing short of a nuclear explosion would halt her, and that wouldn't work until the woman had been leveled into subatomic particles.

Maddie remembered the school movie on Hiroshima when people were blasted into dark smudges. Gruesome memorials forever burned into the sidewalks. She choked down a laugh as she pictured Clair's shadow still talking up a blue streak. Finally, Clair ended with, "I haven't heard from your mom in quite a spell. And where have you been, young lady?"

Maddie used the brief silence to hang up, cringing from the anticipated lecture she'd surely get when Mom did get back. *Children belong out of sight and, to adults, must be polite. Learn this rhyme and learn it well, or be a brat and burn in Hell.*

Despite what the nurse had told her regarding the perverted cop, she called the police. Maddie decided not to give her name, but thought maybe she could get some information. Sergeant whoever asked how long her mother had been missing.

"I'm not certain, sir," she replied.

From there, the conversation definitely took a downward swing. He asked, "Is there an adult in the house, sweetheart? Do you know how incredibly busy we are trying to answer important calls? Are you a little girl or boy? Could it be that mommy's gone to buy you a present?"

Maddie slammed down the phone. Could it be that he was an idiot? If she could fix up the sergeant with Clair, they'd make the perfect couple. A blabbermouth and a retard.

Her cheeks still burned from the little kid remarks. Looking down at her dress and shoes, she went running into the kitchen, stripped off the offending garments, and stuffed them in the trash bin. Then, on second thought, she tossed the socks as well, trying to shed the past with her soiled clothing.

Her stomach rumbled. Things were not going at all the way she pictured. Her mom never left the house open and she couldn't figure out how to deal with it.

Who could she trust? She looked at the front window. It was getting dark, and that left checking Jesus' house out of the question.

Clair had related a graphic account of when the police found Ralph's body. "I swear child, his head was puffed up like a giant balloon! With ping-pong sized eyeballs popped clear out!" Yuck! Yuck! Yuck! She absolutely would not go over there with night coming. Maddie pushed the explicit pictures out of her mind and rubbed her belly.

Her tummy sounded like it wanted to attack and eat her backbone. Going outside, however, remained out of the question. There could be large gold bags over there free for the taking; those and the world's largest flashlight wouldn't budge her.

Nope. Not for all the Abba Zabbas in California. Or where ever it was that they made her favorite candy bars. She had developed a specific protocol for eating the taffy treats, first hiding one in a nice sunny spot and guarded it for, oh, say, twenty minutes.

The bright yellow bars could be spotted a block off by bigger kids, so proper concealment became the first key to pleasure. The final test involved waiting until the candy was soft to the touch, and presto! Party time! Nothing finer in life than sitting on the sidewalk with the warm candy, stretching it twenty feet or so, and eating it bit by bit.

Both she and Jesus shared the philosophy that the only proper way to truly enjoy an Abba Zabba was to let it sit in your mouth, gently suck out the peanut butter, and let the taffy slowly dissolve. Zen-Zabba!

Their favorite pastime was each starting at opposite ends and meeting in the middle. Her best trick happened once they reached the last foot or so. Maddie would suck up the rest and plant a hot kiss on him before he could get away. She knew in her heart that he didn't want to, not with that big smile on his face. The same goofy, expectant smile always appeared within the last couple of feet. He'd even slow down and watch her.

Pulling her thoughts back to the present, she opened the Cookie Jar and ate two of her favorites. Walking over to the fridge, she smelled the milk, wrinkled her nose and settled on Kool-Aide.

Maddie turned to go upstairs and her reflection caught in the hall mirror. She whispered, "who's the beautiful woman?" Realization dawned on her, none other than Maddie Mae Bridger! Over the years, she could pass mirrors all day and simply see an ugly little girl, and sometimes no one at all. Now, she felt kinship with the woman in the mirror.

She stood looking at herself and ran her hands over her body, carefully inspecting. For the first time actually feeling her hands as they moved over her skin, connecting the visual with the tactile. Her checks flushed. Not from any feelings of guilt, but from self-recognition and happiness with the girl in the mirror. For the first time in her life, Maddie felt pretty.

Maddie bolted up the stairs, found some clothes, and headed to the bathroom. Cleaning out the tub, she cranked the water on lobster hot, and added bubbles. When steam wafted over the top, she tested it with her toe and slowly slid into the aromatic bubbles, omitting multi-syllable sounds of content all the way down. "Oh-oh-oh-oh, ah-ah-ah-ah-ahhhhh!"

Maddie no sooner got comfortable when she realized that not once on her bizarre journey had she considered masturbation. Before she could ponder the thought, *Kazaam!* The pilot to her pelvic furnace, lit with a body-rocking explosion. Maddie held tight to a visual picture of Jesus and experienced orgasms until her legs felt rubbery.

Climbing out of the tub, she washed her hair in the sink, and brushed her teeth. Why did it feel so incredibly long ago since the argument with Jesus? So much seemed different. Recent events had dramatically altered her life. She walked down the stairs to raid the fridge. Why did the house look so small? Where could her mom be? A wave of fatigue overtook her. After eating a piece of cold chicken, she went back upstairs and into her room.

Her mom had positioned her doll collection all over the bed as usual. Maddie went over to the closet and pulled out a small trunk. With silk scarves, she carefully wrapped them. She touched them lovingly and kissed each one goodbye. Finding a small padlock, she locked it, replaced it, and hid the key.

Moving back to her bed, she pulled the covers down. Patting her pillow, she looked at her room. Something didn't feel right, but her eyes felt heavy and her thoughts stumbled under the accumulated weight of circumstance.

Maddie climbed into bed and pulled the covers up to her chin. Right before falling asleep, she wondered if she remembered to lock the door. Searching her brain... she... thought... so.

38

George answered the phone. "Yes sir, Mr. Saurian, hot meat fresh off the street, not a problem. What? No. I'm not bringing food. Yes, '*me bring offering.*' I got the point. Just trying to put some get-down-rhyme to the fucked-up-crime. Tell you what. I'll cool the jokes and you try talking. You know. With words and shit. Fuck this mumbling bullshit."

He slammed the phone down. Good thing Mr. Sicko had bucks. The crazy bastard had started speaking mostly nonsense. And the shitty part was that he could understand him.

George laughed. Were things working out or what? He'd received a call earlier in the day and scheduled to meet the late Fat Tony's brother. That could only mean one thing: more money. *Money.* Just the word gave him wood.

He pulled out his mirror and found eye contact. His blacksnake grew hard against his leg. If he had a twin, he'd be gobbling tube steak. All this and money, too. Not a woman on the planet could compare with his fine ass. Ah, if only he had a twin... Didn't everyone have an exact opposite somewhere? George made a mental note to look into that.

The meeting would be at sundown thirty miles from town. Fucking gangsters. Full of cloak and dagger shit, but he'd play it their way. Mega-money wafted in the air and he could smell it.

The last time he received a call, Fat Tony wanted him to make a hit. The family handled most problems in house. But, in sensitive issues, he got the call. He still remembered the fat gangster's words, "once the heat's on, even trusted associates turn rat. Not you, stickman."

George grinned. He felt proud of that reputation, and he despised people who flipped. Fucking pussies. There was nothing wrong with prison, especially when made-men pulled your slack. It was just another place to score. Besides, these guys could reach out and touch you in the federal protection program, or any other place on the planet. Snitching was just another way of begging for a dirt-nap and some grease-ball tucking you in with a shovel.

He went out to his car and drove to the agreed place. Spotting the black sedan, he parked and walked over to the fatly conspicuous mobster. He reminded George of a gigantic wrecking ball in a trench coat. Despite the darkening skies, the gangster wore a hat and sunglasses. George said, "Hey, Chief."

The gangster pointed a fat, ring-covered finger. "Call me Big John, you fucking idiot."

George spread his hands palms outward. "Hey, Big John, there's no one here but us."

For a fat man, Poppelli could really look mean. He said, "let's cut to the fucking chase. The little bitch that you brought us for the Cherry Auction did some nasty things. Normally, I'd just fuck her up. But she killed my brother. Rumors are flying around the establishment and I can't have this one fall back on me. I want her death to be painful and totally unrelated to my operation. Up until earlier today, I had tabs on her. Now, I'm not sure where she's at. I figured if you found her once, you can find her again, and soon, before she brings more heat. If she starts spitting out what she knows. I could end up with a wet face–so do the cunt– capisce, stickman? Twenty-large if the job gets done right."

Poppelli slapped a fat envelope in George's chest. "Half the money now and the rest upon completion–or in this case, deletion."

George couldn't believe his luck. He tried adding the money for the contract together with selling her to Devil Dan. He suffered cerebral vapor-lock before he could reach the correct figure. Shit! This would be a big fucking payday and he knew exactly where to find her. "Chi… Big John, I need to bring Bobby Bones."

The gangster's voice dropped to a dangerous pitch. "Why do you think I went out of house on this one, George?" Without waiting for an answer, he said, "because little mice squeak every chance they get."

"Trust me, Big John. Bobby's going on a one-way trip. I've used him too much. It's the same as that old saying, 'two chickens in the bush with one rock in the hand thing'. You know, take care of them both and save a stitch in time?" He placed a hand over his heart and did his best to look solemn. Shit, he was on the verge of crying.

"I'm a little rusty on the moral thingamajigs, but trust me, boss man. I'll protect your interests or take a bullet."

Poppelli's black eyes glittered. He poked a sausage-sized finger in George's chest. "You got the last part right." Then turned and went back to his car.

George fingered the money. Being paid for what you truly love doing; did shit get any better? He didn't think so.

So little Miss Hot Body got away. Lame ass gangsters. Now, not only would he be rich, but he'd get to fuck the tight-assed bitch, too. His cock stirred in his pants. Soon he'd loosen the blacksnake.

Bobby had a car stashed with phony plates. The poor bastard couldn't spot his last ride, sitting in the fucking passenger seat. George felt tearing in his eyes. He felt a terrible sorrow. It took a long time to find and break in a new man and now he'd have to do that very thing. Bobby had started slipping back into his old bad habits. Last week he caught him gambling. After George graphically explained how he'd cut his nuts off, the dice-man promised it'd be the last time. He smiled. It sure the fuck would.

George looked at his watch. He could pick up a piece, find Bobby, switch cars, and be at the Garden Street home in less than three hours. He jumped into his car and went to get Bobby.

39

Jesus sat up on the cot. The sun cast a final brilliance and started its descent. He made his way over to the river and drank more water. A multihued sky looked as though a colorful, iridescent paint-filled mortar had exploded across the horizon.

His emotions felt raw and clean. Anxiety flooded his being, but it felt different, not the same old everyday fears, definite change had taken place. He looked forward to seeing his friends again. If panic attacks came, he would no longer try to hide them. Time to face reality.

Jesus quickly cleaned up the campsite and started walking toward Big Momma's. The tennis shoes on his feet felt comfortable, like old friends. All traces of swagger disappeared from his walk; simply the brisk long strides of youth. He squared his shoulders. The wind in his face felt good.

Nearing the bar, a well-dressed woman approached him. She looked familiar. He said, "Hello, Betty."

She looked at him with wet, reddened eyes. "My name's Delilah and I stole your money." Handing him a roll of bills, she began talking as tears streamed down her face. Her words stumbled out one after another in a drunken fashion. "I have news about Maddie. Gangsters kidnapped her in town. She managed to get away… be… before… well… something bad happened. When she escaped, someone… got… a mobster got killed. She ran into the street. Hit by car."

Jesus tried to speak.

Delilah held up her hand. "Let me finish. Although she remained unconscious for a while, my nurse friend says she's o-okay. Just a temporary problem with memory.

Today, she ran off from the hospital. No one knows where she went or where she lives. I'm really sorry I didn't try and find you sooner, but some bad people are looking for both Maddie and me."

Jesus handed her back the money, squeezed her hand, and said, "I think you need this more than I do. Knowing Maddie's okay's enough for me."

Delilah put the money in her purse and hugged him. Stepping back, she said, "Maddie loves you, Jesus. Please ask her to forgive me. She's the bravest young woman that I've ever met."

She looked intently into his eyes. "You've changed. Whatever demon you carried on your back is gone. I know a peaceful face when I see one. Please take care. When you find Maddie, take her somewhere safe."

Watching the woman turn and leave, Jesus' original plans of stopping at the bar evaporated. He headed for Garden Street.

Smiles kept erupting on his face as he hurried along.

A few blocks short of his goal, a familiar voice said, "Well, fuck me, if Sue's not back. Hey, bitch, don't you know it's getting dark and we butt bone little girls? Night fucking's best, that way we don't have to look at your dog-ugly face. How about sucking some bad boy dicks, Suzy?"

Jesus turned and saw the same group of boys who had beat him up before. Without a word, he walked up to the leader and did his two cigarette trick. The bully fell on the ground with blood streaming from his nose, then touched his face and came away with a red hand.

"No bitch bloodies my nose. This cunt needs her ass beat off." The boy now had a waver in his voice as he stood and moved hesitantly forward. Jesus knocked him down for a second time. Now both his lip and eye were cut. Jumping back up he said, "Come on, boys, it's time to kill this punk."

His gang stood there, not moving and looking back and forth at each other. Jesus hit him again. From the ground, the boy put his hands up waving surrender. "I've had enough, Sue."

He picked him up by his collar and slapped him hard. Now he looked ready to cry. "Please don't hit me anymore."

Jesus let him go, and said, "forget my name and we'll do this again." He looked intently at the other boys. They shook their heads, waved him off with their open palms and backed up. Their eyes reflected no more interest in fighting. He started walking off.

The one on the ground yelled after him. "Hang out with us, Jesus. And show me that neat trick." He wondered about the invitation. These boys were the school bullies. Their singular purpose for being was intimidation. Everyone followed the leader; a large, boisterous dark-haired boy. The one he'd just beaten up. They called themselves 'the Ballpark Nine.' In the outdoor baseball stadium, boys were taken, robbed and beaten. Girls were forced into sex.

The gang got away by either intimidation or the victim's shame. The leader spent time in the local reformatory and wore that black mark like a badge of honor. Jesus could not understand why other boys would seek their company. If the price of social acceptance involved harming others, he'd stay a loner. He quickened his pace.

While he walked, a flashback of the earlier attack by the boys when John Henry showed up, replayed in his mind. It was different somehow. The part where the big man pulled the boys off seemed unreal; like waking up in a dream and watching it fade with consciousness. Instead, the bullies beating him until he lay still, curled into fetal ball, replaced the memories.

Even the prized cowboy boots resembled faded photographs left too long in the sun. And his recollections of the night at the campground with John Henry were different. Now all he recalled were images of a heartsick boy, dancing around a burnt-out fire, conversing with the empty night in broken-down shoes.

What really happened? Ever since talking with John Henry at the river, more and more things regarding the reality of their relationship were in question. But not his love. That would never change.

Day departed and stepped through the dark curtains of night as he walked up the steps to Maddie's house.

He started to knock on the door and it slid open. His heart beat hard in his chest. Neither Mrs. Bridger nor Maddie left doors open.

He stepped into a silent house. Some vague warning stood hairs up on the back of his neck. What did Delilah say about Maddie? Hearing that she loved him loosed such a flood of warm feelings that he didn't pay close attention. All he could remember was gaps in the conversation.

Jesus moved slowly into the kitchen, looking around frantically for some weapon.

On the counter were butcher knives. He grabbed one. He jerked his head from side to side trying to spot anything moving as he started back for the stairs. Gradually, he crept upward. Something felt horribly wrong and dread filled his heart.

He gripped the wooden handle so hard that the blade shook. He had no idea if he could actually use such a weapon under any circumstances. However, the thought of Maddie being hurt brought hot tears. They stung his eyes. With the back of his hand, he cleared his vision.

Before reaching the top of the stairs, one creaked! Jesus heard a male voice followed by a scratching sound. Fearful that he warned whoever was lurking in the dark, he froze. Sudden quiet…

He waited for what seemed forever, straining his ears in the darkness. Nothing followed. Then, as he eased forward, the heavy sound of scraping wood came from Maddie's room! He held the knife up in a stabbing position.

He reached her room and slowly turned the knob. His heart lurched against his chest in an all out effort to escape. Taking a deep breath… he stepped inside.

Something hard hit him on top of his head. *Bonk!* Both he and the knife went flying to the floor.

"Is that you, Jesus?" Light bathed the room as he felt Maddie jump on his back and pummel him with her fists. "Are you trying to scare me to death?"

His head still rang with the force of the original blow but he managed to flip over.

Tears flowed down Maddie's cheeks as her punches subsided. She started kissing him. After what seemed like a blissful forever, he looked into the wet eyes of the most important girl in his life. She inspected his head for damage. "You've got a big lump there." She raised her hips and looked down at his waist, "Make that two."

He looked at the pink scar over her right eye. Jesus could still see holes where the stitches were recently removed. It curved and looked to be in the same place as one of his. Actually, both their scars bore resemblance to the big one on John Henry's face.

He started to comment on this, but she pushed his shoulders back against the floor, and, with considerable wiggling of her hips pinned him. She said, "I couldn't sleep and started playing a record when I heard noise downstairs."

He could see her portable record player still spinning with the needle knocked aside. A small baseball bat lay on the floor, the words, *Louisville Slugger* emblazoned on the wooden handle. He felt thankful that Mrs. Bridger hated firearms. "Where's your mom, Maddie?"

"I don't know. I came home today to an empty house." Then she began explaining all that had happened to her since the playhouse.

He hugged her. His heart was filled with words he couldn't find to express the pride he felt. Jesus said, "Delilah told me you escaped from gangsters and then ran away from the hospital. She wanted to know if you'd forgive her." She moved in his arms and said nothing.

He swallowed hard and started on his own story. Jesus' eyes begged understanding while his tongue faltered, then skipped fleetingly across still sharp memories of his father's death, avoiding at all costs the loose-sutured uncertainty surrounding his mother's fate.

His face lit up while he told her about Big Momma's bar and his friendships with her and Bart.

Jesus' eyes watered and he avoided her gaze while explaining giving her address and ring to George, as well as giving up and throwing it away. She smiled, touched his hair and shook her head.

He couldn't find words to make clear why he believed George when he told him that she hated him, or why he lost hope. And all the very bad things he'd done since... his cheeks burned... Stammering, stuttering, he told her about the other women. Voice cracking, Jesus related the sexually embarrassing parts. Damning his stupidity, he told the plain ugly truth–no avoiding it–she would know if he lied, she always did.

He finished talking.

Maddie's eyes were blazing. She slapped him–hard. "That's for taking drugs." She closed her hand, smacked him in the face, and said, "This one is for having sex with those other girls." Thumping him again even harder she added, "And that's for kissing someone down there. How could you? If you're ever that stupid again, the only person about to die will be you."

Blood trickled from the corner of Jesus' mouth as Maddie broke into convulsive sobbing. Not knowing what to do, he held her in his arms until her tears subsided, even as her body continued to make jerky hiccupping movements.

She used her arms, rose up, and looked at him.

Right then, he noticed how incredibly lovely her eyes were. Long, fine, black curled lashes, quivering like damp, exotic butterflies over immense brown pools.

She put her hands on his cheeks, kissed him softly, and sat back up looking at him. "I still love you, Jesus."

He stared at this bright spot in his troubled life; this special being that had always been there for him. "Maddie, I have no excuse. Everything I did was dreadfully wrong. I regret all of it. Especially the last words I said to you in the playhouse."

She ran her fingers over his face. "Good, my fists were getting sore."

He looked at her hand and then inspected them both. "Your hands look so nice, you even have finger nails!"

Her face broke out into a big grin. "I've been working pretty hard on that. While were on the subject of change, you smell different."

"I took a bath in the river."

Maddie gave him a look of disbelief. "No, Bonehead! Every person has a different smell. And yours has changed. I love it."

She hugged him. Jesus pulled her closer, he smelled her neck, moved up, and did the same thing to her hair. Wow! She did have her own scent. And it was neat. He tried to identify or compare it, the best he could come up with was hot fresh bubblegum stuck to a red rose.

He kept moving his nose and taking whiffs. Her odor comforted him. It swelled his heart with warm emotion. How odd, he thought. When she had left and the void took her place, this was part of what he missed. He would never forget her smell again.

He noticed something else. It excited him. Maddie stirred and moved her hips to cover his growing arousal, with the same results as throwing gasoline on a fire.

She jumped up and tossed off her clothes. With both hands outstretched, she used her gimme gesture. Ever since they were little kids, if Maddie really wanted something from him, she would attract his attention–usually by whacking him or throwing things–then reach out, clasp, and unclasp her small hands and say, "gimme." It never failed in getting her way. Jesus would just keep handing her stuff until she stopped. He could clearly see the child in her when she did this. And he saw something else. The child in Maddie loved him. He reached for her outstretched hand. She pulled him up, let go, and fell back onto the bed.

He stripped off his clothes and joined her. Jesus reached for the light. She pulled his hand back, and said, "No. I want to watch." He sat up and looked at her. The automatic part of his brain sucked in air as he forgot all about breathing. He closed his mouth before drool came out. Her dark hair fanned out on the pillow. She wriggled and arched her body. His eyes went into sensory overload. Loveliness filled his gaze wherever he looked.

She took his hardness and laid it against her groin, the heat and wetness made him shudder. She pulled him down into an urgent kiss.

He felt the hotness of Maddie's building need. It felt as if the rhythm of their bodies slowly transcending the physical plane, reaching for oneness; a merging represented by flesh giving way to spirit. Jesus felt sucked into her being, deep inside the miracle that was uniquely her, Maddie Mae Bridger, the sugar-sweet, Abba-Zabba grabbing, heart-stealing wonder of his entire existence.

Although he had physically joined with other women, they were mere performances from a lost child's efforts to belong. Nothing compared with the connectedness that he felt at this moment, without penetration. It seemed as if every pore in his body matched and melded with hers in nature's heated dance.

He felt honored being held in the embrace of this woman becoming. Her breath raced and her movement quickened. He felt himself falling beyond all bodily restraints as she locked eyes with him and he leaped with his entire being into those dark pools, reflecting love's honest devotion and life's dream realized. Maddie's breath caught as she plummeted off some unseen precipice, and Jesus reached for, and followed his soul mate into absolute bliss.

They lay together in spent ecstasy. For the next hour, they held each other and spoke rarely, communicating instead by hearts achieving synchronicity; the invisible energy transference of mated souls, bodies in absolute harmony; like two hearts joined on a dime-store ring.

Maddie jumped up, grabbed his hand, and pulled him out of bed. "Go start the bath, and use my toothbrush." She grabbed his hair. "Wash it. And someone needs a haircut. I'll take the bedding down and toss it in the washer before mom gets home." She turned off her record player, picked up his clothes and started folding them as she shook her head.

Pointing her finger she said, "Get a move on, Mr. Messy, I'll bring our clothes after I take the laundry downstairs."

Jesus walked into the bathroom and switched on the light. He found what looked like Maddie's toothbrush. Pink with small yellow flowers. He finished cleaning his teeth, grabbed the shampoo, and washed his hair. Before rinsing, he remembered to turn on the water in the tub. He adjusted the water so it would be hot, but not the scalding inferno that Maddie enjoyed. He moved back to the sink and washed the suds off his head.

He looked into the mirror and inspected the new scars on his face. If he didn't learn to duck the way Bart taught him, he would resemble a boxer in no time–one who lost a lot.

Jesus could see Maddie's grinning reflection as her hands were snaking around his waist. He spun around and kissed her. She pulled back, jumped in the tub and crooked her finger. He climbed in behind her and kissed the back of her neck. She handed him a bar of soap, and said, "Wash me."

He rubbed soap into a cloth and began washing her back. She arched her body and he scrubbed harder. Maddie handed him the shampoo and ducked her head under the water.

Using his fingers, he worked the suds around her scalp. She bent forward. Adjusted the water until it steamed, and handed him a cup for rinsing. He poured water over her hair until it rinsed squeaky clean. He piled the hair on her head and marveling at her long neck. He started caressing it. Maddie held up her hand and said, "Whoa there, Tiger, you're about to start another fire."

She scooted around facing him and made a downward twirling motion with her finger. He spun in the tub. She squirted more shampoo on his head. He felt her fingertips massage his scalp and rinse him with the cup.

Maddie washed his back. It felt as though his skin lived implicitly for her soft touch. Her fingers caressed his shoulders and neck. She pulled him back to rest against her breasts. Jesus snuggled his cheek into her softness. Losing himself in the moment and feel of her. Content at last, sweet, silky, wet-hot, rosy bubblegum filled his senses.

She brought him back into awareness by kissing his shoulder.

"You're the best, Maddie."

She rapped him on the head with her knuckles. "And don't you forget that, Mr. Bone Head." Her voice turned somber. "Is there anything else you want to tell me?"

He made a sighing sound.

Maddie's voice implored, "A few small words?"

Jesus felt lost in the bliss of her warmth. His body still tingled from her touch. He sighed again, surely that would convey how especially good he felt right now. He felt her stiffen. Maybe he should say something. "You sure have nice breasts, Maddie."

She shoved him off. Her voice changed, it hardened, "Jesus, I've been thinking about this since I last saw you. I've never loved another boy and I don't think I ever will. But we're not ready to be more than good friends because of where we are in life. Any more would only bring misery."

He felt as if he swallowed an entire tray of ice cubes. "But, Maddie... "

"No, Jesus. M-Maybe in few years, but not now."

He noticed the choke in her voice and turned around. Her eyes were wet with tears. And there was something else, as if she needed... some... ?

The clanging of garbage cans interrupted his thoughts. It must be daylight! The words from Delilah that had been eluding Jesus came blasting into his mind at full volume, *"Take Maddie somewhere safe."*

He said, "Get dressed. We need to get out of here. We can call back for your mom, or send my friends."

He watched her dry off. All of a sudden, the distance between them seemed endless. Maybe she didn't want him after all. He simply wasn't sure.

Jesus dressed in silence. He felt more coldness from her now than ever before in his life. Was something wrong with his compliment? Maybe he should have mentioned her eyes. What did he say?

She avoided looking at him. Quietly, stiffly, Maddie dressed in jeans and a white blouse. Slipping sneakers on she headed toward the stairs.

He followed her downstairs and started for the door, before they reached it, loud running steps sounded behind them.

A familiar voice said, "Hey, little bitch-boy, want me to look up any more people? I killed your girlfriend's mother. Next I'm face-fucking her while I make you watch."

Jesus pushed Maddie toward safety, then turned and hit George, knocking him to the floor. Spinning around, he ran for the door. He could see Maddie's eyes widened with terror as she looked behind him. She opened her mouth to speak.

Stars exploded in his head, and Jesus fell into darkness...

40

George got off the ground and kicked an unconscious Jesus in the side. The little prick busted his lip.

He watched Bobby grab Maddie by the hair, and smack her with the same gun he hit Jesus with. Construction workers were coming over from across the street. Fucking daylight!

He would have been here hours earlier, but he had to track down a drunken dice-man and drag him by the hair out of a sleazy gambling hole. The other players started protesting until he showed them the barrel of his pistol. If Bobby hadn't stopped Jesus, he'd blast his bug-eyed ass right now.

These nosy fucking hard-hats were totally messing up his day. A big man with a yellow hat turned to George and said, "Get the fuck away from those kids."

He pulled out his badge, and said, "This is official police business, get lost, porky."

The man doubled up ham-hock sized fists and walked closer. "Hey, fuck your badge. Oily-headed, dog-faced, cheesy prick. I don't think cops behave that way. And tell your skinny bitch to get away from the girl. Police my ass."

He pulled his gun, shot by the guy's feet, and said, "the next one will be through your big fat head."

Sirens sounded in the distance as George quickly tossed Jesus in the back, and a now-sober Bobby threw the girl in behind him.

The big construction worker regained his nerve and started coming for George. "You ain't a fucking cop, ugly monkey-looking… "

He shot him before he could close the distance, the guy's leg buckled and he went down, holding his knee.

He started pointing the gun at the other workers, each time he moved his arm men hit the ground. If the cops weren't coming he'd have fun making these pricks duck.

Keeping his pistol trained on the men, he made his way around the car and slid behind the wheel. The dice-man jumped in the passenger side. The engine fired and died.

Grinding the starter until the asthmatic engine finally coughed and wheezed to life, they lurched away from the curb. Between clenched teeth he said, "where'd you get this peace of shit, Bobby?" His partner in crime remained wisely silent.

Barely two blocks away, a cruiser with red lights flashing hurtled by. George growled. "You Buckwheat-looking-motherfucker. If we get stopped, I'm blowing your ass into another county."

Bobby mumbled another apology.

He hit the steering wheel with his fist. Fuck! If they were stopped with these kids in the car, they'd be jailed until they were gumming prunes. He fought all impulses to speed and kept the car within the posted limits.

His nerves were close to shot by the time they reached the secluded road leading to Devil Dan's factory of fun. Turning on the dead end road, he traveled passed the old mansion and onto the property.

Stopping at the rusty gate, he jumped out and opened it. When he hopped back in, he could see Bobby visible shaking, if he thought his nerves were shot now, wait until he shot him.

With that thought, George decided to plug the dice-man at close range. Hitting a trembling motherfucker could be tough. Not to mention a skinny, running, long-legged, trembling motherfucker.

His first scheme involved doing the bitch then leaving her for the killer, and snuffing the kid after he rubbed out Bobby. However, that presented complications. He would enjoy nothing better than killing Jesus for hitting him in the face. But, the current level of heat from the cops necessitated dumping both victims with the white-fright.

He pulled out his mirror and assessed the damage to his mouth; a slight cut behind the top lip. George grinned. Nothing time wouldn't heal. He was still the fairest in the land and damn if that didn't make the old blacksnake wiggle.

When they left, he would make Bobby drive, and, if they were stopped, he'd pretend to be a hitchhiker. The dice-man would back his play, or die like a rat. Not that Mr. Death wasn't already in the cards, but if Bobby snitched, he'd dream up something really fucking painful.

He figured Devil Dan may complain, but hey, two for one. Besides, the sick twist needed him to keep the goodies coming.

As for the kid hitting him, if Jesus knew what was soon to be coming around the corner, he'd wet his diaper. So would Miss tight ass. George hated to see a virgin die without the deed, but win some...

He pulled the car up to the crypt. Bobby's eyes were bulged out so far they almost pulsated, he said, "this fucking place is scary. Where'd you find it?"

George replied, "you'd better pray fucking amnesia strikes your black ass and stop asking questions."

The idea of using Bobby's butt for a silencer and blasting him on the spot crossed his mind. But then, he'd have to carry the heavy body and gunshots might freak out you-know-who. Not to mention Bobby's dead ass stinking up the trunk. Nope. The dice-man would see another hour or so of life.

Exiting the car, they carried the kids downstairs and propped them up against the metal chair. Cuffing them through the arm of the chair and then to each other seemed the best bet. They wouldn't be going anywhere unless they gnawed their arms off.

He laughed. Once they got a load of their fate, they might just start chewing.

Remembering his mouth, he kicked Jesus in the ribs again. A soft grunt came from the boy's lips. He knew the kid couldn't hear him but he spoke anyway. "You're either a super-lame motherfucker, or you're a fucking idiot. And your name sucks. I'm pressed for time. If not, I'd face fuck your ugly sister and do you just for sport."

Bobby's eyes bugged out like cue balls.

George looked at the gambler and unconsciously started rubbing his dick.

Bobby said, "Hey man. What the fuck?"

"Only thinking 'bout how nice it'd be to do the bitch."

"Then why you looking at me?"

George smiled, while he daydreamed about snuffing Bobby. Paybacks were on the way and he could barely wait. He winked at Bobby and rubbed his cock again. The dice-man turned, and started running up the stairs.

He spit in Jesus' face and said, "Have fun, kids."

He ran to catch up with his freaked-out associate. "Hey, Bobby. Did you know that your ass jiggles when you run?"

At the car, the dice-man looked ready to bolt for the woods. George tossed him the keys. "Be cool, Bobby, stay under the speed limit and let's dump this piece of shit."

The dice-man backed the car out and followed his instructions. George had a simple plan: switch vehicles and put his crime partner out of his misery. The scheme gave him a hard on. He covered his erection with his hand; he didn't need Bobby running into a tree.

41

Jesus opened his eyes. He was in a dimly-lit building.

Pain grabbed at his shoulders. Looking up, he could see ropes binding his wrists, suspending him from a metal hook. His clothes had been stripped off and piled a few feet away. His head and ribs still hurt from whatever hit him. His thoughts seemed slow in coming.

To his left, Maddie was nude and suspended in the same fashion. Her legs were tied. He looked down at his own legs and found them unfettered; feet hanging mere inches from the cement floor.

A dripping sound caught his attention. Beneath Maddie, a bright pool of blood was forming. She swayed in the chains. Jesus noticed what appeared to be a stick protruding from her side, and a trail of blood trickling down and off her body.

Terror erupted inside him. He whispered her name. She opened her eyes and looked at him. Jesus said, "M-Maddie, I'm so sorry. I-I should have gotten you out of the house s-sooner."

Her eyes filled with tears. "My mom's dead, Jesus. That black guy said he killed her."

"W-Who stabbed you with that s-stick?"

Her grief exploded and snot ran down her nose as she sobbed, "That... thing... it's barely human... My mom, why?... something's wrong between its legs... no hair... powder skin... Mom never hurt anyone... can't understand it... the way it looks at me... wants to kill... burning hate." She looked at him with tear-streaked eyes. "How come?"

Then he saw it half walking, half scrabbling, lurching toward them.

It carried two long metal rods. It placed them under a large round tub and pushed a button. Blue flames roared to life. He saw shimmering silver liquid with smoke wafting off the top. Apparently, the fire had not been out too long. Jesus found the hot liquid beautiful and wondered what purpose it had.

The monster turned around and pointed at Jesus' feet. Incoherent spitting sounds flew from its mouth. It clearly didn't care for his burn scars. It looked both male and female and even though it wasn't tall nor heavy, deadliness emanated from its being. Large muscles danced and quivered as it moved.

The creature looked unlike anything he'd ever seen. Even in the scariest of movies.

It moved passed him out some unseen door. A cold chill came over Jesus. This had to be the serial killer known as 'the Sole Taker.' With this certainty came the horrible realization of his mother's fate. He felt a fiery stinging in his eyes as pent-up grief detonated a jerking, convulsive stream of body-quaking misery.

Maddie started singing. Softly, her words filled his soul and brought comfort. He looked at her. Pale and bloodied, yet she thought of him. Never in his life had he known anyone braver. He felt as though his heart would swell and burst from his chest.

The white monster reentered the door and shrieked at her while holding its ears. Its high-pitched sound had the same effect as eagles screaming at rabbits. Maddie choked in fear and Jesus froze.

It went toward her. He watched as it looked at her vagina and spit. Making clicking, grating sounds with its teeth, it advanced on a visibly shaking Maddie. Like an albino leach, it licked, and sucked the blood trickling down her side, pulling her body as its claw-formed hands embraced her.

She squirmed in the ropes with horror-filled eyes. Jesus found his voice and yelled. The resulting sound seemed minuscule in comparison to the killer's cry.

Rubbing its face in her wound, the monster turned and bared its teeth. Smeared blood gruesomely contrasted a chalk-white face. It looked like a hellish goblin.

Hobbling over, it grabbed another sharpened stick from a pile on a wooden cart. He didn't need to be told what the beast intended. In school, the auto-shop had a chain-hoist on a roller system similar to this one. The other kids left him suspended from it once.

He tried rocking in an effort to swing his body closer. The rollers on the hoist moved precious inches. He swung his legs and gained a little more before the creature loosed another screech. Jesus ignored the sound and continued his efforts.

He watched in horror as it held the stick in a bicep bulging, dagger grip, clawed hand poised to plunge it into Maddie's body. At the last second, Jesus kicked out with his foot and grazed the killers arm. It turned, and with surprising swiftness speared the wood into Jesus' side. He screamed between gritted teeth.

Through a haze of pain, he watched the gruesome thing grab another stick and plunge it into Maddie. She shrieked. He watched her eyes roll up and her head fall limply forward. Jesus' vision faded and he fell into the bottomless abyss of unconsciousness...

42

George watched Bobby Bones concentrate on the road ahead. At his direction, they headed out of town taking every shortcut, dirt road, and cattle trail he could think of. It seemed a safer bet dropping this ride at Honest Abe's Auto Salvage. The owner would take it, no questions asked and give them a cheap exchange. He had dealt with the man before. The swap would be a Junker, but it wouldn't be hot. This car singed the hairs on his ass. Town was outta the fucking question.

His schemes turned back to the dice-man. Soon now, Bobby would be bunking with the earth worms. He had a rather nice ring on his pinky. George made a mental note to take it and frisk the skinny fuck; this could be profitable after all.

He would miss Bobby. Even Dracula needed little dudes to tuck him in at night.

George felt a twinge of disappointment. He would have to drive the car back into town alone. He pulled out his mirror and looked at his reflection, seeking some comfort. Oh well, 'win some, fuck a few, and kill the rest,' or whatever the old adage, but with his looks, he couldn't miss.

He started fantasizing about the actually killing. He felt his cock stir; maybe Bobby would scream for mercy. How exciting. Feeling much better, George whistled his favorite composition by Wagner.

Bobby said, "we got a cop on our tail. Unmarked car."

"Don't turn around you idiot and act normal." He cut his eyes over at the dice-man. "On second thought, say as little as possible."

Bobby said. "Red light's on."

"Fuck! Well, pull over." George started thinking of probable scenarios in his mind. He slid his automatic between the seat and door for easy access. He watched the side mirror. For some reason, the cop headed around to his door.

George remembered seeing a picture of this detective in the newspaper, but couldn't recall the story. He started reaching for his pistol when the cop stuck a baseball-mitt sized hand in and snatched him out the window!

George's face was smashed against the car's hood and cuffs were applied. He felt in shock. He could not believe what just happened to be physically possible. Super pig just yanked him through the car window, like a fucking child.

On the trip back to the cruiser, his feet didn't touch the ground. He felt a small measure of gratitude when the monster cop opened the door before throwing him in.

So this big prick was going into the bad-cop routine. Well, he'd ride it out, and once his attorney got a load of the damage inflicted, there'd be a gigantic fucking law suit.

Thinking about his face brought tears into his eyes. More than anything, George wished he could reach his mirror.

The humongous officer walked back toward the stolen car. Bobby jumped out and assumed the position.

"Fucking pussy," mumbled George, then laughed as his associate's face dented car metal. The maniacal pig picked Bobby up by his hair and blood dripped from a gash on his head.

It occurred to George that all this time the cop hadn't said a word. However, he reasoned that pointing out the flagrant Miranda violation may only be rewarded by super trooper using his head as an auto-customizing tool again.

After chucking Bobby in, the detective got behind the wheel and drove. Not back to town but deeper into the country. Familiar scenery slipped away as George racked his brain, trying to come up with something that might intimidate this weird-ass purveyor of police work.

The more he considered it, the more silence seemed the correct tact. When this detective discovered he wasn't scaring anyone by driving into the fucking sticks, he would head back to town.

George had never been in a hurry to be booked in jail before, but his thoughts were leaning that way–definitely. He clamped his jaw down in determination. Fuck it. He could handle whatever this white monster cock-sucker had in mind.

The car fishtailed down an abandoned-looking dirt road leaving a huge dust plume marking their passage. Old, derelict oil-pumps were on either side. None were operational and two had fallen over. They finally stopped. The remnants of a pumping-rig lay decaying in the dirt.

The Pugnacious pig left the car and opened the trunk. Who did this no-talking motherfucker think he was scaring? He made all kinds of racket with whatever the fuck was in the back of the car. George figured this would be the academy award shit. Hell, maybe he'd just kick their asses and leave them here. He started worrying about Bobby's ability to keep his mouth shut and whispered. "He's playing us. Open your mouth, and it'll be the last fucking time."

Crunching footsteps marked his return. He opened the door, and, with a roll of duct-tape, took several turns around Bobby's mouth and head. What the fuck? Concern turned the corner into horror as George watched the cop toss the dice-man onto the ground with a resounding thump.

Faster than a deranged magician, he slipped garbage bags over each leg and secured each with tape by Bobby's thighs, set Bobby up, covered his upper body with another large bag, and taped the bottom around his waist. Breaths from his terrified crime-partner were causing the bag to suck in and out. George started to tell the cop that Bobby would suffocate, then decided to keep it zipped.

Mind-fucking-reader that he was, the detective took a small knife from his pocket, pulled the bag away from Bobby's face, and cut a round hole. He almost looked maternal in his care to push the bag over the face and around the ears. The result was a bizarre caricature of a nun in plastic. A bug-eyed nun.

With his thumb and forefinger, he dragged Bobby by his nose around the car and out into the field. The stickman had a super view.

Walking back to the trunk, the cop reappeared with a small chainsaw. Then things got way fuckin' strange; weirder than a sack full of motherfuckers strange. Without warning, he started the saw. Beginning at the legs, he made three quick cuts. Bobby broke apart in pieces.

George marveled at how loud and clear the dice-man managed to scream from just his nose.

While this thought shot through his brain, another feeling settled in his stomach, cold and unfamiliar to him. Determined to keep his mouth shut, he clenched his teeth until his jaw hurt. The icy-feeling settled somewhere near the vicinity of his now-shriveled balls.

The demented detective snatched the door open—without so much as a word— taped George's mouth shut and dragged him by his hair over by his now much shorter partner.

Reality started slowly shifting. He'd killed many people and ravaged multiple others, but seeing the blood fly as the noisy saw sliced through Bobby's neck changed something deep inside him. George had awaken in a nightmare where the monster was real; a homicidal, racist-hillbilly disguised as a no talking cop.

The cop snatched his do, pulled his face close and looked at him. The detective's eyes were black and empty, void of spark or expression. George shuddered. Why didn't this pig at least threaten him? This shit was unreal. The cop ripped the tape from his mouth and removed the handcuffs, and casually walked back to the trunk.

Maybe he could make a run for it. Before his legs would respond, a shovel bounced off his knees. "Dig," Said the cop.

"I'm not burying that motherfucker, and you haven't read me my rights."

The chainsaw engine shattered the late morning air.

George discovered he had a natural knack with a shovel. As he dug he said, "look man. Can't we just get along?" The humorless cop pointed back at the saw. In no time, the hole was finished.

The detective tossed the assorted parts of his associate into the pit.

George looked up at blood-spattered pants worn by the detective; the cop glanced down and peeled them off, emptied the pockets, and tossed them in with the body. The maniac wasn't wearing underwear.

George's mind took a hard left on the highway to Normal-Ville. Could this guy be excited? Did he want to... ? All of the sudden, the red blood dripping all over the fucking place, the cold body at his feet, also all over the fucking place, and the big-cocked policeman were more than he could bear. His bladder let go and he started weeping.

The killer cop got right in his face and breathed one word. Riding on the wind of his hot breath, the word bespoke finality; prelude to funky time, game the fuck over, redneck with a saw. He said, "Talk."

George started confessing every sin he'd ever done, and a few he hadn't. He fabricated a realistic sounding, tear-jerking story about being raised by a sadistic, abusive older brother, his newfound hopes of doing God's will, and turning his life around and helping others.

He felt miserable. He explained the Poppelli's, the hit put on the girl, the prostitution ring, the deviant killer, and delivering Maddie and Jesus. As soon as George mentioned the kids, the detective slapped him–super fucking hard–and said, "show me."

No sooner had George finished giving directions when the detective grabbed his hair again, snatched him out of the hole, cuffed him and tossed him back in the car. If he lived through this shit, he was shaving his fucking head.

George watched him gather stuff and walk to the trunk. He returned with clean pants on, started the cruiser, and flew toward town. George started to compliment the cop on organizing his trunk so well, but lost the thought as the car slid off the road in a tire-frying screech. He now had legitimate concerns about dying in a blazing heap of twisted metal. George sought comfort by holding his now shriveled cock.

The lunatic law-man passed other drivers without looking and forced oncoming traffic off the road. Stop lights went by in a blur as they sped toward the cemetery.

They crashed the gate at high speed and came to an abrupt G-force stop at the crypt.

George's face pressed hard against the security screen between the seats. It felt as though he'd be mashed through the wire like black gouda through some huge cheese grater.

The administrator of mayhem opened his door, re-taped his mouth, and gave him a super-duper close up of his mallet-sized fist. The blow caused everything to go dark...

43

Jesus opened his eyes. The only noise in the vast room sounded like a cat lapping milk. As his vision cleared, he looked over. The killer licked at Maddie's blood. Her head remained slumped over.

Without thought or plan, he continued rocking his body, ever-slowly gaining precious inches toward her.

The ghoul either didn't notice or care. Resembling a pale, grisly, hairless leach, it focused on her blood. Until red-faced, suckled, and sated, it turned back toward the cart and grabbed another stick.

Before it could reach her, Jesus kicked with all his might. His foot caught the thing on its chin. For a second, it stood with a vacant look, then fell in a heap on the floor.

Jesus looked up at his bonds. If he could take the weight off his wrists, he could slip the ropes off the hook and get free. He flipped upside down trying to scissor the chain with his legs. He squeezed as hard as he could but sweat prevented a tight grip. He slid down the chain without sufficient resistance. The resulting jerk on his shoulders felt excruciatingly painful.

He studied the problem. The chain-lengths were large. If he could get his big-toe wedged in a link, he could pull the ropes out of the hook and grab the chain. With considerable effort, he swung back up and tried sticking his left toe in a link. It wouldn't go.

Another agonizing jolt...

He felt his strength fading. Panting with exertion, he gathered himself. The creature made grunting sounds and started moving. If he failed now, all was lost. With an adrenaline charged flip, he tried inserting his deformed toe. It fit perfectly!

Like some bizarre flesh and bone key forged and formed by fiery adversity and waiting in loathed silence for this one-time application, he shifted his weight and it held.

Quickly, he removed his hands from the hook, grabbed the chain to free his toe, and flipped onto the floor.

The creature raised its head. Jesus kicked hard and it went limp. Blood mixed with drool foamed from its mouth. He waited long enough to ensure it wouldn't be getting up and ran over to a still unconscious Maddie.

He snatched the sticks from her side. Pulling the one from his body was harder. Just touching it felt unbearable. His sweaty hand slipped on the first attempt. The resulting pain made him lightheaded. With second effort, it pulled free. Jesus reasoned that it hurt far less coming out than going in. He lowered Maddie to the floor.

She opened her eyes and took in the scene. Smiling at Jesus she said, "that's my best boy."

He found a small knife on the cart and cut their bonds. Dropping it, he tried picking her up. She pushed him away and said, "I can walk." She stumbled over, started digging through the clothing pile, and got dressed.

He hadn't considered being nude in his haste to be away from the killer. Following her lead, he slipped on his pants, shirt, and sneakers. He pulled her arm and said, "we need to get out of this place." Blood seeped through the white shirt she was wearing. Wincing, Maddie pulled it up and tied it above the wounds on her waist.

There were two ways to leave the area: down a long corridor or out the door the creature had used before. He chose the latter and pulled her along.

They reached the door and Jesus looked back. His wallet lay on the floor. He started to retrieve it, and the white monster started moving. Without further hesitation he opened, and pulled Maddie into the doorway.

He looked inside what used to be a huge house. There was no evidence of furniture or windows, just a dark, stained, dirty floor littered with food wrappers and what looked to be piles of human bowel excretion. Boards covered what must have been windows. Cockroaches scurried across a sink containing something putrid-smelling.

Jesus closed the door and fear started churning in his gut. They were standing in pitch blackness. He could smell a strong odor of decay and the air carried a chill, not exactly cold, even though goose bumps were forming on his body. This was evil. Like an icy hand, it gripped him.

He turned to run from this dank, stinky place. The creature screamed. Jesus could hear it coming. Spinning back around, he gripped Maddie so hard that she cried out in pain. He pulled her deeper into the black abyss. He could feel his whole body trembling. They walked holding hands.

He held on tightly and reached out with his free hand, feeling for obstacles. He swung his fingers in an arc, looking for some hiding place. Then he bumped her outstretched arm. Maddie shrieked, stretching his already shot nerves to the limit.

Locating another doorway, they stepped inside, finding, then sliding down a wall. Jesus and Maddie huddled in a corner.

*

The Sole Taker opened feral eyes. No longer human, but beast.; pissed-off beast with a grudge. George Jones was to blame for this! Not only were there two offerings left at the chair, but when it undressed and hoisted them up, one was sole-less! Disgusting. Glass-shiny feet, void of humanity's mark. It loathed touching or tying them.

Its body shook in anger. Looking toward the door, it caught a glimpse of them. It peeled back lips, exposing razor sharp teeth; canines grown long by either chance or perverse ambition; jaw muscles bunched as it opened its fetid maw and shrieked.

They picked the wrong exit... trapped! Every door was carefully sealed. Time to rip, slash, tear, and smear the floor and walls with blood. Rubbing its jaw where the sole-less-one hurt him, it trembled in anger. This time, the results would be different.

Primal hunting instincts focused its senses. Grabbing the razor-sharp boning knife from the cart, it advanced on its prey.

Body quivering with pleasured anticipation, it silently stepped through the door. And yanked it shut.

*

Besides Jesus' heart pounding, he could only hear rapid breathing...

A door slamming! By the sound, it had to be the same one they first entered. He strained his ears listening. Nothing... Stillness... And the stinky smell.

Skittering feet ran by them. Rats! Not regular rats. These were large and they were spitting and hissing. Cat-sized monsters! Another stretch of silence...

Maddie's head rested on his shoulder. Her breathing came in shallow gasps. He wondered if she had lost consciousness again. A slapping wet sound started. It seemed nearby. He reached around her waist to pull her closer. His hand touched a furry body. It growled! He struck blindly and missed. The thing scurried away, hissing like a small demon.

With shaky legs, he lifted Maddie and carried her, using his shoulders as a buffer between her and obstacles. He figured that, if they kept moving, there must be a way out. Finding another doorway, he stepped through. His foot slipped in something. Jesus gagged and tried dragging his shoe to get it off. It was stinky monster shit!

Rats squeaked in anticipation! How could they see in total darkness? He stopped against another wall and whispered to Maddie, "are you all right?"

In a hesitant weak voice she answered. "y-yes, Jesus, but I'm afraid."

*

George regained semi-consciousness in what he imagined to be an interrogation room. Now they would read him his rights. He smiled. This cop was in big trouble.

*

Jesus' fear escalated. He grew silent trying to determine the whereabouts of the killer. The patter of small feet raced all around them, ever getting closer. It sounded like they were in a rat's nest. One ran up his leg. He reached to slap it and almost dropped Maddie.

She whimpered and jerked in his arms. Reaching around her side, he found a rat feeding off her blood. He hit it and felt sharp pain. The small fiend moved mere inches and hissed at him. Her body jerked, another one was at her.

Determined to keep them at bay, he covered her injuries with one hand and kept it there. The rats were smart. They would attack his open wound trying to distract him, while others went for hers. He felt one stick its head into the hole in his side. Tiny razor-sharp teeth gobbled at his guts. It gave Jesus the willies more than it hurt.

He grabbed and tossed the thing across the room. It hit the wall, screeched, and scrabbled back toward them like a deranged cat with a petting fixation. Didn't these rats feel pain? He never wanted anything more in his life than to be out of this horrible place.

*

The Sole Taker glided without sound, accustomed to the dark and its lair. It could smell the girl. Her blood was still wet on its lips. It would eat her guts and sacrifice her in ritual. But killing the trembling, terrified boy came first. It moved within inches of them.

Stark terror was etched on the face of the boy, reminiscent of some vague loathsome thing, from an old, frayed nightmare.

Anger churned in its gut, erupting into seething, blood-dripping rage, sending uncontrolled spasms throughout its body.

A rat ventured too close. Baring teeth, the Sole Taker voiced its claim.

*

Getting a better grip on Maddie, Jesus started to move. A bone-chilling scream froze him in his tracks. It shook the very floor they were standing on!

He could feel the monster's hot breath!

Rats ran away shrieking. It dawned on Jesus that the killer challenged them for its prey. They weren't bold enough even in their great numbers. Only one predator reigned here and lesser vermin ran for their lives.

He could hear his own heart skipping beats. His thoughts started freezing up. To know the killer was close felt bad enough, but he couldn't see where, and that made it worse—horribly worse.

It grew quiet again. Maddie squirmed to the floor and stood on shaky legs. A sound stopped Jesus. He couldn't identify it at first, then he knew. The killer was gnashing its teeth together! He felt his skin crawl. More time passed and another sound: a rapid whooshing. It took minutes for Jesus to understand that it was his own ragged breathing.

WHOOSH, WHOOSH, WHOOSH...

Silence...

*

The Sole Taker pulled the knife back over its head, then stabbed repeatedly.

*

Pulling Maddie's arm, Jesus moved several feet. Another noise. This time he knew the source immediately. The knife! It stabbed the floor with the razor sharp blade. THUNK, THUNK, THUNK...

WHOOSH, WHOOSH, WHOOSH.

It spoke. Not in words but in a guttural chanting, almost understandable but not quite. It continued striking the floor and repeating the chant. The sounds of its voice combined with the inky blackness were taking their toll. Jesus felt his whole body quaking. The cottony taste of fear filled his mouth.

He tightened his grip on Maddie. Something cold brushed his cheek. He absently reached for his face as his mind labored to identify the sensation, not wanting to accept the obvious: the monster had touched him! It toyed with him.

His teeth start to chatter and Jesus felt completely defeated.

WHOOSH... WHOOSH... WHOOSH.

This thing had a knife. *It could see in the dark!*

All the terrors from his infancy came rushing back. The killer chanted again. This time Jesus understood. The message rang clear. It only wanted Maddie and would let him go.

Jesus moved again. He could see a dim strip of light! His panic-soaked mind had trouble comprehending, then he realized it was daylight from under a doorway! Precious, life-giving, wonderful light, but it appeared far away and the killer in between.

More strange sounds... BOOM... BOOM... BOOM... What? His heart slammed against his ribcage in an all-out effort to escape, rattling his body and beating like doors slamming in his ears.

Thrust back into the closet of his childhood, Jesus felt as helpless now as he did then.

BOOM... WHOOSH... BOOM

It made a growling sound and repeated its offer. Jesus felt so confused. The prolonged horror of this place had numbed his mind. He could not feel Maddie in his grasp. It seemed as though she wasn't there. The light became the most important thing in his life. He stood slowly and turned toward it. More growling from the killer.

He heard Maddie gasp, and closed his hand. She was gone! Was this a dream?

BOOM... WHOOSH...

Jesus stopped and grabbed his head... Fear froze his thoughts... His legs began jerking uncontrollably... The beast roared a final challenge.

The door... Had to find the door... Get away. Nothing existed but the light; sweet, wonderful light. He focused on it...

BOOM.

Then it happened. In one trembling word, Maddie expressed her doubt, fear, and love; she said, "Jesus?"

Her voice broke through his terror, replacing it with something fire-hot. It burned inside his body like a raging volcanic river. Anger erupted into his chest. Jesus opened his mouth and his own ears couldn't believe the sound. *An explosive roar!* The cry reverberated off the walls.

The killer shrieked in fear.

Jesus repeated the challenge. In it the explicit message, *"Touch her and I will kill you."*

He walked with sure steps toward the killer. It scrabbled away. Lickety, clickety, split.

Hands balled into fists, he advanced. If he found the thing anywhere near her, he would beat it to death.

He laughed; a harsh course sound. Jesus wanted to fight. A red blood-lust filled him. If the Sole Taker had touched Maddie, he would hunt it down and rip the skin from its body.

Darkness could no longer hide the thing; he could sense its location and knew that it was afraid. And it had better be. Maddie was his girl.

He heard splashing and smelled urine. The killer peed itself.

Jesus found Maddie.

Gently lifting her, he moved slowly, confidently toward the light; shoulders squared, swaggering, daring the creature to come for him–wanting it to. In his arms was the absolute greatest treasure in his life, and nothing would harm her again–EVER.

The door was barred with boards. It took unhurried minutes to open it, and, even then, the hinges squeaked loudly in protest.

Dazzling sunlight flooded the room.

44

Harlan walked down a long narrow cement passageway. Knocking George Jones out proved costly. It took precious time finding the concealed opening and figuring out the mechanism to open the door. He carried his chainsaw.

Covered windows gave the place a shadowy look. His eyes took in details at a glance. He entered a large factory.

Heat from the lead smelt brought a sick feeling to his stomach. Gas fire gave the surrounding area a flickering glow. A large skeletal boat frame seemed to meld with nearby darkness.

He spotted something on the floor. A look of sorrow crossed his face. He picked up a wallet. In it, he found the missing Bridger girl's picture. It was a twin to the one given him by her mother.

Blood pooled on the floor. He reached down and touched it; still fluid with a trace of warmth.

Looking at the photograph, tears slid down his face. She was so young and he was late again. Bloody sticks lay on the floor among cut ropes. The killer apparently tortured them before death.

He wondered how Martha met her end. Hair samples matched those sent to forensics with her skinned, butchered foot. A loose-mouthed George Jones had confessed to dropping off someone matching her description.

When Harlan stopped the fugitives, the lab had already matched the prints lifted at the Bridger house to George Jones. The ex-felon had a reputation for doing time and never cooperating with police. And no prior crime partner had ever provided any useful information to convict him.

Bobby Bones was also an ex-convict; a lesser criminal, but the ink on his rap sheet ran red with innocuous blood.

Still, killing him was simply a ploy in a race against time to break George Jones; apparently unsuccessful. He clenched his fist. Maybe he could have gotten the man to talk sooner.

Putting the wallet into his pocket, he started walking for the connecting house. A scream stopped him. Something was coming his way and it didn't sound human.

Moving slowly into the shadows, Harlan concealed himself behind the boat keel and waited...

The van fire flashed across his memory and the beautiful brown-eyed child with the long curly hair. When he kicked the door open and pulled her from the fire, his hand turned bright red from blood on her legs caused by the unconscious scumbag lying thirty feet away on the ground. He cradled the girl and checked the pervert's pulse; strong even and regular. Just knocked out. It seemed this was his lucky day.

Suspicion crossed his mind then as it did now, regarding how the slime-ball managed to find his way out of the wreck, leaving the little girl locked in to burn to death.

With the distant wail of sirens growing near, he placed his boot over the pervert's neck with just enough pressure to stop the blood flow, held it there until the body did that final funky dance and the bastard lie still. Harlan didn't move. There wouldn't be an additional chance for another child. Not this time.

The girl put her tiny hand on his shoulder and looked at him. She trembled and mouthed silent words trying to describe the unthinkable. Her big eyes were unfocused. He doubted they'd ever regain the sparkle of innocence, now that she'd awakened in a nightmare, where monsters hid under the skin of normal-appearing people, and little girls were their prey. He hummed softly and rubbed her back as tears slid freely down his face.

Paramedics arrived and he moved his boot. They prepared to start resuscitation and he waved them off. Would have yanked them off if they'd insisted on starting. Looking at his watch he said, "too long." Indicating the child with his eyes he added, "help her."

The medics tried to take the girl and she screamed. Harlan rode along with her to the hospital and held her in his arms until her mother came. The look on the mother's face mirrored her daughter's and he'd never forget either; they were imprinted on his memory, in the indelible blood of innocence...

The door opened, then slammed, interrupting his thoughts.

45

Jesus carried Maddie into bright afternoon sunlight kicking the door shut behind him. He felt born again. The day felt like seeing it for the first time. It looked vivid, bright, and brought a peaceful feeling into his heart, and made the contrasting journey into the darkness seem almost dreamlike–make that a nightmare. He smiled.

Maddie looked up at him and said, "you're my best boy, Jesus."

He said, "and don't you forget that." Looking at her, he became dumbstruck with her absolute beauty. A tear slid down his cheek as his emotions found voice, "Maddie, I love you."

She punched him in the face. "Put me down."

He laid her gently on the lawn, she looked up at him with tears streaming from her eyes. He couldn't gage the look on her face, but he'd never seen Maddie this upset before. She reached out with her hands making her gimme sign, and said, "pick me up."

He scooped her back up and she punched him again.

"Maddie I... "

"Damn you, Jesus. You wait until we're almost killed by God only knows what before telling me that. Do you know how long I've waited to hear those words? Big... bone-headed... "

"Maddie, I've loved you since I first laid eyes on you and every minute in between."

Her face screwed up and she fired off another punch. It lost steam before reaching him as she passed back out.

He placed her back on the grass. Taking off his shirt, he tore it into strips and wrapped her wounds tightly. Her breathing was shallow but even. Was that a smile on her face? He felt somewhat dizzy. He bandaged his own side and carried her out past the broken gate by the road.

Jesus sat down in the grass and cradled her in the warm sun. He couldn't understand her anger. Was there ever a question? Of course he loved her. Jeeze, everyone knew that.

He touched his face. It still stung from her punches. Maddie packed a wallop. If he kept making her mad, he would need to duck quicker. Even with his recent people experience, nothing prepared him for Maddie. He reckoned it would take a while to know her. Maybe forever. She'd been confusing him since they were both children. He leaned over and kissed her softly. Then dizziness took him...

46

Harlan watched as the albino came into view. It tore at its flesh while making rasping, agitated sounds. So this was the sick fiend known as the Sole Taker. It didn't look human and he doubted that it ever had. It was a freak of nature; a sick, twisted joke with a murderous punch line; a blight on the world.

He watched it pulling and rending its own body in angry display. A noise distracted the creature; George Jones must be waking up.

The albino went into practiced movements: grabbing a wooden cart and pulling it toward where the detective had left the black man. Its screeching returned as it found him. 'Must be a labor dispute between supplier and management, thought Harlan.

George Jones, for his part, did a fair job communicating through his nose. The word "sorry" still clear, despite the missing S, repeated over and over with abundant sincerity by the criminal. He heard a wooden *thunk*, then silence, followed by the returning cart.

The killer reappeared, pulled a small knife from the cart, and cut the clothes off George. The Sole Taker positioned the cart under a chain-hoist and placed a hook between his tied wrists.

With quick pulls on the chain, it suspended him off the floor, and the show began. It grabbed a sharp stick and jabbed it into his side. George Jones screamed; a shrill, shrieking, nasal sound, and his head fell limply forward.

The albino didn't seem at all happy with this development. It started jumping up and down, grabbed a water hose, and sprayed the body.

From his hiding place, Harlan could see a revived George Jones shaking and trying to communicate with his ex-boss through his nose. He did his best to plead without the use of his mouth.

The albino pointed at the pool of blood that Harlan had spotted when he first came in and yelled, pointing first at George Jones' feet and then its own, and repeated unintelligible words over and over.

George Jones vigorously nodded his head, as though he understood the horrible mistake he had made, and, from the whining coming out his nose, was extremely remorseful. The albino went back to the cart and, in a blur of motion, cut him.

Harlan didn't see the actual slash but could clearly see the albino waving George's severed penis in his face. His body convulsed as he loosed a raise-the-dead, piercing, nasal shriek. Harlan stood. It was time to end this thing.

Before he could cross the floor, the albino grabbed a metal rod from the forge and stabbed the glowing end up George's ass. The resulting scream lessened as death closed its arms around him. In a final shudder, he slumped over, bearing macabre audible witness to his demise was screaming blistering flesh as the albino shoved the metal deeper up his ass.

Harlan started his saw. The killer uttered a laughing sound, fell onto his back on the cement, and waited. Horrified, Harlan stood over the bleached white thing. Scars crisscrossed its entire body. The sex was mixed.

He brought the spinning blade close to its neck and the albino's lips peeled back in what may have been a smile. The flap of skin covering its groin became erect. This appalled Harlan. He would not send this twisted creature closer to whatever evil that spawned it by masochism.

Turning off the chainsaw, Harlan smiled. Confused, disappointed pink eyes looked back at him. He said, "I forgive you," and, with a powerful flick of his wrists, hit the killer with the flat saw blade, snapping its neck with an audible pop.

Harlan carefully slid the albino into the pot. Molten metal churned and swirled around the body in a bubbling conflagration. Repeating the procedure with George Jones, he waited for the flaming skeletons to finish their bizarre dance; two silver coated lovers grooving to a smoky, eternal waltz; two cancers burned from the body of humanity.

He lowered his saw into the vat with the bodies.

Using the chain-hoist, he closed the heavy lid.

Harlan turned off the gas to the pilot light and cooled the entire shielded area around the furnace with the water hose. Turning the gas back on full force, he walked out of the warehouse. A thousand unseen vipers followed Harlan down the tunnel.

Checking the door mechanism, he opened it and made his way up the stairs. Stepping from the crypt, the bright sun caused him to squint. Harlan filled his lungs with fresh air. The dankness below seemed toxic in comparison; perhaps a remnant of murdered spirits.

He opened his trunk, found what he needed, and started back. Walking back inside the crypt and down the stairs, it struck him as ironic that a hallowed place of final resting turned out to be death's doorway. The great crying angel, standing a mute witness over the threshold to Hell added a gruesome twist.

Returning to the metal chair, he ignited a road-flare and laid it on the cement by the chair leg, placing the second unlit flare at a right angle near the bottom of the first. He constructed a rudimentary fuse. He considered checking the house, but discarded the idea.

The albino depended on outside help, and, with its small size, unconscious and bound were the only ways victims would leave the chair. George had told him quite a story about this mislabeled killer. He stepped outside the door and re-engaged the door lock. After it shut, he returned to his car and drove back toward the street.

Clearing the downed gate, he noticed two people on the roadside. He recognized the girl right away. Stopping his car, he went over to them. Harlan checked each one. The boy seemed to have the weaker pulse, but both had good color. Assessing the wounds, he went to his trunk and found pressure bandages. With expert hands, he administered first aide.

Carrying the boy into the cruiser, he returned and prepared to lift the girl. She was lovely and looked remarkably like his daughter. While lifting her, he found himself the subject of her scrutiny. She said, "who are you?"

"Harlan. I can help."

She doubled up her fist. "I've been hearing that a lot lately, Mr., put me down."

He smiled and held her. "It's okay, kid."

"Harlan?"

"Yes."

"I'm not a kid"

"Sorry."

She shook her finger at him. "And don't be forgetting that."

He almost tweaked her nose the same way he used to do Sara. She acted a lot like her.

"Where to?" asked Harlan.

"Take us to Big Black Fat Momma's."

"Is it safe?"

"That's affirmative, Harlan."

He carried her without further protest and placed her in the back seat. Handing her the dropped wallet, he shut her door, moved around, climbed behind the wheel and pulled away. Adjusting his rear view mirror he saw her looking at him. She said, "where's that white monster thingy, Harlan?"

"Somewhere hot."

"What about George?"

"Him, too."

He looked back at her. She caught his eye and said, "good for them."

"You're very brave."

She cradled the boy in her arms and replied, "No, Harlan, but Jesus is."

He wondered once more about the genesis of evil and if he was headed there. Each new killing seemed less justified than the one before. Could there be some dim demarcation that once crossed forfeited his place in humanity? Leaving him forever cursed and kin with the albino? Harlan felt drained.

His eyes found the mirror again. The girl held Jesus' head cradled on her breast, as her hands were stroking his hair. He grinned. The Bridger woman was right, this kid... young woman, clearly loved him.

Harlan's memories journeyed back to his wife and daughter. With his grief lessening, he remembered each wondrous moment; all the days filled with laughter and love.

Maybe the answer was to lay aside his anger and be thankful for what he still had. His thoughts turned to his son. The boy would need him, but not nearly as much as he needed the boy. Now, maybe, he could see his son without looking through blood-spattered flashbacks and give him a father's true love, not a mannequin's touch from grief-hardened hands.

A few more loose ends and he'd be free. His daughter's image sitting in the back seat deserved a better start than her current reality. Harlan rolled down his window and let the warm air blow into the car. He remembered happier times as he drove toward their destination.

He pulled the cruiser up to the bar. A number of bikers were standing out front. One with a tattooed head noticed his cargo and sent others running inside. Soon the sidewalk filled.

A large smiling black woman ran out from the bar and straight to his passengers. Harlan flipped the car's security locks and got out as she opened the back door. The woman's eyes filled with concern looking at the girl. "Maddie, you're as pretty as your picture, and all Jesus could talk about. Is that blood on your side?"

Reaching in, the big woman effortlessly scooped the girl up. "Don't worry none, child. Big Momma's got you now."

Maddie looped her arms around the big woman's neck and nuzzled her cheek against her.

Harlan walked around to talk with the biker, who was holding Jesus. The look in his eyes told him all he needed to know regarding their safety. He told the biker what he required and turned to leave.

The big woman grabbed him in a hug. Looking him in the eyes she said, "thanks for bringing my family home. We can handle it from here." He felt comfort from her embrace. She had warmth about her. Impulsively kissing her cheek, he returned to his cruiser. Before he drove off, she blew him a kiss...

In another time and place, he would have stayed awhile. There was something good about these people; something warm in their eyes when they saw the kids. Harlan figured it was love.

47

Jesus opened his eyes. He was in a small bed with chrome rails. Maddie was next to him. She sat on another bed identical to his playing cards with Mace and Bart. Each person flipped a card up and Maddie yelled, "war!" After a card-slinging ritual, Mace exclaimed, "I won!"

He smiled. Maddie was doing her usual soul collecting. She could gather people faster than sucking snot up a Hoover. He remembered the last movie they watched together. Arriving a few minutes early was all she needed to strike up intimate conversations with several rows of people. Following the show, two women came over and hugged her goodbye. One had tears in her eyes.

Maddie had a way about her. Looking at her now, he could clearly see the glow around her. She touched people's hands, used their first names and made them feel special, as if she had known them always. She was a corker for sure, his Maddie. He also noticed something else. She didn't look the same. The girl he'd always known was giving way to a woman. A beautiful one. Jesus said, "where is this?"

Bart looked over and said, "hey, everyone, Jimmy Pod's awake." Then, answering his question, he said, "you're in the hospital and have been for two days. How are you feeling?"

"I feel okay." Jesus noticed a plastic bracelet on his wrist. It did indeed identify him as Jimmy Pod. "What the...?"

"Harlan's idea. Problems with gangsters. That's your alias. Harlan's the guy who found you and Maddie. Didn't say much. But, you would have liked him. I bet you can't guess who dreamed the name up?" Bart mimed polishing his fingernails on his vest and pointed at Maddie, "call her Suzie

Pod. You're related. Here read this," Bart tossed him a newspaper.

Bold headlines covered the front page, *GANGLAND WARFARE!* Jesus read the story, it seemed that 12 people were killed in a shootout and two of them were police officers. Taking a shotgun blast to the crotch, Chief of Police John Poppelli died in seconds. The article presumed missing Detective Harlan Prophet to be the second law-enforcement fatality in what was described as a lengthy and heated gun battle with enough explosives used to wage war on a small nation.

Crime scene investigators found Prophet's shoulder holsters and empty revolvers along with his police cruiser in the alley. There was a picture of an empty cop car with doors open and the trunk lid up. Assorted weapons, munitions, and clothes were found in a trail leading away from the scene.

The acting Chief cited Poppelli and Prophet as a heroes, and said, "the whole thing smacked of gangland warfare and it wouldn't be tolerated in Cottondale." It was presumed that the two officers happened upon foul play and lost their lives in the massive shootout. In an unrelated story, the mansion of deceased yacht building magnate, Madison Saurian, was consumed by fire from an explosion that rocked the entire coastline. The second article brought a smile to Jesus' face.

He looked over at Maddie, who appeared to be engrossed in her card game. She sat cross-legged on top of the bed with her gown tucked under her. It looked as though she wore shorts. Maddie had cute legs. Jesus thought he saw Mace looking at them more than once. He wasn't sure how he felt about it either. People always looked at her and it never bothered him before, but something seemed different this time. A warm feeling swirled in his head and he didn't much care for it.

His own legs were uncovered. He studied them, wondering about all these emotions loosed in his body. Something had changed between him and Maddie. And it confused him.

A knock came at the door. Big Momma and Honey came in. Behind them in the hall, he could see more bikers sitting by the door. Both women ran over and hugged him. Big Momma said, "Child, it's so good to see you and we finally got to meet your wonderful girlfriend." Big Momma turned and hugged Maddie while Honey gave him her first proper sister-like hug. Jesus felt strangely pleased that Maddie observed with some interest.

Honey spun around, ran over, jumped on the bed, kissed Maddie's cheeks and hugged her. They were whispering in each other's ears and laughing. It was as though they'd been friends forever.

Mace said, "hey, you're messing up the cards."

"Stick a sock in it," Honey replied. Then, she ran for some large bags they'd carried in. Holding up a blue dress for Maddie's inspection, she said, "This is for you, sis, what do you think?"

Maddie's eyes lit up. "I love it!" She crooked her finger and when Honey got close, she snatched her in another hug. Jesus started feeling left out. Big Momma opened a shoebox and took out some matching high heels. Maddie began shaking with excitement. "Wow! Those are beautiful!" She bounded off the bed and jumped right into Big Momma's arms.

The big woman's cheeks were wet. She said, "land's sakes, child, they're only shoes."

Mace said, "damn-it! I was starting to win."

"I just love a man who can say what's on his mind," Maddie remarked.

Big Momma looked over at Jesus and said, "speaking of the devil, we didn't forget you, son." She handed him a bag. His friends watched as he opened it. There in the bottom were some spiffy, new, black high-top sneakers.

He reached for Big Momma and she came into his arms. He whispered in her ear, "I love you, Big Momma."

She came away with more tears in her eyes, fanned her face with her hand, and said, "if you kids don't stop I'll get dehydrated."

Bart reached under Jesus' bed and pulled out the worn tennis shoes. He held them away from his body with two fingers and wrinkled his nose. Walking slowly to the trashcan as if he carried bombs, he suspended them above the can and, with a flourish, dropped them. Everyone in the room clapped their hands.

Jesus placed his new shoes under the bed. Maddie was ignoring him again, and he wished she'd stop it.

All of the sudden, he felt very unsure about his relationship with her. She couldn't possibly care about someone as pig-headed as Mace, but... He caught Bart's eye and motioned for him. Bart came over and he pulled him down and whispered in his ear.

Bart stood and cleared his throat. With an unusually loud voice he said, "okay you guys, everyone out. Jesus needs to talk with Maddie." It seemed to Jesus that his friends were doing an awful lot of grinning at his expense as they slowly filed out and shut the door.

Maddie turned, crossed her arms, and started tapping her foot. Now Jesus felt on the spot. He wished Bart hadn't made such a big production out of this, the big idiot. His cheeks warmed.

He pointed at his right foot and wiggled his big toe. "That's the best darn toe, Maddie."

She gave him a big smile and said, "It sure is, Jesus."

Panic took hold of his heart. He'd almost lost this girl once from not speaking his mind. Remembering a movie he once saw, he got off his bed and dropped to his knees before her. He took both her hands and softly kissed each one. Looking up into her eyes, he said, "Maddie Mae, will you marry me?"

She looked startled. Trembling, her lower lip came out as her eyes filled with tears. Almost imperceptibly, she nodded.

He grew excited and added, "Maddie, I know I'll still be afraid sometimes, but that won't stop me from being there for you. We'll probably need to finish school and get our lives straightened out. But we can do everything together like a big adventure. I want us to know all about each other... I have so much to tell you."

While formulating his next statement, he released her hands, stood up, and carefully watched her shoulders. "And I promise to tell you each and every day that I love you, for the rest of our lives."

She stood, gave her gimme signal, and broke down crying. Jesus could hear cheers and applause from the hallway as he took her in his arms and felt complete for the first time in his life...

Epilogue

FIVE YEARS LATER

John Henry glanced at his chess opponent. They were sitting atop a grassy peak, hunched over a white marble table with white puffy clouds directly below them, this being the latest of several complete scenery changes within the past hour.

God's chess-pieces were fashioned after heroes of the world. John Henry had villains. The creator always demanded white.

God started the body-shifting thing again. This behavior usually occurred when he was falling behind. John Henry concentrated hard, but each time he looked up, someone else appeared. One minute a boy, the next a girl. Sometimes, the creator seemed everywhere at the same time, including looking over his shoulder. This was the precise reason that he refused to play poker.

Currently, The Ubiquitous One inhabited his favorite human form: long shaggy gray hair, bushy white eyebrows, and piercing blue eyes.

John Henry figured he had checkmate in four moves.

Upon reaching this conclusion, he looked up at the most unbelievably beautiful woman he'd ever imagined, or he should say women. It was like watching an incredibly erotic moving picture. First, a black woman with silky skin and pouting red lips, melding into a lovely Caucasian with long curly hair, and eyes that looked like the sky on a summer's day. Then, came the other races of the earth, each one different, yet stunning.

He felt speechless. It seemed as though God was testing his reaction to each one.

Finally, the black beauty remained, pursing her lips in a promised kiss that made John Henry's senses reel. His brain quit working. Seemingly, all tactics were lost, and his subsequent move put an immense smile on the face of the now gray-haired man. The ending appeared anything but certain.

He'd worked for God eons now. In all that time, he became certain of two things: the Omnipresent One cheated at chess and possessed a rotten sense of humor.

Learning to dimension warp wasn't without incident. When first assigned, The Creator put the target's image in his head, and, once he made contact, John Henry linked with the person's chemical signature. He still remembered the first travel instructions. With a big smile, God said, "picture the objective in your imagination, then, go there."

He did as instructed and, upon landing, he looked around. *And the earth was without form, and void; and darkness was upon the face of the deep.*

John Henry said, "well, blank this."

God's booming laughter rang in his head and the destination was corrected. He didn't think it one bit coincidental that he'd won the chess match earlier in the day.

The Creator could be a true wonder, but, when it came to chess, he was sneakier than a monkey in a produce market. John Henry pondered his next move.

He rubbed his scar and sighed. Of late, his thoughts often returned to Cottondale.

God said, "Okay, before you go completely brain dead, let's have a look at things, shall we?"

✳

John Henry walked the darkened streets of Cottondale as God related bright, colorful progress reports: Jesus and Maddie were playing a concert at the fairgrounds. The young couple had become international sensations. Fans claimed that the piano melodies and Maddie's heavenly voice changed them somehow. Some say healings took place, but all loved the music.

Big Momma, acting as their agent, had shows sold out in advance. Maddie insisted that they tour only four months in any one year, and the rest of their time was spread out among friends and new family.

Bart provided security at all events, and the same saying applied to him and Jesus as did the one that Big Momma pointed out about Maddie and Honey; "if you're looking for one of them, simply find the other. They're two goobers in the same shell."

God concluded the update, but John Henry wanted to see it with his own parched eyes. The-Scourge-Of-The-Chess-Board possessed never-ending love, optimism, and hope for humankind. And that soft spot painted broad, soft, stokes on the canvas of reality.

Adopting a Missouri-like attitude, he turned to the ache in his heart. The thing affecting him the most was missing the kid. When he was first sent to help Jesus, they grew close fast. There was a magic about him. Clients are the only humans that can physically see a seeker. Then, after either failure or successful catharsis like Jesus had, all memories slowly fade from awareness. Sometimes, being a seeker had setbacks, this being one of them.

Jesus would never need him again in the same fashion. When he reintegrated the lost horrors from his childhood, he unearthed the root of his fear; very much the same as restoring a missing chunk of himself.

The reason panic attacks had plagued Jesus was a baby's normal response to inconceivable abuse, especially from a parent, was unconsciously repressing it into his subconscious. Then, whenever anxiety found him later in life, his awareness would switch off because of fragmentation from repression, leaving him frozen, unable to react, lost in an emotional black hole created by his horrific past.

Ironically, to find his courage, he first needed to revisit the seat of his fears. The events consciously relived on the cot restored the missing parts and allowed the healing process to begin. By now, he would be adept at handling the stressors of life. John Henry knew that, with his new family's help, Jesus would never return to the fragmented being of his youth.

He rubbed his scar. He must be getting old. He should be feeling only joy and happiness, and yet, he felt bad about having been forgotten. Well, occupational hazards, he guessed, but one thing he knew for blanking sure was he would never forget Jesus.

God was doing the woman-melding thing again. Flowing gown and full high heels, The Creator was a vision.

Several men had already made the mistake of making sexually inappropriate remarks. They vanished shortly thereafter. It wasn't so much their disappearance that bothered John Henry, but the way they left. Each appeared as a thin candle flame, then snuffed out, leaving a wisp of smoke dissipating in their place. If this trend continued the census would clearly be impacted.

God smiled. John Henry tried a quick tooth count. No one could possibly have that many teeth. She winked at him. He grumbled, "must be planning a chess match."

God bumped him with a shoulder. "I may have to stop letting you win."

John Henry started wondering if they would make it by show time. No sooner had the thought crossed his mind then, magically, they were there; right up front, one row back from the podium.

He looked around. The crowd spilled clear up into the foothills around the fairgrounds; tiny dots in the distance. Every face looked toward the dais. A warm summer's night breeze gently fanned his face. Uncountable, brilliant stars filled the sky and framed the stage in celestial splendor.

Soft music began and a spotlight clicked on. Big Momma came out and introduced Jesus and Maddie. Both came on stage in matching shorts and shirts, and each was barefoot.

They held hands as they approached the microphone, bowed as one, and welcomed the crowd. Receiving a thunderous applause, Jesus kissed Maddie, whispered something in her ear, and walked over to the concert piano as she waited.

Spotlights silhouetted each and the music began.

As Jesus played, the music cut right through John Henry's heart. Around him, the crowd swayed as one with the composition. Maddie's voice seemed to rise from the notes and dance around the melody like a verbal butterfly, unequaled by anything that he'd ever heard. Her song and the haunting piano were one. Chills went up his spine as her vocal range crested and ebbed, washing over his soul in soothing waves.

Bart and Honey were right in front of them. John Henry could see them both holding children. The Creator had left out this little detail. He looked at her with questioning eyes.

God flashed a super toothy smile as she motioned for him to lean closer. She whispered in his ear and lightly punched him on the arm. He turned back to look at the kids with a smile matching God's.

Perched on the biker's shoulders were Jesus and Maddie's three-year-old son and his namesake, John Henry. The boy looked at him and he reached out and tweaked his nose. Peering around Honey's neck and watching intently with sky-blue eyes was his two-year-old sister, Angel. The children looked like carbon copies of their parents.

A new song started and people held hands and swayed, lost in the spell cast by the magical duo. John Henry took the black haired beauty's hand and said, "well, what do you think?"

God wiped tears from her eyes and said, "I just love happy endings."